"Yo
D0831355

"Oh," Hannah said, lowering her gaze. "No, I'm not."

"Forgive me, but do you know what I'm asking?"

"I think so." Her cheeks grew pinker. "Don't apologize; it's a perfectly rational question under the circumstances."

"Thank you," Ian said with relief. "You agree we can have a sensible marriage then? I promise I won't bother you with my lovemaking."

"You are a celibate?"

"No. But surely you know ours will be a marriage of convenience. I won't trouble you to make love to me."

"Oh, no!" she said, her hand on her heart, her expression filled with horror. "You don't understand. I *must* make love to you."

F
Layton, Edith
A bride for his convenience

MID-CONTINENT PUBLIC LIBRARY
Raytown Branch
6131 Raytown Road
Raytown, MO 64133

RT

Other **AVON ROMANCES**

ATTENTION: ORGANIZATIONS AND CORPORATIONS
Most Avon Books paperbacks are available at special quantity
discounts for bulk purchases for sales promotions, premiums,
or fund raising. For information, please call or write:

**Special Markets Department, HarperCollins Publishers,
10 East 53rd Street, New York, New York 10022-5299.
Telephone: (212) 207-7528.   Fax: (212) 207-7222.**

A BRIDE FOR HIS CONVENIENCE

EDITH LAYTON

AVON

An Imprint of HarperCollinsPublishers

MID-CONTINENT PUBLIC LIBRARY - BTM

3 0003 00792091 9

This is a work of fiction. Names, characters, places, and incidents are drawn from the author's imagination or are used fictitiously and are not to be construed as real. Any resemblance to actual events, locales, organizations, or persons, living or dead, is entirely coincidental.

AVON BOOKS
An Imprint of HarperCollins*Publishers*
10 East 53rd Street
New York, New York 10022-5299

Copyright © 2008 by Edith Felber
ISBN 978-0-06-125367-6
www.avonromance.com

All rights reserved. No part of this book may be used or reproduced in any manner whatsoever without written permission, except in the case of brief quotations embodied in critical articles and reviews. For information, address Avon Books, an Imprint of HarperCollins Publishers.

First Avon Books paperback printing: December 2008

Avon Trademark Reg. U.S. Pat. Off. and in Other Countries, Marca Registrada, Hecho en U.S.A.
HarperCollins® is a registered trademark of HarperCollins Publishers.

Printed in the U.S.A.

10 9 8 7 6 5 4 3 2 1

If you purchased this book without a cover, you should be aware that this book is stolen property. It was reported as "unsold and destroyed" to the publisher, and neither the author nor the publisher has received any payment for this "stripped book."

MID-CONTINENT PUBLIC LIBRARY
Raytown Branch
6131 Raytown Road
Raytown, MO 64133

RT

To Sebastian (Baz) Q. Felber, my newest beamish grandbabyboy!

Acknowledgments

To Joan and Joseph Wolf, good friends indeed, in words and deeds.

A Bride For His
Convenience

Chapter 1

"**T**hen what you're saying is that I have to sell myself," the gentleman said.

"Good Heavens, my lord!" the stout middle-aged man answered. "What a dreadful way to look at it."

"Honest, not dreadful, Mr. Foster," the gentleman replied. He didn't move a muscle in his face, nor did his long, lean body stir in his chair. But his still posture and the look in his cold gray eyes made the other man nervous.

"Finding someone to marry is nothing like a sale," Mr. Foster quickly said.

"Then you've never been to Almacks, or to a *ton* party, I suppose?" the gentleman asked. "There, I assure you, it is the females who are on sale, apart from a few desperate gentleman paupers with nothing to their names but their names." He paused. "I realize I'm now one of them, but I don't want to be."

"It is tradition that the lady's family provide her

with a dowry and make a settlement—" the other man began to say.

He was ruthlessly cut off. "The dowry is standard, the settlement is an act of good faith offered to a gentleman who has equal or more funds of his own. As a successful man-of-business you should know this, Mr. Foster. And as you also know, I have nothing to offer."

Mr. Foster took in a deep breath. "That's true, so far as money goes. Your estate and town house is entailed. There's little left in them anyway except for those heirlooms you refuse to part with. Nor can I blame you for it. Worthy as they are, they wouldn't fetch enough to help you over the long term. Your coffers are empty. You didn't empty them, but in trying to fill them after your father's depredations . . ."

"My *stepmother's* depredations," the gentleman corrected him.

"Both then. And yours."

"I see," the gentleman said coldly. "I should have left my brother to die here in England when I was told the air on the warmer shores of Italy might help him live? And it is. He is healing, and breathing freely again. That was and is an unavoidable expense. I grant I made some bad investments. But I neither gambled nor wenched nor drank my fortunes away. My ancestors took care of most of that. My stepmother wasted what was left. Now you tell me my only recourse is to marry for money?"

Lord Ian Sutcombe, Marquis Sutcombe, stood up and paced, keeping his high-nosed profile averted from the other man as he did. "The ladies of the *ton* don't want me now. They know my financial condition and set their sights higher. I can't blame them. Am I to marry someone whose family is desperate to have her married? Perhaps a wealthy half-wit or deranged woman? Or maybe a commoner, someone with no manners or intelligence? No, Mr. Foster, I care too much for my name to burden it with idiots and fools. We've had enough of them."

"Then you have your eye on some suitable female?" his man of business asked eagerly. "Perhaps there's still a chance . . ."

"Suitable? None, because I never looked to marry. I had hoped to leave that to my brother."

Mr. Foster sighed. He studied his client carefully, noting the well-cut blue jacket that had been brushed once too often, the clean linen that had been washed too frequently to be absolutely snowy, the well-made boots that still took a shine, but showed their age. The gentleman was dressed elegantly, with care and taste, but that elegance was strained. The marquis's hard-edged face showed none of this. Though he had thick, dark gold hair and clear gray eyes, his lordship was not a handsome man in the current poetical style. It was a face of crags and planes, the only softening feature, the cleft in his determined chin. He looked more like a Roman Centurion than a nobleman. But females found him wildly attractive. They flocked to him to win one smile from that firm mouth. The long thin scar that ran from his ear down his cheek to his jaw, earned in the wars before he inherited his title and had to come home, made him appear even more dashing.

The man looked every inch a member of the aristocracy. Unfortunately, Mr. Foster thought, his tastes followed suit. He was high in the instep and low in his regard for other people's intelligence. While never rude without meaning to be, his eyes and his silences nevertheless spoke volumes about his opinions.

"Then there is only one solution," Mr. Foster said. "You can't learn a new career quickly."

"As well I know," the gentleman said softly.

"And you cannot go into Trade."

Now Lord Sutcombe smiled. "I have nothing to trade, nothing to stock and nothing to sell."

"So. My lord, you have obligations, and must have a roof over your head as well as over your brother's. And you must maintain your holdings and their staffs. There's nothing for it except to marry well. Though you have no money, you have a great deal to offer even so. You have a fine ancient title and are accepted everywhere. You have the estate, and it is noteworthy. Your house in London is magnificent."

"Or would be if it had furnishings," Lord Sutcombe murmured.

"Precisely. You have other holdings in the countryside and a charming cottage in the West Country, all sadly entailed as well. But as for yourself, you're relatively young, healthy, considered well-enough-looking, and clever. If you'd only hold your famous scathing remarks, my lord . . ." He saw his guest's face and hurriedly added, "I don't mean you must demean yourself, or bend out of shape in order to be endearing."

"*Endearing?*" the marquis echoed, his eyes opening wide.

"Engaging, is what I meant to say. If you tried to be more conciliatory, we could find you a charming female, and a new fortune that would come with her."

"A commoner?" the marquis asked flatly.

"I believe that would be our best choice. I would not ask you to marry a madwoman or an idiot, and at present, every other female of the gentry is either spoken for, or clamored for. Titled ladies often find themselves in the same difficulties as you do now and solve it in the same fashion. Wealthy titled men and women always have first choice. But common men are making money these days. They can win a title for themselves if they make enough money to do favors for the Prince or one of his brothers' mistresses. Failing that, at least they can see their grandchildren reach heights they can't. Hence, a trade, my lord: money for a title. It has ever been so."

"No other choices?"

"None."

The marquis strode the window and stared out. His hands were clenched at his sides. "I suppose the only other option is to hang a sign about my neck," he said curtly, "and go begging on a street corner the way some of the poor devils I fought beside before my father passed away are doing."

Mr. Foster didn't deign to answer this.

"Then find me a rich woman to wed," the marquis snapped, turning around abruptly to face the other man. "Find me a bride that can speak coherently and knows her place. Find me one I can bear to look at and talk to, if only for the time it takes to get my fortunes back in tune again."

"Done," Mr. Foster said, and thought: *God help the poor woman, no matter how rich she is.*

Chapter 2

She ran through the fields, holding up the hem of her skirts as she did. The grasses whipped her ankles; her hair ribbon gone, the sun teased gold from her tumbling brown hair and blushed her cheeks. Her gown was in disarray from her haste. She looked like a young woman freshly risen from a bed of love, fleeing an irate parent. But she was rushing toward her love, if not her lover. She'd change *that* this very day, Hannah thought, her heart beating doubly hard from excitement and effort. She ran on, laughing aloud.

She'd never looked better, though she'd never know it. Hannah wasn't a beauty, and well she thought she knew that. No matter what Timothy said about her being lovely, she knew. A beauty would drift like a sprite through the meadow, not plunge on like a plow horse, she thought as she stumbled, caught her balance, and kept on going. Timothy may have said he liked a female with some flesh on her bones, but a beauty would be sylphlike, rounded only in the pertinent places, with nothing jiggling and bouncing beneath her gown, as she was now. Hannah had to keep her hand on her heart to keep her gown from falling down, because all that jouncing had loosened the strings on her bodice.

A beauty would have a classic face too, with a calm look upon it, whatever she was doing. Hannah was excited and was sure she looked it. She was only passing fair, no matter how vehemently Timothy denied it. She was snub-nosed, pink-cheeked, and cultivated freckles the way beauties did admirers. She wasn't stout, but was never slender. Mostly, she had few illusions about herself. But then, she'd had her illusions teased out of her by her two younger sisters.

What she was, was three and twenty, unwed, unbedded, burdened with an education, and overburdened with morals. That last, she resolved, would change as soon as possible. Today anything was possible, because last night he'd promised her more than the moon and the stars. Last night, he'd begged her to meet him in the glade where he could properly declare himself, at last. Of course, a "proper place" would be her own parlor, but that niggling doubt didn't slow Hannah. A glade was so much more private and poetic.

She'd never met anyone like Timothy Adkins. Though she supposed she'd known him all her life, she'd only come to really know him this spring, and now she wanted to know no other man. Because she was the eldest, her sisters chaffed at her to find a man and marry so that their father would let them go too. But she'd been reluctant. Any suitors she'd met were too eager for her father's approval. In fact, she didn't know if they even looked at her.

Timothy knew her father wouldn't approve of his poverty or his expectations, and he didn't care. He cared, he said, only for her. He made her feel absurdly young. He made her feel the one thing she'd never felt for a man before. She desired him, not only for his handsome face and form but also because he always made her so intensely aware of how much he desired her.

Hannah was out of breath as she ducked beneath the trees and ran into the home forest. And when, at last, her breathing slowed, there he stood in the dappled shade, waiting for her. She stopped. The thrill of it almost stopped her heart as well.

Timothy Adkins stood waiting for her. When he saw her, he snatched his hat off his curly black hair. As usual, one inky strand escaped to ornament his high forehead. But as she approached him, he bowed.

She wondered at that. Though she wanted to throw herself into his arms, he didn't open them to her. She saw he wanted to play a different game today, so she stopped in front of him, swept a bobbling curtsy, and laughed up into his handsome face. Her own face fell. His deep blue eyes were solemn, and there was no humor in his expression.

He was taking this proposal business very seriously, she thought, and so then, she would as well. He was right; marriage was a solemn business. She stifled a grin, folded her hands in front of herself, slowed her breathing, and waited, while her pulses kept drumming like a blacksmith's hammer beats.

"Nan," he said. "Our time together is brief today, and we'll have none at all tomorrow."

She stared.

He shrugged. Then he began to pace the little mossy space beneath the trees.

"You're not joking?" she asked nervously. She half expected him to swing around and catch her up in his arms and laugh. Then they'd begin the delicious business of kissing again.

But he didn't stop pacing.

"Not joking, no," he said, head down.

"What's happened?" she asked in alarm.

"I've come to my senses," he said.

"Has my father found out? Has anyone threatened you?"

His head came up. He looked as though she'd stung him. "No one's threatened me. Much good it would do them to try," he muttered. "The thing is, Hannah, there's no future for us. I've come to see that clearly. I haven't compromised you, yet. Nor have you compromised me. Though lord knows you've tried."

"What?" she said stupidly. "But you're the one who wanted to kiss and . . . suchlike. I'm the one who always stops you."

" 'Deed, I know that, I do, full well, and I see it for what it is now," he said bluntly. "If I laid a hand on you, I'd be bound to wed you, and dammit, Hannah, but I'm not ready yet. I have a lifetime ahead of me."

"But," she blurted, "you have laid a hand on me."

He shook his head. "A female isn't ruined by a touch."

"Well," she said, hanging her head and growing as red-faced as if she was still running, "no one ever touched me in those places before."

She remembered the night before, his touch might not have ruined her, but it had certainly awakened her. She'd squirmed, now used to his caresses, her breasts tingling with anticipation of his kisses. But then she'd been as embarrassed as excited when he'd finally put his hand in a place forbidden even to her. She'd stiffened. He'd chuckled. "Steady," he'd whispered.

She'd been astonished when he'd moved his fingers and the way it made her feel. "Hush," he'd said in her ear. "Isn't this nice?"

Beyond that, she'd thought, unable to speak. She'd felt a rising, a longing, and a promise of unknown rapture. She'd closed her eyes and raised herself to him. It had ended abruptly when he suddenly drew away from her and threw himself back on the haymow with an arm flung over his eyes.

She'd lain there, alone, coming to her senses, feeling mortified. She'd looked down at how her gown was rucked up and drawn half down, and shuddered. When she started fumbling to get herself in order again, he'd swiftly turned, covered her with his own body and whispered, "No, don't be shamed. It's just not time. Not now, not yet, but soon, Hannah. Now, let's get you home."

He'd helped her straighten herself, taken her hand and led her back through the night shadows toward the safety of her house. Then he'd kissed her once more, and said, "Tomorrow. At noon in the glade. Then."

He didn't seem to remember that passion now. "That wasn't ruination," he told her. "Look you, Hannah, you're a good sort, and we've had fun, but the summer is almost over, and so is our sport."

"*Sport?*" She gasped. "But the things you said. Our embraces, the secret meetings . . ."

"Did I ask you to marry me?" he asked with challenge.

She shook her head, took a breath and looked him straight in the eye. "But you said you'd ask my father's permission first."

He visibly shuddered as though shaking off a bad dream. "I didn't. I shouldn't have said I would. I was carried away. But the thought of actually doing it sobered me up. Thing is Hannah, apart from needing more time to establish myself, the truth is that I've met someone else."

She froze in the warmth of the day.

He began pacing again. "She's a beauty: charming, smart and rich too, for a wonder. And me without a penny piece, as you know. But it don't matter to her, or her family," he added, shooting her a bright look. "I met her at a cousin's house and can't forget her. Nor has she forgot me. We've been exchanging letters, and she's invited me to her home near Dover. I'm leaving tomorrow. I'm sorry if I misled you. But I did you no harm, did I? Come, you can't claim I harmed you, can you?"

She shook her head. She had no idea of what to say. She wanted to hit him; she wanted to cry, she wanted to run away. She'd never been rejected before. It wasn't because she was such a great beauty. She knew that. But this was a small village. Her father was the richest man in the district because his mill sat on a broad river not far from the great road that wound up toward the north or down to London itself. He was a clever businessman, and used the funds he made from his mill to invest in more profitable enterprises. He had an eye for the future. The world was opening up for such men. He owned mines and ships as well as the mill now, and kept buying more. He was bound upward in the world beyond the London road itself.

Timothy was the son of the local draper. His family wasn't poor, but neither were they wealthy, and it wasn't likely he'd ever be that, since he was indolent by nature. He hadn't much of an education either, or a skill or craft. But he was clever and as glib as he was handsome. All the village girls were mad for him. Hannah never thought he'd come courting her, or care if he did. But he had, this summer, in spite of her father's obvious disapproval. She'd been surprised, and then, delighted first by his gentility, then by his ardor.

Now he looked at her as though he hated her. And yet, just last night they'd met in that empty barn, by secret and moonlight. She'd lain in his arms and returned his kisses as his hands slipped down to places she'd been taught to ignore, but now knew she never again could. What had she done? Was she so repellent in her need? Had he been shocked by her reckless shamelessness? She knew she had been.

"Sorry," he said, seeing her expression. "We got on very well, Nan. It's just that I didn't know my own mind. Now I do."

"What can I say?" she asked, hoping it was still some monstrous jest.

"Good-bye and best of luck," he said.

He bowed, abruptly turned, and left her there alone in the glade, feeling lost, and stupid.

Chapter 3

I an stared at the assortment of new, snowy fresh linens laid out on the dressing table before him. He looked up into the glass at the reflection of his valet standing behind him.

"Baker. Where the devil did you get those neck-cloths?" he demanded.

His valet smirked. "I got my ways, sir."

"You *stole* them?"

"Of course not," the man said, looking offended. "This ain't Spain, m'lord. I traded."

"What do we have to trade?"

"Nothing you want, sir. Stuff you told me to clear out. Stuff you tossed in the trash. I been saving them against the day."

"*Stuff?* Such as?" Ian asked, fascinated.

"Stuff and nonsense, sir. You said it yourself. Remember when you came home? That cupid setting on that inkwell you found in a bedchamber and threw out the window?"

"My stepmother's," Ian said bitterly. "Base

metal, not worth a farthing. She sold off every-thing of worth before she left us."

"Well, begging your pardon, but that's where you're out. Base metal, it is. But appealing, is what it also is. I picked it out of the shrubbery after you tossed it. Now, there's a valet I met at a pub. He works for some jumped-up fribble. The valet's got a lady's maid in his eye, and where he wants her is in his bed. Whether that inkwell is gold or lead, he thinks it's just the thing to melt her heart. So we made a bargain. Fair trading is what it is."

"Six neckcloths for that paltry inkwell? You did well," Ian said as he raised his chin and began to wrap the cloth around his neck.

"Naw. That's just him showing good faith, is what I told him," his valet said, watching as his employer deftly wrapped and then knotted the cloth into a simple style.

Ian stood and examined himself in the glass.

"Your pearl stickpin, sir? It's small, but looks good."

"Have I a choice?" Ian said, nodding.

"As for that valet, don't worry," the man said as he thrust the pin in the neckcloth to secure it. "We'll have you togged out fine before I finally let go of that cupid."

"I don't know why you stay with a pauper, Baker," Ian said seriously. "You could make your own fortune in Trade, you know."

"Wouldn't be as interesting. Anyway," Baker said as he looked at his employer critically, "trade never saved my life, did it?"

"That was my job," Ian said.

"Aye, and this's mine."

Ian forced a thin smile. "Good. Done, then," he said. "I'm ready for the auction block. Will a female think she's getting her money's worth?"

"Bah," Baker said, scowling. "That ain't no attitude when a man's going courting."

"But I'm not," Ian said. "I'm going selling. Cheer up. I may be for sale, but I'll try to bargain as well as you do."

"Good luck, milord," his valet said, bending to pick up the unused neckcloths so he wouldn't see his employer set his jaw tight and stride from the room.

"Three in one day?" Ian asked his man of business when he settled into Foster's carriage.

"Yes," Foster said. "Simply because I know you, my lord. If today doesn't go well you'll never come with me again on such an errand. So I sifted through many prospects and then chose three of the best for you to meet today."

"How did you find them?"

"It's simple, my lord. It's my business to know what my clients need. Some have daughters, and want to elevate themselves in the world. Miss Cheswick, to whom we go first, has a father who became wealthy in the mining trade. Don't worry, there's no dirt under his fingernails now, but there's gold enough. Miss Nicholson, whom we next visit, has a grandfather who invented a part for carriage wheels. A flourishing business now, can you believe that? And Miss Leeds's father was a miller and is now an owner and investor in many trades. They are all anxious to meet you."

"Me? Or my title?"

"Both, my lord. Ah, here we are. Miss Cheswick lives close, in a very good district, as you can see."

Miss Cheswick lived in a fine house in the middle of a crescent of similar homes. The gentlemen were shown into a well-furnished salon, where Miss Cheswick and her mother and father were awaiting them.

Ian was announced, but not invited to sit down. Instead, Miss Cheswick rose from her chair after hearing his name and came straight to him.

Ian was pleased. It showed her to be a young woman of spirit and nerve. He admired her looks as well. She was of medium height, medium weight, dressed in something gray, and had cropped her curly black hair into a modish new hairstyle. It showed off her cool blue eyes. She looked at him and put up her chin. He was vastly relieved. This wasn't going to be difficult for him at all.

But instead of greeting him, she only walked until she was close to him. She ignored his inquiring gaze. Instead, she looked him up and down, and began to slowly circle him, one finger tapping her lip, as though she were silently evaluating him. He didn't know whether to laugh or turn on his heel and leave the room.

Mr. Foster grew red-faced.

"Everything you said about him is true?" she asked Mr. Foster.

He could only nod.

"Well then, yes," Miss Cheswick finally said, turning from Ian at last to look at her father. "Much better than the others. Still young, and good-enough-looking, and a marquis. I do believe he'll do. Now we can talk about settlements. Papa?"

Ian broke from his astonished immobility. He bowed. "Good morning to you too, Miss Cheswick," he said. "I regret I've another appointment I must get to, instantly. And," he added, as he snatched his hat back from a footman, "I refuse to show you my teeth. Good day," he said as he strode from the room.

Mr. Foster came trotting after him, babbling apologies.

"Now I know how the horses at Tattersalls must feel," Ian said as he settled back in the carriage again. He gave a short bark of a laugh. "Good gods, but she was terrifying."

"I was entirely surprised," Mr. Foster said, taking out a handkerchief and mopping his brow. "What a thing to do to a nobleman!"

"What a thing to do to anyone," Ian said. "If a man did that to a female, he'd be a cad. But who knows? Maybe she didn't want to marry and found a novel way to get out of it. In that case, bravo to her. But in any case, I don't want to see her again."

"You never shall. Our next visit will be different. Miss Nicholson is nothing like Miss Cheswick," Mr. Foster said hurriedly.

Ian said nothing.

"You *are* coming?" Mr. Foster asked nervously. "I told them you would."

"My word's good even if my financial situation isn't," Ian said. "I will."

"The Nicholsons haven't bought a London house yet," Mr. Foster said as the carriage stopped in front of another fine London hotel. "They've put up here while they look for one."

"And a son-in-law," Ian muttered.

"Yes," Mr. Foster said as he showed Ian to the front door of the hotel. "I haven't met Miss Nicholson, but I have seen a portrait of her. She's very beautiful."

Ian sighed.

Liveried footmen opened the door of the hotel to them. Mr. Foster presented his card, and another footman showed them to a spiral stair that led to the second floor and the Nicholson suite. Ian climbed the stair, paused in front to a door, and braced himself. Mr. Foster glanced up at him as they waited. Nothing of Ian's unease showed on his face.

The door swung upon and a florid gentleman met them, arms open.

"My dear Mr. Foster," he said warmly. "And this must be my Lord Sutcombe. Welcome, welcome, my lord," he said, bowing, and gesturing to them to enter the hotel sitting room. "Do have a seat," he added, addressing Ian. "Some sherry? Or a glass of something more bracing, my lord? I think that would be best. I'm sure this must be difficult for you, sir, because I know it is for me." His laughter was rich and hearty. "Come, do sit down please. My angel will be right in. She's that anxious to meet you. Forgive her if she's a bit shy. The situation is not easy for her, you see."

"Yes," Ian said as he sat in the chair his host indicated. "I certainly understand."

"Of course, it might have been easier if you could have come to our home," the gentleman went on, as he poured a goblet of brown sherry for his guests. "We've a fine place in Surrey. Used to be the gem of the countryside, but it fell to wrack and ruin. I bought it up cheap, and now it is once again the magnificent place it deserves to be. The old Powell place, don't you know. The Duke, he gambled it away. He had no direct kin when he passed, so I was able to snap it up for taxes. Not that it was a bargain, mind. Falling to bits. I had to put in new walls, floors, furniture and whatnots, everywhere. I didn't stint, though. I did it up grand. The money I poured into the place staggered my friends. They thought I'd run mad. Who cares? What's money when it comes to happiness, eh?"

Ian didn't get a chance to answer. He soon realized he wasn't expected to. During the next several minutes, he was regaled with stories of his host's cleverness at investing, his love of property, and his immense fortune.

"My poor motherless chick," Mr. Nicholson finally said, pulling a sad face. "What good is it to her? She's lonely. She needs a family of her own. And a man of her own choosing, because believe me, my lord, the minute you clap eyes on her you'll see she could have anyone. Anyone. But who is there for her deep in the countryside? That's why we're in London, she deserves a gentleman of quality."

Mr. Nicholson went on and on. Ian found himself listening with half attention, since no reply was expected of him. He'd been subjected to rudeness at the last call. Now he was being buried in flattery. He wondered what ghastly defect the girl in this house had.

But when he saw her, he tilted his head to the side and smiled in spite of his cynicism. Simply put, Clarissa Nicholson was lovely. She had long golden ringlets, and deep brown eyes, a lovely figure, and clear, white skin. She was dressed in pink and white, and looked liked she belonged on top of a pastry, or in a dollhouse.

Ian rose to his feet to greet her. Her father rose as well, and rocked on his heels, beaming. Mr. Foster audibly sighed his relief.

"Good morning, my lord," she said softly, curtsying low after she was introduced to Ian.

Ian bowed. "And good morning to you, Miss Nicholson," he said.

She rose and gazed at him.

"And how are you this morning?" Ian asked.

She put a hand to her pretty pink lips, blushed, and giggled.

"This is awkward, isn't it?" he said with fellow feeling.

She giggled again.

And so it went.

Ian had seen violent warfare up close, but in a half hour, his nerves were stretched to their breaking points. Mr. Nicholson kept talking. His daughter scarcely uttered a word. When she did, she giggled. At first, Ian persisted, trying to draw her out. After all, shyness was a curse. But whether the subject was weather, London, or her favorite book, her answers were simple, and her giggling constant.

A clock somewhere in the rooms chimed. Ian shot up from his chair, made his bows and excuses, and headed for the door.

"She's not simple!" her father told Ian at the

door. "Not precisely. She's just not sharp-witted. But a more charming, docile creature you'll never meet. I'll wager none come with more money."

"I expect not," Ian said.

"But she isn't for you, eh?" her father asked bluntly.

"Not for any amount," Ian said. "I'm sorry, but that's the truth. A younger man, perhaps?"

He got a slap on the back for his comment. "Don't try to gild it. It isn't a matter of age. You're a man of honor and you're right, sorry to say. Good luck to you, my lord. Should you change your mind you can always return."

"Never," Ian muttered, when he sat back in the carriage again. He put his head back on the squabs, and closed his eyes. "Did you know about this, Foster?"

"Not I, my lord. I only saw her portrait. Had I known I'd never have dragged you here."

"Of course you would have," Ian said, still with his eyes closed. "She's swimming in money. How could you know that though I'm up against the wall, I wear no blindfold? How could you know that I have limits? Damn me for them, but I do. Poor creature needs a nursemaid, not a husband. I've had enough, Foster. I may have to emigrate after all. A new world might present new opportunities for me, and I don't mean for marriage."

"You promised, my lord," Foster said mournfully, sounding like a forlorn child.

"So I did. Then drive on." Ian opened one eye. "Are you being a clever horse trader, Foster; showing me the broken-down nags and saving the best for last?"

"I hope so, my lord."

"So do I."

The town house they drove to was in a good part of Town. As they waited for the door to be opened, Ian's agitation showed only in the way he tapped his gloves against his thigh.

The door opened, and he and Mr. Foster were shown into a well-furnished front parlor.

"Good afternoon," a rotund, balding gentleman said, greeting them. He showed his nervousness by talking too quickly. "Do come in, Mr. Foster," he said. "I take it this is the marquis? How do you do, my lord? I'm Wallace Leeds. My daughter, Hannah, will be here directly. Would you care for some tea?"

They sat, accepted tea and a tray of little cakes, and made desultory comments about the tea and the weather. Finally, when Ian was ready to make some excuse, to rise and leave, the young woman he'd come to see came into the room.

She was, Ian thought, as he stood to greet her, passing fair. Not a great beauty, but pleasant to look at. Of middle height, her modish russet gown showed a gracious figure; a bit plump, but not unseemly so. Her hair was brown with a gold sheen wherever the sunlight touched it. She had a small nose with freckles on it. Her eyes were fine, he thought: brown and gold, large and long lashed, and intelligent and watchful, until she politely cast her gaze down after she greeted him.

"This is awkward, I know," Ian said softly, as they all sat down again.

She flashed a look at him. "Yes," she whispered, looking down again, "So it is, my lord."

She didn't say much more, but when she spoke her voice was low and educated, and what she said was proper. If anything, Ian thought as he put down his empty teacup, she was a bit too proper for him. He checked. *If anything?* If anything, he never meant to marry, and certainly never where his heart was not. But he remembered his circumstances. Hers, he imagined, were that of an obedient daughter. Her father wasn't rough spoken, but would never be taken for a gentleman of birth. And she had two younger sisters. His title wasn't just for her; it would doubtless advance her sisters and benefit the whole family.

They'd be getting a bargain in buying him, Ian thought with resignation. And it was possible. In sum: face, form, and demeanor, she was acceptable. If the money was right, she could have him. If they married his brother could continue to prosper on sunnier shores for the rest of his life. And it could be a long life too. The estate could be put to rights. The girl wasn't bad at all. God knew, Ian thought, he could do worse.

As he relaxed, he supposed his expression did too. Because both Foster and Mr. Leeds were smiling more freely now. Ian knew he could sometimes look forbidding. But the young woman, Hannah was her name, he remembered, didn't look a whit happier than when she'd entered the room. It wasn't that she was sad; rather she was still, and looked sober and concerned.

But if he was signing his life away, Ian thought, so was she. And he had more cause to do it. Or did he? He should and would insist on at least a six-month engagement before any actual ceremony. If this marriage was a necessity for her, he should be able to see it after that long a time. He didn't care about her virginity, but he didn't need an heir, especially not one fathered by someone else.

"My lord, Hannah, why don't you two go for a stroll in the garden?" her father suggested after a while. "We can see you from here and perhaps you can talk a bit more privately."

She rose at once, and so did Ian. He offered her his arm; she bent her head and walked with him to a door set in between the long windows. It opened onto a small London-sized garden that nevertheless boasted a terrace and carefully shaped shrubbery, and in the middle, a statue of Cupid pouring a marble pitcher into the middle of a splashing fountain.

Ian winced at the sight. He didn't seem to be able to escape the damned symbol of love today.

It seemed to be mocking him. He waited for his companion to say something, anything, and yet he found he liked her quiet ways. After having just met one female who sized him up like a side of beef hanging in a butcher's window, and another who giggled at motes of dust in the sunlight, he appreciated the sense of peace he felt as he strolled beside her. He wasn't sure of what to talk about with her. Still, he wanted to know what she was thinking, and why she was agreeing to a sham of a marriage.

They walked in silence, and then turned to stroll back the way they came. She kept her head down and seemed lost in thought, miles away.

"I have to marry, and for money. You know that," Ian finally said. "I suspect you don't have to marry for any reason other than to please your father. If I don't please you, please say so, and save us both time."

She looked up at him at that, as though remembering he was there. "Oh. Yes. You're right. No, you don't displease me—or please me, actually. But I can't see any harm in you. Is there any? Would you tell me if there were?"

He frowned. She backed up a step. He realized he'd frightened her. "Why the devil are you agreeing to this meeting, Miss Leeds?" he asked, "much less marriage to a stranger?"

She tilted her head to one side. "Because it will make everyone in my family happy. We have looked into your background and seen nothing amiss. If I marry a gentleman with a title, my sisters will be able to marry well. I'll be able to sponsor their come-outs and introduce them to the *ton*. With your recommendations, my father may have entrée to business opportunities he couldn't have any other way. My family will certainly gain stature in the world, apart from our riches. My father is right. Money isn't everything, and a title is not nothing either. Someone has to advance us even further now. And I am, after all, three and twenty, well past the age of wedlock."

"Why are you still unwed?"

"You are to the point. Well, good." She smiled, sadly. "The truth is that I wagered on the wrong horse, my lord. I harbored a preference for someone who didn't deserve it. I can't and won't say more. But I'm done with silly dreams." She gestured toward the cupid on the fountain. "That sort of nonsense."

"You aren't . . ." he hesitated, searching for words that wouldn't insult her but would save him six months of waiting.

"Oh," she said, lowering her gaze again. "No, I'm not."

"Forgive me, but do you know what I'm asking?"

"I think so. I was foolish, my lord. But not that foolish." Her cheeks grew pinker. "I am not with child. Don't apologize; it's a perfectly rational question under the circumstances. I'd hoped there'd be no nonsense between us."

"Thank you," he said with relief. "So did I. You agree we can have a sensible marriage then, the two of us? Don't worry about the young Eros over there. He won't be a factor with us. In fact, I promise I won't bother you with my lovemaking."

"You are a celibate?" she asked, stopping to look at him, her eyes wide. "Or have some other preferences, or difficulty with females?"

"No," he said, scowling. "But surely you know ours will be a marriage of convenience. I mean," he said patiently as she gaped at him, "I won't trouble you to make love to me. I already have my heir: my brother."

"Oh no!" she said, her hand on her heart, her expression filled with horror. "You don't understand. You *must* make love to me."

Chapter 4

There was silence in the little garden. Ian's face showed no expression. Hannah was so horrified by what she'd said she actually reached out and touched his sleeve. He looked down in puzzlement. She drew her hand back as though she'd touched a hot stove.

Though there was no one to hear them, she whispered, "It's *not* what you think."

His eyebrow went up.

"The point is that if I'm to marry someone I don't know," she said quickly, "I want something out of it. But not what you're thinking!"

"You don't know what I'm thinking."

"I'll wager I do," she said. "And that's not it. I'm not asking for lovemaking because I'm so madly attracted to you. Nor do I think it necessary for my happiness. *Quite* the contrary. But if I'm to marry without love or passion, or even liking, I need something for myself from the bargain. Why should I marry you and then live just as I might have if I'd never married at all? A title doesn't impress me. That's my father's idea and for his benefit. I already have a fine home. Where's the benefit for me? The point is that I don't want to be a doting auntie to my sisters' children someday. Well, I do. But I want more than that. Were I to remain a spinster that would be all I'd ever have. I want babes of my own. I want children."

He sighed. "With all the best intentions in the world, there's still no guarantee I can assist you with that," he said, ". . . even if I agreed."

"But in such a case, I could take in children," she said. "A maiden lady can't, without being considered odd. You'd like adoption even better, actually, because an adopted child can't inherit your title."

She saw him pondering what she'd said, and added, "But I'd like some of my own children, if possible. With all my father's money, it's the only thing I can't have on my own. I'll marry to please him. But I'd do it for myself as well. I'd marry so that I could have my own family. If I don't have love, I do insist on babies."

"You're very outspoken," he murmured. "I wouldn't have thought it."

"Well, I wouldn't have believed I'd marry a stranger," she said sadly, falling back into her usual calm demeanor. "So there you are."

"So then," he asked, looking down at her intently, "why not wait for love to come along?"

"Because I no longer believe in it. And I don't want to suffer for my illusions anymore."

He stayed still a moment. "Miss Leeds," he finally said. "You've obviously been badly hurt and aren't thinking straight. I've seen this in men just come from battle. I think, therefore, it would be best if we didn't wed."

"You don't want me?" she asked.

"It has nothing to do with me," he said, taking her hands in his. "You need time."

"You don't want me," she said.

He inclined his head. She saw a small smile on his lips. But all he said was, "Be grateful, Miss Leeds."

The couple seen in silhouette from the parlor window was observed to be standing close, holding hands, and talking quietly. Both gentlemen inside, having completed their preliminary negotiations, looked out the window, turned to each other, smiled, and shook hands.

The couple strolled back to the house.

"You know," Hannah said carefully, walking with her head down as though watching her step, "any female you do marry, under the circumstances, will want and expect a child. You do realize that, don't you?"

Ian stopped walking.

"Well yes," she said, pausing by his side. "She would want one, and certainly so would her father. The bargain is not made just so a father can brag about a titled son-in-law. I don't know what Mr. Foster told you, but such a pact is made so that the child of a common man . . . although I think my father uncommon, of course . . . can herself have children who *are* titled. Otherwise, what's the point? In fact, I liked you because you seemed to have a brain. I had heard some extremely dim aristocratic gentlemen are nevertheless chosen for sons-in-law. They are pleased to go to the highest bidder for the purpose of improving the line, like prime livestock bought to improve the quality of a herd. In humans it's done in respect to titles, at least."

Ian smiled. "You're trying to get back at me, aren't you? You're doing a good job of it. But," he said slowly, "of course, you're right. I should have thought of it before. My financial situation has stolen more than my pride. It's addled my wits."

They moved on. Ian stopped again. "*If* we were to marry, should I expect to have the fact that I was purchased, like livestock, so to speak, be thrown up at me every time I annoyed you? That could get tiresome."

"No," she said, blushing. "In fact, I'm sorry I said it. But I was angry. I wouldn't say it again because that would be cruel, and I suspect you then would constantly remind me that I had to buy a husband." She looked up at him. "Can we both agree that whatever happens, those are subjects we ought never to bring up again?"

"Agreed," he said. "What extremely dull-witted gentlemen were you talking about? Or did you just make that up?"

"I heard about the Viscount Wooton and his marriage to Miss Hadley."

"Oh. Yes. He's a simpleton; the poor lady probably didn't realize it."

"No, the *rich* lady. But she wasn't a 'lady' before she met him," Hannah murmured. "Which is why she married him. Of course she knows what she got. Who could not?"

"By the way," Ian said, "did you meet poor Lord Wooton, or any other prospective grooms? Or am I the first?"

"The first," she said. "At least, the first I've met. I was told that my father or his man of business must first recommend suitors for me."

"Your father's man of business met with Mr. Foster? And that was enough of a recommendation to your father?"

"Oh yes. He has excellent judgment. You're the only one they've asked me to see."

"I should be flattered."

"So you should," she said seriously.

"And you learned things about me?" he persisted. "Anything I should know about?"

"Everything you already know. You have an excellent service record, and would have stayed in the military if your father hadn't died and passed the title and its responsibilities on to you. That military record was a point in your favor. Many titled gentlemen are layabouts or fribbles. You are thought to be intelligent, devoted to your king, country, and family, and are generally well liked. You are respectable in your education, and your physical condition is good. Mr. Foster thought you a good-looking gentleman, or at least not one to repel a young woman."

"And you find this so too?"

She lowered her gaze and her voice. "As you saw; I was not repelled." Then she spoke with more spirit. "More important to both my father and Mr. Foster, your current state of finances isn't because of any vices on your part. There was nothing to dismay in anything they discovered about you. You were considered eminently suitable, if unfortunate in your present situation."

He nodded. Then he took a deep breath. "Well then, Miss Leeds, since you did agree to see me, and have reminded me of certain realities which I ought to have considered, do you want me to go down on one knee? I'm sorry, but I forgot a rose to present you with. I can't write poetry to read to you either. Isn't that the usual procedure?"

"I wouldn't know. I've never been proposed to," she said with a trace of sadness. "Is that what you're doing?"

"I believe I am. I'll marry you, promise of infants and all. What do you say, Miss Leeds? A wedding in the spring?"

"Yes," she said. "That would suit me."

"That would also give you time to reconsider," he said, "should you find fault with me or more delight in another."

"Not likely," she said. "But it will give you the same option as well."

"No. I'm a man of my word. So then, agreed?"

"Yes," she said.

"This," he said as he bent his head toward hers, "is expected as well, I believe."

He kissed her lips, lightly, fleetingly.

She felt a slight electrifying shock at the touch of his mouth, and her lips tingled as he moved away.

He only drew back, and smiled. "Done, then," he said.

The elder gentlemen were waiting with champagne when the couple came back into the house.

"Congratulations, my lord," Mr. Leeds said, handing Ian a glass.

"Well done, Miss Leeds," Foster said, handing Hannah one. "I don't think you'll ever regret this day's work."

"How did you know?" Hannah asked.

"By your expression, my dear," he said.

"I'm sorry your mother didn't survive to see this," her father said. "It was her greatest wish that her girls marry well. You must meet Hannah's sisters too," he told Ian. "And of course, I must put the notice in the papers."

"I've saved you the trouble, my lord," Mr. Foster said smugly. "I've already written it up and will send in the notice first thing in the morning. Then I suggest you introduce your fiancée to the *ton* as soon as you can."

"Where would you suggest we go?" Ian asked.

"A ball," Foster said thoughtfully, "a musicale, a dinner at a statesman's house, perhaps even the Palace itself; anywhere the elite are gathered."

"I'm no longer invited to such places," Ian said calmly.

"I'll wager you are," Foster said with a smug smile. "I'll wager the invitations are already piled high in your front hall. Well, in all honesty, I mustn't wager. I asked your valet. He says you've not even looked at them."

"It would be rude not to reciprocate," Ian said simply. "I was unable."

"Well, no fear of that now," Foster said merrily. "And see what happens after the engagement notice is placed in the papers. You'll have to wade through invitations to get into your house."

"Then I shall," Ian said. "Although the other truth is that I was uninterested. That will change if Miss Leeds wishes. I don't know if you'll care for the denizens of the *ton*," he told Hannah. "Nor do I much care if they care for you, any more than I cared if they approved of me. But if you want to see them, I'll show you the invitations and we'll go to wherever you please. I suggest we make an appearance and then move on. Cruel things may be said until the novelty of our arrangement wears off."

"*'Arrangement!'*" Mr. Leeds exclaimed. "Certainly there'll be gossip if you refer to your engagement to marry as such!"

Ian leveled a cool stare at his future father-in-law. "Mr. Leeds," he said, "my financial problems are well known. Your financial success will be equally known by the time we meet the people concerned. No matter how charming your daughter, there isn't a sane person who'll believe our arrangement to be anything but what it is. What you want for your daughter is acceptance in my world. That will take patience, familiarity, and time."

"Then why bother to go meet them at all?" Mr. Leeds demanded angrily.

"So Society can meet my future wife," Ian said. "And she, them. But there's no need for her to hang about, waiting for insult. It won't be within my hearing, of course. But I can't be at her elbow every second. After we're wed, there'll be less chance of it."

"You're saying they'll forget?" Hannah's father asked incredulously.

"Never," Ian said patiently. "Those who care about such things remember for generations. But as time passes, even they care less and it matters less."

Mr. Leeds pulled on his lower lip. "I don't

know," he said, looking at Hannah. "I expected snobbery, but this? Now I don't know if the whole idea makes any sense."

"Nothing has changed, Mr. Leeds!" Foster exclaimed. "His lordship is merely trying to be sure your daughter is protected from gossip."

Hannah looked at the marquis, and suddenly felt a pang of remorse for someone other than herself. Nothing showed in his expression, the man seemed made of stone. Although he maintained his calm demeanor, he did have human feelings. She'd detected strain in his manner toward her when they'd met, and had accepted that it was likely that he was uncomfortable. Certainly it must have been difficult for a man of his stripe to place himself on the marriage market for financial gain. But now, after he'd agreed to the marriage, to be openly reevaluated as to his ultimate worth as a husband? She didn't know how he restrained himself from turning and striding from her house without another word. He'd agreed to be part of the marriage market, not be cattle on the auction block.

"Papa," she said evenly. "If you don't approve of the marquis, I must tell you that I'm done with it. I'll no longer be available to any other gentleman of the *ton*."

"You love him?" her father asked in confusion.

She could feel her face growing warm. "Certainly not!" she snapped.

"Well, but you were always going on about love and such with me before you agreed to this," her father said, looking aggravated. "I could've made a suitable match for you years ago if love had nothing to do with it."

"I don't know the marquis," she said through clenched teeth. "How can I feel love for him? I agreed to come to London to let you make a match to your liking, so we could elevate the family. It was an uncomfortable idea for me. But I did it. I accepted the marquis. I tell you I can't go through this again. If you don't want me to marry him, then I'm well out of it. I'll go home and find my own match."

She tapped her foot, and waited for his answer as his face grew redder. She knew her answer didn't please him. He'd disapproved of Timothy, and had done, for years. That's why she and Timothy had to meet in secret. But he couldn't know that Timothy had sheared off. Just thinking of her handsome blue-eyed former suitor upset her. Hannah didn't have to pretend a reason to reach for a handkerchief. She sniffed, wiped her eyes, and then dared peer up at the marquis. He stood rigid, unmoving. He must feel absolutely humiliated now. She knew she did, for him. She didn't know whom she felt sorrier for, him or herself.

"I'll leave, then," Ian finally said. He bowed. "It was . . ." He hesitated. A half smile lifted a corner of his hard mouth. "It was interesting meeting you, Miss Leeds. Good day."

"Wait!" Hannah's father cried. "Don't leave. Forgive my manners. If she agrees, of course I do. Nothing wrong with you, my lord. Nothing to do with you at all. I had a momentary misgiving, but it wasn't on account of you. I just didn't want her shunned or insulted. When you have a daughter, I don't doubt you'll feel the same way about her. Please stay on. Foster here has drawn up the papers, all to do with financial matters. Why, the first payment has already been drawn against my bank. All that's needed is your signature. And your forgiveness," he added with an embarrassed smile.

Hannah saw the marquis take a long breath. Mr. Foster was red-faced, obviously holding his breath as well. For that matter, she thought, so was she.

The marquis's slate-colored eyes showed nothing. But a tiny muscle unclenched in his jaw. "Thank you," he said carefully. "Then if all is in order, I'll stay, and sign. But if you'll forgive me, I have another appointment and must leave soon after."

Ian left the Leeds's house at twilight. There had been a great many papers to sign. But it meant a great deal of money would come to him in order to pull together his estate again. In fact, there was enough to restore and invest too. The money would also help to ensure his brother might live to marry one day too. The rest would help Ian to clear his other properties and cleanse the Sutcombe name. He'd sell his soul for that. And perhaps, he thought, he had.

"Done," he told Baker when he returned to his rented rooms. He pulled off his jacket, stripped off his neckcloth and threw it on a chair. "Signed, sealed, and I think delivered, at least from my debtors. I'll be able to pay you your back wages tomorrow."

"Who is the lucky lass?" his valet asked as he picked up the jacket and the used neckcloth. "And what's she like, if you don't mind me asking."

Ian lifted his shoulders, but not in a shrug. He was rotating his neck now that it was freed of the binding starched cloth. "She's actually a pleasant creature," he said absently, as his hand went to the back of his neck and massaged it. "Not bad to look at and intelligent. Well spoken, sensible, quiet and reserved. I was in luck. She's marrying to suit her father, so it's clear she's an obedient female too. That was a relief. You ought to have seen the gorgons that Foster made me meet first!"

Baker chuckled. "An old horse trader, is he?"

"You'd think so," Ian said. "But he needn't have bothered. The future Lady Sutcombe isn't bad at all, and not just in comparison to the others. I think we'll rub on together very well. It could have been far worse."

"And the father?"

"Rich as Croesus. And not a bad sort either," Ian said, rising and going over to a sideboard, lifting a decanter and pouring himself a healthy jot of tawny liquid. He drank it down, and grimaced, looking at the glass. "Not the best Scotland has ever produced," he said, "but better days are coming, Baker, be sure of that."

"Congratulations, my lord."

"Come to think on it, pour yourself some too," Ian said, offering the decanter to his man. "You've put up with a lot. Turfed out a lot of clamoring shopkeepers and mortgage holders and yet kept your insolvent employer looking civilized all the while."

"Thank you, my lord, I'll have a swallow of that Scotch gold with you, to toast your success and future happiness. As to putting up with things, I'm happy to have done it."

Baker poured himself a glass. He raised it to his employer. "To better days," he said.

Ian drank to that, and then flung himself down in a comfortable old chair. He laid his head against the back of the chair and closed his eyes.

"I'm staying in tonight," he said. "See what you can get us for dinner, will you?"

Baker bowed, and left the room.

Of course he was staying in, Ian thought. Some things couldn't change yet. He hadn't the funds to visit a club, or a gaming Hell, or even a pub. Which was, he reflected, just as well. He didn't enjoy gambling, and a club or a pub weren't amusing places to pass an evening if you had no friends with you. Poverty had cost him all his old friendships. Or if it hadn't, then it was his pride that had done it. In future, he thought, it might do the same. Because it would soon be widely known that he'd sold his name, and married a commoner.

That was a thing he'd thought he'd never be capable of. If he'd been in comfortable circumstances, he wondered what he'd have thought of a friend who'd done the same. He grimaced. That was bad enough. Pray God, he thought, that he hadn't sold far more. He rose, and went back to pour himself another glass. He knew he was being ungrateful. He knew he was lucky.

He just wished he felt it.

Chapter 5

They went for walks and drives. They took tea together, and sometimes dinner. After a week, Hannah was sure of three things: her fiancé had excellent table manners, could discourse pleasantly on every topic she could bring up, and had a light hand on the reins. The rest, if there was any more, went unsaid and undone.

He was so well bred and controlled it was hard to discover what he really felt. So she watched his eyes. They responded to her even when his only comments were calm and polite congratulations on how well she looked. His eyes told her more. He was attracted to her, she'd bet on that. But when he said good night his lips were cool on hers. He either had great control or not much fire in his belly, at least, as concerned her. Tonight, she wanted more. No, she needed it.

"We're going home," Hannah announced.

Even in the darkened interior of the coach, she saw her fiancé tilt his head to the side.

"Right now?" he asked.

"Of course not," she said, smiling at the nonsense of his question. Even her father, sitting in the carriage opposite them, chuckled. They were on their way to the opera. "We'll go as soon as you can accompany us," she went on as they drove through London's dark streets. "The thing is that Father decided that it would be best for you to meet the family before I make my formal appearance in London Society. We'll go home and then my family can come back with us."

"That way," her father said eagerly, "when she makes her formal bows to London Society, we can all be there at her side, so she won't be so uneasy."

Ian was silent for a portentous moment.

It was strange how the man's silences were often as commanding as other men's voices, Hannah thought. *The man she was promised to marry*, she corrected herself.

"Oh!" she exclaimed as though stung, sitting up straight. "That is to say, we will, if you don't mind." Bad enough he was being forced to marry by circumstances, she didn't want him thinking she and her father now had the ordering of his life. No wonder he'd grown so still!

"But Society will see Hannah tonight," Ian told her father. "Although," he went on thoughtfully, "I can try to ensure that tonight they'll *only* see her. I'll make sure she won't be subjected to anything but speculation. We won't stop to speak to anyone, and we won't have to. Speculation may actually work for us; they'll be that much more eager to meet her. An excellent suggestion, Mr. Leeds."

Hannah relaxed. He hadn't been brooding about what she'd thought had bothered him. "I hope you don't think we're being high-handed in asking you to leave London and come with us," she added. "We just thought it would be for the best that you meet my sisters."

"I don't doubt it," he said. He wore no expression, or at least none Hannah could see in the flickering flare of the carriage lamp as he pointedly turned his head to gaze out the window at the blackness of the night.

Hannah sighed. Of course he'd agreed; he had to. The man had been purchased, like a silver candlestick. He must resent that, and so her as well, she thought. Although he'd been unfailingly polite to her in the week since he'd signed the betrothal agreement, he hadn't been anything else, at least, not to her. Not loving, or flattering, or eager to extend their goodnight kiss. What could she do? And since she'd known what she was doing, as had he, why should she do anything?

Because it will be hellish living with a polite stranger for the rest of your life, she silently answered herself.

Still, what had she expected? And why did it

bother her so much now when she'd been content to go through with the soulless arrangement in the first place?

She knew too well. After she'd exposed her body and her soul to Timothy, and he had rejected her, she'd felt so scorned and humiliated she'd thought she'd die of it. She'd felt she could never love again. That hadn't changed. But now she also felt great empathy with the man she'd soon marry. She wondered how such an aristocratic fellow as the marquis kept his dignity in light of the circumstances, and admired him for it. Or was it that he had no problems because he had no dignity beyond that which every nobleman must show?

Hannah was glad for the coach's interior darkness. She didn't want anyone seeing her face. She was no longer sure of her decision. Making a decision in the full flush of first mortification was very different from trying to live with it when your emotions calmed down. The marquis's insolvency and debt, however, were authentic and constant things. He had no choice but to do as he'd done, or else lose what little else he had. Was her reason to marry and her resolve as real and steady as his? Should it be?

She could still shear off. Her father had enough money to be generous; he could afford to settle the matter by offering the marquis funds to placate him. Still, if she did renege, what would she do? She felt as numb as she'd been after Timothy had left her, though it was true that London had diverted her. But she'd discovered that dealing with a live fiancé was far different than agreeing to marry one just because she wanted to leave her home and feel no more pain. Plus there was the fact that even on short acquaintance, she'd begun to respect Ian Sutcombe. He was a pleasant companion and seemed a decent fellow. Would that be enough for her? Fortunately, she'd months to decide.

In the meanwhile, she'd made sure he'd nothing to be ashamed of in her but her name and lineage. If she found he thought there was anything else, she'd end the farce of their proposed marriage before it became a fact. She wouldn't be insulted again, and ending this engagement wouldn't distress her. She'd gone somewhere in her heart that was beyond such trivial hurt.

Hannah smoothed her gloves and looked down at herself with pride. At least she looked the part she was playing; she looked as if she deserved a titled husband. Tonight she wore a new blue cape. Beneath she had on a long-sleeved, low-necked dark rose-colored gown sashed high under her breasts, and a string of pearls around her neck. She wore no tiara or flowers in her hair, but a filmy net dotted with tiny pearls glowed in her welter of curls. Her father had stared at her when she'd come down the stair. She didn't blame him. It was astonishing even to herself; doubly so be-

cause of how interested she'd become in fashion
since she'd got to London and met her fiancé.

Tonight, he was elegant in black and white.
The only color that showed was in a small pearl
stickpin in his neckcloth, and the gold pattern in
his black waistcoat, and of course, the dark gold
curls beneath his high beaver hat. He looked, as
ever, correct and formidable. But now he was
also dressed in the latest style and his clothing
was clearly expensive and new, making it equally
clear to her that part of the settlement her father
had made on him had already been used to good
effect.

She kept as silent as he was and waited for the
coach to deliver them to the opera house. She
hoped her father would say nothing more. He'd
always been gregarious, but had begun to posi-
tively prattle these days. She was silent because of
her nerves. Perhaps her father was reacting in the
opposite way, so overwhelmed by his prospective
son-in-law that it made him gabble.

The marquis exited first, and held out a hand
for Hannah. She stepped out of the coach and into
her new world. She'd never been to the London
Opera, and had never seen such a terrifyingly
well-dressed crowd as now was streaming into
the ornate opera house. Her father stepped out
too, and for once, was absolutely silent with
awe.

The men wore high hats and black cloaks. The

women shone out from among them, some with huge egret plumes rising from their high-dressed hair, some with lavish jeweled tiaras and combs adorning theirs.

Ian took Hannah's arm, placed it on his, and walked into the thick of the crowd. Her father followed. No one seemed to notice them as they hurried into the theater to take their seats.

But once Hannah had removed her cape and settled into her chair, high up in a red trimmed box to the side of the theater, she at last had a chance to relax, and look down—into a sea of uplifted faces that all seemed to be staring back at her.

She shrank back into her seat, blinded by the sparkling crowd.

"They're staring at everyone," Ian remarked. "From the benches to the boxes. It's why they come here. Some listen to the music. Most disregard it. Some sleep. The *company's* the thing here, not the opera company. Lift your chin and smile. Isn't that why you came here?"

"I came because you asked me to," she whispered.

"I was the one who wanted you here," her father said quickly. "I thought it would be a good place for you to take your place amongst these people. After all, they're going to be your people."

Hannah turned to Ian. "You don't like the opera?"

"Not very much," he said. "But your father is correct. Once we're married it will be your right to attend."

"They're hard tickets to get," her father put in with obvious relish. "And a box like this! Only a marquis could get such, I'm told." He breathed, staring down at the faces staring up at them.

"Actually," Ian said, "only a duke. An old friend of the family."

Soon, but not soon enough for Hannah, the opera began. She sat still, feeling foolish for thinking herself well dressed. True, she'd never dress as elaborately as any of the dowagers she'd seen, or as plainly as any of the young misses in their white, similarly boring gowns. But she boasted no feathers or tiara. And she was too old to wear or to look charming in pure white. So what exactly was she now?

She watched. Some stout people in garish masquerade costumes took the stage and began to howl at each other. She frowned and tried to concentrate on what language they were using so she might get a glimmer of what they were saying.

She felt a warm breath on her ear. "You don't like opera either?" her fiancé said softly as he leaned toward her.

She startled. Then she quickly calmed herself and answered in an even lower whisper. "I don't know. I've never seen it before. Is that a shameful thing to admit? We get some theater from the touring companies that stop near home, and that's great fun. But no opera. Does that appall you?"

He chuckled. "It's an acquired taste. I've never acquired it. Neither have half the people here. But it's a place to be seen and to see, so they're all here."

"What are they singing about?" she whispered.

Again, that rich chuckle against her ear. "I've no idea."

"At least," she said in a small voice, "can you tell me what language they're singing in?"

He shrugged. "It hardly matters. Most of the singers are foreign and so even if they sang in English you wouldn't understand it. That's not the point. I'm not sure what the point is."

The point, she thought, is that I'm perishing to ask about that wonderful scent you use. You smell like lemon and ferns and the forest at home. She sighed, and used that sigh to say instead, "I fear this is lost on me."

He patted her hand. "Good, I'd hate for you to insist on dragging me to the opera for the rest of our lives."

"But it's not a true test," she quickly added. "I'm too overwhelmed by this place and the people here to pay attention."

"Relax," he said softly, "the lights are only on the stage now."

"Yes. But I don't want to call attention to myself."

"So shy?" he asked, amused.

"No, I feel like a fish out of water."

"Then join me here on the beach," he said.

She suppressed giggles. But this was going to be her natural place, she reminded herself, and all thoughts of levity fled. She stole a glance at her father. He was watching everything on stage and in the audience, and there seemed to be a permanent smile of vast content on his face.

She sighed again. "Even so," she whispered to Ian, "I don't think this is going to be one of my favorite pastimes."

"Thank God," Ian said, a smile in his voice.

Then he sat back. She felt both abandoned and relieved. Close proximity to her fiancé seemed to muddle her thoughts.

Hannah braced herself at intermission when the lights in the house came up again.

"This is the time when the audience promenades to get a closer look at the others here," Ian said. "We'll forgo that, so you can dazzle them another time. Feel better?"

"Much," she said, and then glanced over to her father. He looked crestfallen."

"Should you like to stretch your legs, Mr. Leeds?" Ian asked. "This is a private box. I'll leave orders that no one is to enter until we return.

Footmen here make their livings guarding these boxes," he explained.

"I'd love to," Hannah's father said, rising from his chair.

Ian handed Hannah a paper. "Here's a program of the night's entertainment," he told her. "It will confuse you even more. But I expect you to have it memorized by the time we return."

She smiled as he opened the door and left the box with her father.

Ian had a word with a nearby footman, slipped some coins into his hand, and waited until the man took up a station, standing cross-armed in front of the box they'd just left.

"I'm sorry your daughter can't stroll with us," he told Mr. Leeds as they walked away. "But soon enough, she will. Although I don't know that she'll ever enjoy it."

"She'll enjoy whatever she deems proper," his future father-in-law said quickly.

They hadn't taken two steps before they heard someone coming up behind them. "Wait!" Hannah said breathlessly. "I'd rather be with you than be alone, whatever happens. Once you left, I swear I thought everyone below was staring at me, and when they began to leave their seats I thought they were planning to come up and greet me. May I come with you? Because if anyone does accost me, at least you'll know what to say."

Ian frowned.

Hannah's eyes opened wide. Was he protecting her, or ashamed of her?

"She's right," Ian said to her father. He offered her his arm. "Of course. Forgive me. I should have thought of that."

They strolled on. The halls were so crowded they decided not to go down the long staircase. Instead, they stood by the railing in silence, watching hordes of opera-goers ascending and descending the staircases.

"Ho!" a voice called. "As I live and barely breathe! It's Sutcombe!"

They turned to see a beaming, fattish young man trailing a group of lively-looking people.

Ian bowed. "So it is, Rathborne. How have you been?"

"I?" asked the young man, as though astonished. "I'm always the same. But look at you! Togged out to beat the devil. I'm glad to see your fortunes have changed. Friends, here is the brave Major Sutcombe, late of His Majesty's fourteenth. You know Dollard, Pickens, Fezel, and Lady Fezel, my lord? Well, here they are. And this is my wife, Lady Rathborne, and my mama and her sister, Lady Ogilvy, all of us out for a night on the town. And this is?" He was staring fixedly at Hannah and her father.

"Mr. Leeds, Hannah," Ian said smoothly. "May I present George Rathborne, his friends and family? George, here is my fiancée, Hannah Leeds, and her father, Wallace Leeds."

"I saw it in the *Times*," an older lady said. She raised her lorgnette to stare at Hannah. "The Sussex Leeds?"

"The Northampton Leeds," Ian said smoothly.

"You getting married, Sutcombe?" George asked. "This *is* news. I don't read much. Congratulations."

"News, indeed," one of the women behind him murmured loudly enough to be heard over the general din. "Never heard of the Northampton Leeds."

"Pulling our legs," George's mother answered in the shrill voice of a deaf woman. "Northampton Leeds, my foot! The father must be well greased, I'd say. Everyone knows Sutcombe hasn't a penny piece to his name."

Ian bowed. "We'll take our leave now. Good evening." He turned his back and walked Hannah and her father back the way they'd come. But they could still hear the muttering behind them.

"Now you've gone and insulted them," George was saying in annoyance as Ian and his party moved away.

"*Mushrooms,*" the old lady said with a sniff. "There's no insulting them. The girl's papa's obviously got funds. She ain't no raving beauty, and we never heard of her. Sutcombe's fallen into gravy. Good for him."

"They're fools," Ian told Hannah, and her father continued on. "I apologize *for* them."

"They can't truly be friends of yours," Hannah exclaimed.

Ian's smile was tight. "They believe they are. That's how they react to anyone they don't know, and don't fear. They have no manners because they were brought up to believe they can afford not to have them."

"But you have manners," Hannah protested.

He inclined his head, as though in thanks, and said nothing.

Hannah ducked her own head, and realized her mistake. He might only have manners because he couldn't afford not to, at least, not yet.

"They just have to get used to us," her father said heavily. "I mean, get used to you, Nan, of course. I've been around some and I've found that money is a great equalizer. Don't you think so, my lord?" he asked Ian.

Ian smiled. "I have found it so," he said.

Hannah's father looked pleased. But Hannah winced. It was the kind of answer that was no answer. Unless, of course, her fiancé meant that he had found her money to be acceptable enough for him to get used to her.

She didn't try to understand the opera when it started again. Instead, she considered what had happened in the corridor and puzzled over how it might influence her future, and if it had hurt the marquis's feelings, if he had any. But then, she finally realized, letting it go, the marquis was no worse off than she was. Because she was marrying for convenience, at least her family's convenience as well.

After the opera ended, they waited in the shadows of their box until the crush of the audiences' exit was over. Hannah felt that they were skulking, but there was no help for it. She didn't want to face any of her fiancé's so-called friends again. She didn't know if she could hold her tongue if she did. But when the corridors were empty, they left the Opera House.

Their ride home was done in a thoughtful silence until Ian finally spoke. "I apologize again for my acquaintances," he said softly. "You're right, Hannah. I can no longer call them 'friends,' of course."

"Do you really think familiarity will make it easier for them, and for us, my lord?"

"They say familiarity breeds contempt," Ian said. "But in this case, it will breed content. My class of people always fear the new."

"Ah, here we are," Wallace Leeds said with relief. "Home again."

They left the coach and entered the town house as a footman opened the door for them.

"Care to come in and join me in something warming, my lord?" Wallace asked.

"At any other time, I'd say yes," Ian said. "But not

this evening. I think I must speak with Hannah, alone. May I have your permission?"

"Of course, of course," Wallace said as he motioned for the footman to leave the hallway. "But only a few minutes, mind. Don't want more gossip, do we?" he joked.

"Good night," Ian told him, and waited for his footsteps to die away. He looked down at Hannah. "I'm sorry," he told her simply. "I'll see it never happens again."

She shook her head. "It wasn't all bad. Because it made me think," she said, looking up at the hard expression on his face. "You'll receive as much insult as I do, won't you? Are you still sure, my lord, that this arrangement really suits you?"

"I may have lost my money," he said, reaching out to touch a curl on her cheek. "But not my wits. We'll get past this. You have to harden your heart, Hannah. Still sure this is what *you* want?"

"I am."

"You still wish to marry me?"

"I do," she said.

"Well said," he said with a smile, and lowered his head to hers. "Remember that phrase please." He kissed her lightly on her lips.

She felt her mouth tingle at his brief touch. She might not know or understand him, but it seemed to her that her body was reacting to him beautifully.

"Good night," he said again, bowed, and left her.

"Well," her father said, as she entered the salon. "All is well?"

"Yes," she said slowly.

His expression grew troubled. "Look you, Nan," he said. "He's a good fellow, or so I think. And you seemed willing enough. But you've been as close as a clam, and just about as warm as one too, come to think of it, since you met him. Since you left home, in fact. It isn't like you, my dear." He sighed. "You seemed to be languishing; I thought this marriage would be a cure. But now I realize that marriage is never that. Sometimes it only makes matters worse. I don't want you to find yourself lost in regret. It isn't too late. We can still call the thing off, and I won't make the fellow give back a penny. I only gave him a taste, so to speak, anyway, so he could take care of pressing matters until you were wed. So tell me. Are you marrying just to be able to forget . . . someone else?"

She lowered her gaze, wondering how much he knew about her dreams of marrying Timothy. She thought their rendezvous had been secret, but she should have known it was well nigh impossible to keep secrets in her family. Her sisters were always covertly watching her. It was the price of being the eldest.

She looked up at her father seriously. "You can never forget anyone you never really knew," she said with a smile that was a little askew. "But I don't want to spend my life trying to remember.

The marquis seems a little stiff and a bit rigid, true. But he can be charming, and I detect a keen sense of humor. He is careful, though, I admit that. I think it's the weight of his position. And I believe he feels his financial position keenly. I admire him for not wanting to appear to be a beggar. If he spent his time flattering me, I'd worry. Anyway, we're not marrying until spring, and here it is only September. I'll have time to think about it. Don't worry."

Ian worried as he walked to his rooms. He'd planned to move to better quarters soon. But now he thought that maybe the best thing to do would be to marry sooner. Either way, he'd have to avoid certain idiotic acquaintances until after the wedding. And he'd have to make sure that his wife went out into Society as infrequently as possible. Her father might want her to make a splash. But Ian began to think if she did, she'd drown. It was a good thing that they were all going to go to their home in the countryside. It couldn't be soon enough to suit him.

"Good evening, milord," Baker said as Ian came into his rented rooms. "How did it go?"

"Not well," Ian said, letting his man help him out of his tight fitted jacket. "My intended's feelings were hurt by some idiots in the exalted rank of fools that her father wants her to please. Remember Georgie Rathborne? He was there with his friends and some old witches from his family. They're the sort that whisper at the top of their lungs because they don't think it matters what they say, or care if anyone is hurt by it. Miss Leeds was. She's used to being well thought of in her own world. I think that's why she's such a timid little thing here in London," he said as he raised his chin and stripped off his neckcloth.

"And that's bad?" Baker asked.

"For her," Ian said. "She'll never cause me any trouble. But if she remains a meek little mouse, the cats will eat her alive."

"Rethinking the matter?" Baker asked, pausing with the discarded neckcloth in his hand.

"No. I'm actually very lucky. She suits me, at least in my present circumstances," Ian said. He paused. If he sometimes thought of the lovely graceful females he'd seen in the old days at house parties and fetes he'd once been welcomed at when he was young, before all his wealth had gone, he suppressed those thoughts. There had been no particular one. He'd since learned that the world was filled with beautiful, poised females. He'd never be able to wed one of rank, he'd accepted that long since.

He realized Baker was waiting for him to continue.

"She never uses the fact of her money to lord it over me, or pushes herself forward," Ian went on. "She'll be agreeable and easy to deal with. I have to introduce her and her family to the *ton* after we marry, but that's easily done. We're going to her home in the countryside soon. I expect tonight's debacle will make it even sooner. I never said we had to stay on in London after we marry. And so I'm thinking the sooner this wedding is over with, the better for everyone.

"Baker, we have to find masons, roofers, and gentlemen who decorate. The sooner my estate, Hopewell Hall, is ready for us to move into, the better off we'll all be. We'll marry and she'll be able to settle down into a quiet country life, such as she's used to. The landed gentry there are kinder than the cream of Society here. She won't be afraid of the people in the countryside. And I won't have to watch my every step in Town."

Chapter 6

"**Y**ou're the slyest thing in nature, I can't believe I was actually feeling sorry for you," Jessica Leeds said as she threw herself across her sister's bed.

Her sister Anthea was already there. She lay back and stretched her arms out the ceiling. "*So* distinguished," she said on a theatrical sigh. "*So* well bred, and with a title too. He may look a bit craggy, but *so* masculine. He is a bit stiff, but his voice! Like warm gravy. I don't care if he cost more than my dowry, I *so* envy you, Nan. Lucky, lucky girl. Don't you just love him?"

"No, dear, that's the point," Hannah said, looking down at her two sisters with fond amusement. They were at her country home. She was always comfortable here, and now, seeing her home through the marquis's eyes, she was newly pleased by how prosperous the place looked. There was nothing for her to be ashamed of. Her family mightn't be titled, but clearly, they were well educated, well to do, and had taste.

Her sisters had met the marquis, and now that he was resting before dinner, they were discussing him in Hannah's bedchamber. Hannah smiled as she looked at them. Anthea was the youngest, and at seventeen still had some puppy plumpness about her. She was blond and merry, and would one day be, if not beautiful, then charming and bubbly enough for any man. But her father didn't want her marrying just any man.

Jessica was dark and sensible, but also loving, with a strong sense of honesty and loyalty that made her sisters worry for her. She was nineteen, ready to wed. That was the problem. She attracted suitors without trying, and her father didn't want her giving her word, hand, or body to any man except in wedlock, and then only to one of exalted rank.

That was why he was so eager for Hannah to marry the marquis. It would open doors for the girls. It suited Hannah now that she'd given up her own dream, because it would also close the door on any future pain of love for her.

"He is unfailingly polite," Anthea said. "And yet how dreadful it must be to have been sold into wedlock."

"Why, yes," Hannah said dryly. "How extra dreadful considering the ghastly female who bought him."

Anthea sat bolt upright. "I didn't mean that! . . . Oh, you know it," she said, waving a hand as she sank back down to the bed again. "It's just that it must be humiliating for a man of his stature to have been brought so low. Had he been disappointed in love too?"

Now Hannah stood stock-still. "I was *not* disappointed in love," she said.

"Of course not," Jessica said, looking knowingly at Anthea.

"As for the marquis, well, I don't know if he ever loved another," Hannah said. "Or even if he still has a care for someone. It's a good and fair question," she added, looking pensive. *And one I should ask before we go any further,* she thought. The thought made her uneasy. As if she were taking advantage of him, which was ridiculous. He was the winner in this. Or was he? How dreadful if he loved where he could not because he had no money. If that were so, she'd be cuckolded the minute he stepped away from the altar.

"I hope it doesn't turn out to be true," Jessica said anxiously.

"Because if so, knowing your pride, you'll send him away and Papa will murder you," Anthea muttered. "It wouldn't matter to me if I were you," she told Hannah dramatically. "I'd *make* him love me."

"Oh good," Hannah said sourly. "Just what I

always wanted to do. Capture a husband, swear him to marriage, and force him to love me."

"There!" Anthea cried, sitting bolt upright. "There! I just saw a flash of the old Nan again. You've been squashed flat for so long I almost forgot that mischievous look in your eyes. Oh, Nan, where have you been? Is it because of this forced marriage? Then, don't worry, best of sisters. If you don't want him, *I'll* take him!"

Jessica laughed, and though she tried not to do it, soon Hannah was laughing too. Anthea looked highly offended, and then began to giggle.

"Well, he is something to see," Anthea said. "A bolt of lightning in my dull life, at least."

"The point is," Jessica said soberly, "does our sister want or need anything so dramatic in her life? You're young yet, Nan. Or, relatively so at least. You don't have to decide just yet. Why not let some time go by?"

"And how would he feel if I told him that?" Hannah asked. "Poor fellow, now that he's beginning to plan his future again, what would happen to him if I were to suddenly draw back and land him in the suds once more? I can't do it. It wouldn't be kind or fair. In fact, it would be downright mean, and whatever I am, I'm not that."

"Now I feel better," Jessica said triumphantly. "You're not entirely uninvolved, are you? Because no matter how mopish you've been acting since Timothy-the-wretch left you, you're no angel, sister dear. If you were unhappy with your wedding plans, you'd renounce Apollo himself."

"I don't know how I feel anymore," Hannah said on a sigh as she plumped herself down on her bed. "I only know that I set this thing in motion, and I think I should let it spin on."

"Hoorah!" Anthea cried. "Now find me someone just like him!"

Hannah laughed. "Now, shoo," she told them. "I want to rest and then dress for dinner. And I want you to as well. We may be country girls, but it's time to show him that we do know fashion. And," she said with that same mischievous light in her eyes, "I have something to tell you at dinner."

"*No!*" Anthea breathed. "You're not! Is that why you're marrying him? Is the babe his? Or did that wretch Timothy leave you with more than a broken heart? Oh, now so much of this hurry-scurry engagement makes sense. Now I feel sorry for both you and the marquis."

Hannah leapt from the bed. "How dare you!" she cried. "No, and no, and no! And you should be put over Papa's knee for even thinking such a thing." She stopped, looking aghast. "Is anyone else saying such a thing? Is it a rumor around here?"

"No, and no, and no," Jessica said, rising and putting her arms around Hannah. "No one but your idiotic sister was even thinking that. Pay no mind to Anthea. She's always been fanciful, and," she added, turning her head to glower at the luckless Anthea, "never knows when to close her mouth. I didn't hear such a rumor. And I will personally slay Anthea if she ever says such a thing again. Anyway," she went on, looking into Hannah's eyes again, "I know you too well. You'd never do such a thing. I'm not saying you'd never lose yourself in passion, which is why I so very much disliked Timothy, because he wasn't worthy of you. But I know you'd never burden an innocent man with such a scheme."

She hesitated. "But now that it's been brought up . . . if such a thing happened, and was going to happen, with the marquis's knowledge, I'm not sure it would be a good thing for either of you. I know it's done, but—"

She never got to finish her sentence.

Hannah pulled away from her. "It didn't happen. In fact, to be sure there isn't anyone doltish or evil-minded enough to think so, we aren't being married until the spring. Because if I were in such dire straits I'd be waddling down the aisle by then. Oh," she said wearily, "go away." She waved a hand. "I'm all out of patience with the both of you. I expect I'll have forgiven you by dinner. Just go now."

"We will," Jessica said, hauling her sister up by her arm. "And we do know you. Which is why we worry so much about you."

As do I, Hannah thought as her sisters scurried out of her room.

* * *

Hannah took great care dressing for dinner and was pleased to see that her sisters had done the same. She wore a simple but elegant rose-colored gown that she'd had made for her in London. The modiste had assured her the cut and color lent color to her face, and brightened her looks. It did more. It ought to widen Ian's eyes. She'd never worn a neckline so low. It looked rather well, she thought smugly, falling as it did in a straight column from under her high breasts, down to her slippers. Still, as always, she felt she couldn't compete with the vivid beauty of her sisters. Their gowns came from the local seamstress, and even so, they looked charming.

Jessica had on a soft yellow gown that contrasted with her dark good looks, and Anthea's peach-colored frock complemented her fair hair and complexion. They looked like fresh spring flowers that chill autumn evening. Even their father, dressed as he usually was in the countryside, wore his best—or at least his cleanest shirt, waistcoat, breeches, and jacket.

But their guest overshadowed them all, even in his casual attire.

He wore no high crisp white neckcloth; instead, his strong neck was covered with a softly folded one. In his dark blue jacket and dun breeches, he looked both casual and correct. And, to judge by Jessica and Anthea's widened eyes, he also looked

magnificent. He'd surely be the most elegant male
to ever share their dinner table, Hannah thought.
She couldn't feel guilty about thinking that, because she couldn't compare him to Timothy. Timothy had never been invited to break bread with
them, nor would he ever have been. That realiza-
tion turned her moment of surprised pleasure
into forlorn memory. Timothy had rejected her.
Since then, her every attempt at seductive splendor turned to mockery in her mind.

"Good evening," Ian said, rising from his chair
as his host's daughters entered the salon, but hesi-
tating as he saw the look in Hannah's eyes grow
suddenly bleak. "Is all well?" he asked her at
once.

She startled. "Oh! Yes. I suppose I was just thinking about the weather," she invented quickly. "It
looks like rain. And here I was looking forward to
showing you our village tomorrow."

"If not tomorrow, then surely he can see it the
next day," his host said. "That is, unless you're set
on leaving immediately?"

"*Leaving?*" Hannah asked as she sat down near
the hearth, and accepted a glass of wine from her
fiancé. Had the marquis changed his mind? Then
she was safe. Or lost. She didn't know exactly
what she felt as she raised her face to his. The first
time she'd been rejected as a possible wife had
been a calamity. This time she had the uneasy
thought that it might hurt even more.

"Aye," her father said. "Sorry to say, but he's got the right of it. The bad weather will be setting in soon, and the marquis wants to get his house in order before your wedding in the spring."

"*Literally* in order," Ian said as he stood before the hearth and looked down at Hannah. "The place, as you may have imagined, is a shambles. It's not just a question of suitable furnishings being missing. The structure of the Hall itself must be mended before it is livable again. There are missing tiles and rot in some of the roofing, there are windows to be fixed and basic carpentry everywhere that must be mended. And that's not even mentioning the peeling paint and paper that must be scraped away and redone."

"Oh," Hannah said, raising her eyes to his. "So I'll be going too?"

"Oh, no," he said.

"I thought I might have a say as to the colors and modes," she said, sitting up straight. "I can bring my sisters as chaperones. . . ." She heard their surprised murmurs of delight, and added, "I suppose not. Of course they're too young. But I can find a worthy chaperone soon enough."

"No doubt," he said with a faint smile. "But no need. Not now. When I'm done with the repairs, I want you to come and have a hand in it. Or if I do it and it's not to your liking, it can always be redone. Just let me know your favorite colors."

Hannah tried to keep from frowning. Of course

he didn't know her favorite colors, flowers, or scents. They never talked about such things. They were to be companions in life, but they weren't lovers who asked each other about such simple, silly, important things. Timothy had loved the color red, and didn't pay much attention to flowers, but loved it when she wore attar of roses.

"I like soft, bright shades," she said dreamily. "Springtime shades of yellow, pink, gold and green. And the blue of the sky."

"I'll remember. But I'm not just talking about design and color here," the marquis was saying. "There are holes in floors and walls, damage from the wainscoting to the eaves. There's masonry work to do, stonecutting, brickwork, in fact, right now the mice have more of a say about my home than you or I do. There's no place I'd feel safe for you to sit or sleep but the local inn, and that's miles away. Never fear, when the Hall is clean and solid again, I promise I'll send for you, and as I said, you can have your pick of furniture and draperies, and such, if you don't care for what I've done. I'm just going to put it back the way it was before I bring you to my home. Then I'll be happy to turn you loose on the project of making it more to your liking."

"I see," Hannah said softly.

"But she *wants* to go," Anthea said.

Ian raised an eyebrow.

Hannah laughed, and relaxed. "Anthea speaks true. I do want to go. I'm not a pampered lady," she added, and winced, instantly sorry to be reminding him of her lack of noble ancestry again. "I'm itching to see the place, and seeing it remade might be exciting."

"Exciting?" Ian asked quizzically. "You do remember we're doing this all autumn and into winter . . . in spite of possible snow and storm? And that the Hall isn't far from the sea? That's probably how it got tumbled down so quickly. It has to be kept up. The salt air and wind take a toll. If you insist, I'll take you. But I'd rather you stayed safe and warm until our wedding in the spring."

She opened her mouth, and closed it again.

"You know?" Ian said, "I think you and I should walk before dinner. Can you get a wrap? I find a stroll before dinner does wonders for the appetite."

"Yes!" Hannah said, bouncing up from her chair. "A fine idea."

"I'll get my wrap too!" Anthea cried.

Hannah wheeled around. "That you won't. I mean, I'd rather just walk with the marquis."

"Anthea, use some discretion," her father said. "Let them have a moment or two to talk alone."

"Oh," Anthea said, looking crushed.

"*Oh*, indeed," Jessica said. "They haven't had a second alone together since he arrived."

"But it's not as if they're in love or anything like that—" Whatever else Anthea was about to say was suddenly cut off as she put her hand over her lips. Her eyes grew big.

"We'll be back before dinner," Hannah said quickly, taking Ian's proffered arm and leaving the room with him.

They walked out into the fresh air, took the front stair in silence, and moved along the circular gravel drive that led from the house. It was late afternoon, and the autumn sunset hadn't dimmed the light so much that they couldn't see at all.

"She was right," Ian finally said. "It isn't as if we were lovers longing to see each other. But you're obviously angry. Did you want me to pretend we were?"

"No," Hannah said, shaking her lowered head. "Our arrangement is no secret to my family. Anthea's just young. Anyone else would have understood that two persons about to get married do have things to discuss in private even if it isn't snuggling and cooing they're after."

"What a relief!" he said. "I'm not sure I could muster a 'coo.' Never done one, you see."

She smiled, and looked up at him. "The thing is that I would like to come with you to Hopewell Hall. It sounds like you'll have to pass a lot of time there overseeing the work. Winter's coming. You might not be back until our wedding in the spring." She took a deep breath, stopped and looked up at him. "That way, I really will be marrying a stranger. I'd hoped to know you better by the time we actually were married."

"Ah, I see," he said lightly. "That's sensible. But since we aren't marrying for love, there's also the possibility that as you came to know me better you'd change your mind and call the whole thing off. I didn't think of that when I made my plans, but now I'm entertaining the notion. Hannah," he said seriously, stopping to look at her, "there's a real and pressing reason for my wanting to marry you, I've never denied it. I need money. I thought you wanted a titled husband for your family's sake. It surprised me, but I gladly accepted that reason as a suitable one. Should I have?

"You're attractive and educated," he went on. "You're a very marriageable young woman, in fact. You have no reason to marry for anything less than your heart's desire. I think you may have accepted this plan when your feelings were freshly wounded. That would have been a bad decision on your part. My fault was when I eagerly accepted what obviously couldn't be true. Hannah, if it's love you're looking for, after all, I can't say I can ever give you that. I don't know. I can and will provide you with loyalty, kindness, and care. But if in your innermost heart you're still looking for a lover to marry, you've made a serious mistake. I won't blame you and will, of course, let you end this whole matter without recrimination."

He stood straight and still. She couldn't make out his exact expression in the growing gloom. But he wasn't frowning. Again, she was struck by his absolute composure, his utter control. Here he was, talking about the possibility of ending their bargain, and so, surely, his plans for the future. His whole life could be altered in the next moments, and yet nothing in his voice or affect suggested it.

"I haven't changed my mind," she said.

"Perhaps you should," he said in a calm flat voice.

She searched for words, wondering why she didn't accept his generous offer and let the arrangement be broken. Now, here, at her home again, she realized the full absurdity of agreeing to marry a stranger, especially when she'd still been feeling baffled, hurt, and enraged by Timothy's strange desertion. Worse, now she realized she might have agreed to this marriage to show a man she'd likely never see again that someone worthy wanted her.

And yet she felt that ending it all now would be an even worse decision.

Although she didn't know Ian Sutcombe, and maybe never would, she liked him. She liked his courage and his behavior. She liked the way he was sacrificing his own life to a stranger in order to put his home and his family to rights again. And yet even so, he was willing to undergo all the humiliation of putting himself on the market again because he thought she might be doing something she'd later regret.

If she did take him up on his generous offer, she'd be free. Her family would be surprised, but not furious with her, or at least, not for too long. She understood that though he'd be cruelly disappointed, the marquis would never blame her for it either. But, in truth, the more she knew him, the more she liked him. He was right, that might change on better acquaintance. But she thought she could do far worse than to marry such a man.

"Well," she said in a stronger voice, "I repeat: I haven't changed my mind."

"Very well then, thank you," he said, and began to walk with her again.

"No. Don't!" she said, spinning around to face him directly again. "Don't thank me any more than I intend to thank you. You're right. We made a bargain. That's what marriage is, after all. And who knows? Without infatuation and passion fogging up our brains, we may do a better job of it than many others." She hesitated and then blurted, "But now that we're at this point, I find there is a question that's been troubling me."

He tilted his head to the side. "Then ask it."

"You thought I agreed to marry because of some disappointment in my past. Have you had one? Do you have one? That is to say, if you had all the funds you require, and weren't burdened with our bargain, would you marry another? I know it's a personal question, but our relationship will be a personal one. And if I don't ask you now, I'll always wonder."

"You have the right to ask personal questions," he said. "You should. Ours is a sane and logical connection. No. I haven't loved another. That is to say, not with my whole heart."

He suddenly remembered the women he'd entertained or entertained fantasies of. He couldn't have married a titled heiress; he'd known that since he'd come of age. But Lady Samantha had tempted him to make a fool of himself, once upon a long time ago. Nor could he have wed "a bit o' muslin," as the kept women of his class were called. He thanked the fates that he'd happened to see, by chance, his sometimes mistress, Felicia, with another gentleman before he'd wrecked his life offering to save her from the one she was so obviously enjoying.

"I can't claim saintliness," he said carefully. "I've known women in a physical sense, but always fleetingly, and for no other reason than for fleeting pleasures. I don't love another. I never have. I don't know if I can. That's one of the reasons why I can't honestly promise you more than devotion."

"I see," she said, nodding. "Nor I. So we begin this equally. That's not bad at all."

His laughter was real. "You're a remarkable woman."

She smiled and strolled on with him. And if her smile slipped after a moment or two, she didn't worry because it was now too dark for him to see it. But she realized she was inordinately pleased by his small compliment and found herself wishing it had been a bigger one.

"So, when are you leaving?" she eventually asked.

"As soon as I can," he said. "The artisans, carpenters, masons, and the architect have already been contracted, and will be there before I can, whenever I go."

"What if I'd said we should abort this wedding?" she asked impulsively.

"I'd have found myself in more debt," he answered smoothly.

"I'm sorry, I shouldn't have asked that. I don't know what made me do it," Hannah said.

"You resent the fact that I couldn't say I adore you, I imagine," he said. "Again, are you sure? I've been in debt for a long while. I'll find a way out. So don't take pity on me. My God," he said, turning around, "it isn't because you feel sorry for me? I won't have that."

"Do you pity me?" she asked.

"No, not in the least," he said. Then he laughed again. "You're the buyer. No one ever feels sorry for the buyer."

She nodded. "Yes. True. But it was cruel, so we're even. Shall we do this, or not, my lord?"

"I will," he said, "and you're right. I regret my words."

"But I deserved them. And I'll keep to mine too."

He bent and dropped a light kiss on her cheek. "Brave girl. This is a difficult thing we're edging into."

"Wish us luck," she said flippantly, to make him laugh, feeling her face tingling where those cool lips had touched it, wishing he'd kissed her lips instead of her cheek.

Chapter 7

The sleet stopped striking against the windows and was replaced by driving gusts of snow. Wind whistled down the chimney and stirred the crumbles of burning wood in the fireplace, sending the flames flying up and out, everywhere, it seemed, but toward heating the room. Two men sat there and rested quietly.

"It's cold as bedamned in here," Ian said as he laid his head back in his chair by the fireside. "But I'm too tired to shiver."

"I'll throw more wood on the fire," Baker said from an adjoining chair.

Ian raised a hand wearily. "No, don't. It will only smother whatever heat we do have. Next on my agenda after repairing all the holes in the roof will be fixing the flues and getting every hearth in this house working again. If you want work, pour me some more brandy. At least I'll be warm on the inside. Pour one for yourself too."

His valet went to a sideboard, poured two generous glasses, and gave one to his master. "Some holiday for you, milord, ain't it?"

"Yes," Ian said, accepting the glass, "actually it is."

"Tsk!" Baker said, halting and staring at the hand that took the glass. It was wrapped in gauze, and there were red stains on the palm it covered. "Look at that hand of yours! The bandage's seeping. Let me rewrap it. You oughtn't to be working with the workers. You've chewed your hands to bits."

Ian waved him away. "Later. My hands were too soft. They'll harden. I want to work. The job will get done faster if the men see me working too. Besides, this is a labor of love for me."

Ian was dressed in worn clothes. He wore no jacket; his shirt was not fine linen but warm wool. He wore no cravat, only a scarf at his opened collar, and his moleskin breeches were rubbed into thin patches at the knees. His boots were scuffed. He didn't wear the standard rough garments of a workingman; but it was plain that he'd done hard work in what he wore.

"You've been at it weeks now," Baker said. "The job's harder than being at war. The more you work, the less chance you give them hands to heal up."

"The more I work the better I feel, whatever the state of my hands."

"Still, some Christmas holiday for you," Baker grumbled.

"Actually, it is," Ian said, after taking a swallow of brandy. "We're getting the old place to rights, at last. I'm repairing the past for the sake of the future. This is the best way I can imagine bringing in a new year."

"Aye. But Christmas? That's another matter."

"Did you want to go home for Christmas?" Ian asked. "You should have said. I had help. You could have gone."

"So I could. But I'm staying the course until I see you're set: this Hall, wife, and all. Then, mebbe, it will be time for me to go home to my little village on the sea. I miss the sea. Yet I joined the army. That's life. But you?"

"My brother's latest letter was encouraging," Ian said, closing his eyes. "What more could I want?"

He closed his eyes. The silence was only broken by the crackling sound of wood in the hearth. Ian opened his eyes again. "What a disapproving silence. Yes. My fiancée. But she's home with her family. I've been working too hard to think of her except when I write to her, which is once a week, as promised. She doesn't know me well enough to miss me."

Another silence fell until Baker said, "A damned shame anyway for you two to be apart at Christmas, no matter what your arrangement, if you don't mind me saying it."

"I don't mind," Ian said. "It may be difficult for

her, I suppose, if she wants to show me off. But not for me. I have all I want now, the funds to Hall to set to rights at last." He realized how that sounded and sighed. "Damme, but you know the way of it. She's got what her father wants, and I have what I want. Not that she's averse to the bargain. But if you're thinking of lovers parted, that's not the way of it."

"Aye, but that's the pity of it."

"And the way it is," Ian said. "Let's hear no more."

He felt guilty because he didn't miss his fiancé. But then, Ian realized with surprise, the mere thought of her set his body to remembering her well enough. Aside from certain nocturnal yearnings, he usually blocked all such thoughts. That way he could cope with his celibacy. It wasn't the first time he had done it. He didn't like sex with strangers. Since the first fumbling experience he'd had with what passed for love when he'd been a boy, he'd trained himself to ignore prostitutes.

Ian had known women since, with whom he'd shared pleasure. But for the past year and more he hadn't had the money to pass his time with any available, willing women. He did believe there were good women who had to earn their livings with their bodies. If they didn't sell themselves on street corners or in brothels, they accepted "gifts" for their company. He didn't blame them. Life was hard for females without money.

Morality was for the well fed, and "good" was a term only the well-off dared apply. There were also many worthy women in situations such as he faced, who'd had to marry for money, and lacked love and pleasure. He'd known them too, and supplied them that pleasure without shame for it.

Some nights he dreamed of rounded, heated, silken bodies sliding against his own urgent one, and he'd wake, remembering warm, eager hands and mouths. Still, he was in his own manor now. However pressing his bodily needs, he wouldn't do anything to disgrace his future wife in what would be her own backyard. And he had no time to travel to London.

He and his fiancée were essentially strangers and he wondered if they'd ever really be much to their marriage, especially in matters of intimacy. If so, after he was married he hoped to find a handsome, understanding woman and maybe even share a sort of love with her. For now, sex and love were as distant to him as the cold winter's moon above, and so then was any kind of sexual relief. He lived with need, and accepted it. He'd done it before.

But Baker was right, he thought, it was a damned shame.

The two men didn't speak for a while, and then Baker spoke up again. "Actually, the locals like that you're working with them. At first they were shocked to see a lordship getting his hands dirty. Then they started liking it. They respect your love for this place. It gives them hope that you'll take care of them and the village too. That's what they say at the tavern in the village. They go there at the end of the day. I do too."

"I know," Ian said. "I've often wanted to go down to the tavern. But it's a fine line. I can work with them, but not socialize. My grandfather told me that I owed a responsibility to the people on my land, from time out of mind. They helped build this place at the beginning on the promise that we'd protect them in times of need. We gave them land to farm, and they gave us a share of the profits of their toil and a promise to stand with us if we asked it of them. We've kept to that compact all these years. But I can't be one of them. They need to think of me as the one in control, and would even when I was a pauper. Now that I've come into money again they know I'll help them fix their cottages after the great house is rebuilt. But we don't take tea together, or lift a pint, except on special occasions. That's how it's done."

He stretched aching limbs. "Things are changing now. Our bargain may not be as important in the future. But for me it still is. I want to take care of my tenants, see to my obligations to them, and restore this Hall to its previous state and employ as many locals as I can. That's why I'm so glad to be back and doing what I was born to do."

"Huh," Baker said. "It's still important. Else why would your father-in-law come down so handsome for your hand? Begging your pardon for my frankness," he added, when Ian didn't answer.

Ian waved a hand. "No pardon needed. It's not the land, or the bargain with those that work it that Mr. Leeds is wise enough to want from me. It's the influence of my name and title. That's still there."

They sat in companionable silence until they heard a sudden echoing, booming sound. The knocker on the great oaken front door was being used. They looked at each other. It was getting on to be Christmas Eve, they were in a half-ruined mansion, sitting in one of the few habitable rooms, and yet there was a summons at the door. Ian hadn't any household help except for his valet, because there was no place to put them yet. As it was, his man did the cooking, and there was nothing in the manor house to keep clean.

Baker rose and left the room to answer the door.

Ian heard male voices at the door. He rose just in time to see his valet returning with a group of men, hats in hand, following behind him. Baker was beaming.

"Your tenants, my lord," Baker said. "They've come to wish you a happy Christmas."

"We didn't plan nothing in time," one of the men said. "We was sitting in the inn, having a pint afore we went home to the wife and kiddies, and we remembered. It's coming on Christmas Eve, and you all alone in the Hall, my lord. So we come to bring the spirit of the year to you."

"It's the other way round," Ian said as he looked at the dozen or so roughly dressed men, all of whom he'd worked with. "If I had a whole house, I'd have had you all in for a cup of cheer. That's the way it's supposed to be. Still, I do have one whole room, and that, because of your help. Join me in a glass, fellows, if you would."

"Nay," said one of the men. "Thanks to you, my lord, but we come prepared. You gave us extra coins afore Christmas, 'stead of waiting for Boxing Day. That bought us our leisure, so we brung you a whole barrel of ale, my lord."

There was much laughter as the men rolled in a huge barrel, and set it up on a makeshift trestle they'd also dragged in.

The first toast was raised to their lord and benefactor.

"You coming back has changed our fortunes, so we wish you the happiness of the Season," the leader of the group said. "We're only that sorry your good lady isn't here yet."

From the way the other men shuffled their feet and looked down at them, Ian knew they'd heard the whole of his story. It was obvious they didn't blame him for the sale of his name, because it was the saving of them.

"Although she isn't here," one of the men said, "we'll drink to her too."

Ian solemnly raised his glass. "Thank you. And we'll drink the second glass to your good ladies."

"And a third," Baker said, "to the bad ones."

That caused much laughter. Ian smiled. It was a strange holiday celebration. But in all, he thought, one of the best he'd ever had. And perhaps, he thought with a twinge of regret, one of the best he'd ever have.

Hannah drew back the drapes and looked out the frosty window again. "The snow's stopped falling. Still, how cold it must be where he is."

Her sisters didn't answer. She had harbored a faint hope that Ian would come to London to surprise her at Christmas. He wrote her a letter every week. One simple page a week, filled with the details of the reconstruction of his home. He wrote that it was hard going because of the bitter winter. Still, he would soon have a surprise for her, he said. She didn't know what it was, but her nonsensical hope had been that it would be himself, on her doorstep, for Christmas. Her family had gone to London for the holiday, thinking that traveling there would be easier for him than going east, where their family home was. They rented a fine town house, complete with staff, and waited for Society to notice. It seemed clear that they had not.

Ian had not come. Now the dull winter day was turning to a darker twilight. Hannah had dressed carefully today. She'd put on a new, long-sleeved yellow morning gown, brightened by a gold locket at her throat, in hopes that she'd be gloriously surprised. If he had come today, Ian would have nothing to be ashamed of in her.

The day had worn on, without any visitors. They had no relatives in London, and didn't know many people there. An engaged female with no fiancé in sight, especially if she were a commoner, and he, a lord, occasioned much talk if she went out without him. Or so Hannah believed the few times she'd gone with her family to a restaurant and heard the whispers they left in their wake. Or when she went to a modiste or a hat shop, or anyplace where those in the *ton* might appear. She wasn't foolish enough to think they were admiring her face, her form, or her gown. There was nothing else about her to account for the many covert stares and murmurs, except for the fact that she'd been publicly declared a marquis's fiancée, and then he'd completely disappeared from sight.

So they didn't go out socially. The few invitations they got were for the engaged couple, not Miss Hannah Leeds or her family. Now here it was, Christmas passing, and still was no sign of her fiancée. At home, they'd at least had a village to celebrate with, even if it stormed. Here, no one came. The whole land was ice-locked. Her father and sisters had given up all their friends. Hannah felt terrible about that.

She sighed heavily as she let the drapes fall back.

Her sisters looked at each other. Her father looked dour.

"Ah well," Hannah said on a faint smile, "I guess you all know what I was hoping for this past week. I know he had no plans to see me before his work is done, but Christmas, after all . . ." Her voice trailed off. "It's a sentimental time," she added, rallying. "Still, just as well. The truth of it is that I haven't seen him in so long I'm not sure I'd recognize him if he did come."

"Nonsense," Anthea said bravely. "*I* haven't been able to forget him."

"*You*," her sister Jessica said, "never forget *any* gentleman. Papa, we have to get the chit married off soon, or she'll run away with a chimney sweep."

"She hasn't *seen* any other gentlemen," Hannah said as she sat down again.

"That will all change when you marry," Anthea said brightly.

"So I hope," Hannah said.

"Did he say anything about his friends?" Anthea asked.

"Or his plans?" Jessica added.

Her father shot them a dark look.

"Disregard it, Papa," Hannah said. "It's a fair question. My dears, I tell you everything he says in his letters. I withhold nothing. Don't frown, Papa. There's nothing embarrassing in any of them. They're all to do with lumber and the scarcity of good tiles, the need for another mason, or they are questions about what color paper, paint, and type of wood I prefer. He has no time for friends; at least he never mentions them. I suppose his finances had something to do with that too. He's a very proud man.

"There's never a personal word to me either," she went on, "because our friendship isn't a personal one. In fact," she said glumly, "it isn't even a friendship. We're acquaintances. His letters would be foolish if they were filled with loving nothings, because there's nothing loving about our plans. And no, Papa, even so, I don't want to change a thing."

"Maybe if you had a chance to go out and meet new gentlemen, you might rethink things," he said quietly.

"You think so?" she asked him. "Because, believe me, I don't. I've no interest in meeting new men or dreaming of wedded bliss with a sudden new love. I believe I'll be happy enough with the marquis. He's a decent man, and no fool. I'd think less of him if he sent me passionate letters filled with rosy promises. Let be, Papa. I'm happy enough."

"No one is ever happy enough," Anthea said passionately.

Everyone ignored that.

"But will he come to see you and spend time with you before spring, and before the wedding?" her father asked. "Otherwise you will truly be marrying a stranger."

"I never thought otherwise," Hannah said. "He says he hopes to see me long before then. But he wants the Hall finished. To tell the truth I don't fancy living in a home that's under construction. The weather's been holding him back. Who can say how long it will take?"

"He sends me an account of every penny spent, though I never said he should," her father said. "And he writes to me too. All is going as well as can be expected, but it will take longer than he thought."

"But why wait?" Anthea said dreamily. "Even if some places are still dangerous, you could marry earlier than planned and sail off to some beautiful warm tropical island, or someplace else romantic. Then you could come home to a finished house."

Hannah considered that. "So we could," she said slowly. She smiled. "His brother is in Italy. He might leave his work to visit with him. I don't care if the wedding is earlier. No one will think the worst of hurrying the day now, because everyone knows I haven't seen him in months. That's not a bad idea."

Anthea beamed.

"I'll write to him this very night to tell him what you suggest," Hannah said, though in her thoughts she immediately erased the word "romantic." "But first, I must have dinner. Cook has outdone herself, to judge from the savory scents coming from the kitchens." Hannah raised her head, and inhaled with pleasure.

The scent of roasted meats, spices, and puddings, with a faint overlay of gingerbread, filled the house. Cook was obviously preparing a festive dinner for them. It was cozy enough for the family this frigid evening, even if they had no others to share with. Fires blazed in every hearth as night descended as fast as the temperature outside did. Visiting hour was long over. And yet there she still sat, like a stuffed goose, Hannah thought. She'd kept her family grounded with her in the parlor, and all for no real reason, except for one forlorn, foolish hope. She pasted on a smile, and rose in a dignified manner.

"Time to change my gown," she said. "I never planned to get gravy on this one. And if we don't sit down to dinner when it's ready, Cook will start weeping."

She went slowly up the stair to her room. His sisters and her father watched, silent and sad. She wasn't fooling anyone; they knew she was crushed. She didn't care. She had to be alone for a few moments. Once in her room, she closed the door. Then she sat at her dressing table, glad that her maid wasn't awaiting her. Disappointment sat on Hannah's heart like a weight, but she couldn't cry about it. He *wasn't* rejecting her. Clever he was, but he couldn't read minds. He didn't know he was disappointing her; it wasn't as though he didn't want to see her. They were still going to marry. And she was still going to be marrying a stranger. Nothing had changed at all.

What a ninny she'd been, she thought angrily, blinking back suspicious moisture that insisted on clouding her eyes. How could anyone get the present they wanted if they never told Father Christmas what it was? The marquis didn't know how important family holidays were to her. How could he? She stood up. She had to wash her face, change her gown, and try to cheer herself so she didn't dim the holiday for her family.

And then, even through her closed door, she heard the sounds of some commotion downstairs. She heard Jessica and Anthea's glad cries, and then much laughter. There was a silence, and then more laughter. Hannah raised her head, wiped her eyes, and firmly told herself not to be so silly again. They were likely just telling jokes.

She walked to her door and cracked it open. She heard the reverberations of a deep masculine voice. Not her fathers'.

She hesitated. Ian hadn't promised her anything to do with Christmas. He was a grown man with a duty to perform, and the roads were ice from here all the way to where he was. But though she was a grown woman, she couldn't stop herself from flying to the door, flinging it open, racing down the corridor and then the stairs, and whatever her family thought bedamned.

Chapter 8

The man who stood in the parlor was really Ian, Lord Sutcombe; her fiancé. Hannah hung in the doorway, gaping at him, almost not believing her eyes. When he turned from the hearth where he'd been holding his hands over the fire, there was a broad smile on his face.

"I give you greetings of the Season," he said, bowing to her.

His cheeks were scarlet from the wicked cold and his eyes sparkled with amusement. "I surprised myself," he added. "But I couldn't let you pass the Season here without me. It's no time to be without family, and we are to be family soon. I'm lucky; I thought you all might be off at some festive ball or other. Imagine my delight at finding you here."

"Us, and the fire in the fireplace," Anthea said, with a laugh.

"Aye," he said, glancing down at his boots. "I managed to pry off my frozen gloves and now can feel my hands again. But I seem to be melting." He glanced down at his boots, and stepped aside. "I'll stand on the hearthstone to spare your carpet. As it is, I apologize for tracking in half the road with me, and it all ice and dead cinders. But I'm glad London throws ashes on its streets to make it easier for weary travelers. We made much better time once we rode in under the north gate. And it was lucky for us that we followed the mail coach all the way here. His Majesty sees to it that the mail has passable roads. But I doubt they'll stay that way with the wind howling and surfaces icing. Hannah? Are you all right?"

She broke from her silence and went straight to him. She took one of his icy hands and gazed up at him. He covered her hands with his own.

"You came here," Hannah breathed. "I felt you might; I hoped you might and then I realized you couldn't. But here you are. Oh, thank you, Ian. Thank you."

"But who are 'we'?" Jessica blurted.

Ian raised his gaze from Hannah's, but still held her hand. "We? Oh, Mr. Baker, my man and old friend of mine as well, came with me. We took an extra horse too, in case of accident. We rode from dawn until now; and rode as if possessed. He's in your kitchens, doubtless regaling your staff with his mighty deed. But it was remarkable! For a miracle, we're all here with ankles, fetlocks, and heads intact," he said, smiling as he looked down at Hannah again.

"Then you must join us in dinner immediately," Wallace Leeds said. "Your stomach is doubtless as empty and frozen."

"Thank you. My stomach is empty as my head. Nothing could be more frozen than I am. And it's all my fault, and your daughter's," Ian said, still smiling as he gazed at Hannah. "I know it was a damn fool thing to do. My apologies for the profanity, ladies," he added, as Hannah's sisters grinned. "But I confess, I'm happy to be here. What is that marvelous smell? Fresh gingerbread? Or your new perfume?" he asked Hannah. "Either way, it's delicious. That color you're wearing suits you," he told her more seriously. "There's more sunshine in it than I've seen in weeks."

"Thank you," she said breathlessly. "Thank you," she said again.

"But I must change," Ian said. "I'm in all my dirt from the road."

"Then, hurry," Hannah said. "Please hurry."

He smiled.

"Show the marquis to his room, James," Wallace Leeds ordered a footman.

"And hurry," Hannah added again, knowing she sounded a bit insane by doing it, but too happy to care.

* * *

They dined on roast goose and beef, cutlets, turkey, ham, mince, and fresh bread, ale, and every savory Cook could find in the kitchens. But Hannah didn't taste anything but triumph. He'd come at the risk of his neck, and she hadn't even had to ask him to do it.

His adventure seemed to have loosened his tongue and stripped away that faint air of superiority he often projected. He was relaxed as well as elated, gleeful as a boy because of his daring adventure.

"It's lucky you didn't go to your house in the country," Ian said as he raised yet another toast. "I couldn't have got there from where I was, and wouldn't have dared try. The roads wouldn't have been cleared half so well. So here's to a Happy Christmas," he said, holding his glass high. "And to a daft but happy fellow, who came in from the cold to a warm welcome."

"Hear! Hear!" the girls cried.

"Exactly," Hannah said with vast content, raising her glass to Ian. "You're here, at last."

He drank to her, and then, done with terrifying them with tales of his risky ride, he told them about his celebration with his tenants.

"We had no wassail bowl, and had to make do with ale. It suited very well," he added, smiling. "That was what put me in a fever to be here. They were all going home to their families, and I wasn't. So Baker and I packed that night, chose a few reliable fellows to keep watch on the Hall, and lit out with first light. It wasn't snowing as hard then, and indeed, it didn't snow at all in some places we rode through. Let me tell you what we've been doing at the Hall," he said as the table was being cleared for desserts.

He talked about how he was restoring the red salon and the blue one first, because they faced north and had missing windowpanes, and so had the most damage. "They had the most valuable hangings too, as did the front and back parlors," he added, less joyously. "My stepmother took those paintings last, I think, because they'd been ripped from the walls in haste. My tenants wouldn't have touched them. And besides, she was seen carting off everything she could have pried loose. That left the paint, the murals, and the silk wall coverings in lamentable condition.

"The music room was emptied of instruments and furnishings. It echoes, but it's a resonant echo, so we can easily get it back in tune, as it were. The orangerie had cracked glass everywhere, of course, and is a ruin. We'll leave those repairs for better weather. The ballroom was emptied, but at least the floors were left covered with sheets. The blue bedchamber, the gold, white, and green ones are in relatively good condition. The yellow and rose ones and some others seemed barely touched. No matter, all will be ready for you when you come," he assured Hannah's sisters.

"And the maid's quarters, which are separate from the menservants', will be getting due attention soon," he went on, Hannah's eyes continuing to widen as her father beamed at his recitation. "Men being men, the stables were repaired first, as well as the living quarters for the stable workers," he added apologetically. "But when the weather clears, we'll get delivery of the new oven and sinks for the kitchens, and finish repairs in the breakfast and dining rooms once the kitchens are kitted out. No one tried to haul away the mosaic tiles or marble tubs. All that's needed is some modernizing, a few fresh touches. So the bathing chambers," he assured Hannah, "will be fit for mermaids by the time you see them, I promise."

As the puddings, pies, jellies, nuts, fruits, and sweetmeats were brought in, Ian kept talking about his plans for Hopewell Hall. When he spoke about his home his expression grew brighter and he seemed illuminated, and those listening were charmed as well. Then he said the one thing that jolted Hannah.

"I've spent a deal of money, Mr. Leeds," he told her father seriously, turning to him. "But I think if you go over the books I've kept you'll see that there isn't a penny piece misspent."

"I'm sure not," her father said, flustered. "It's your money, my lord, to do with as you please. I don't need to go over any accounting."

"I only thought you'd want to know that I have not misused any funds," Ian said soberly.

"I doubt you would," Wallace Leeds said. "But if you did, it would be your own pocket you raided. That money is yours now, fairly gotten, and fairly spent, I'm sure." He hesitated, and then added, "Do you need an advance of more funds that you've got coming to you?"

"Good grief! No," Ian said. "I've sufficient to my needs, as I thought I would when we made our bargain."

The other piece of their bargain sat suddenly still, watching them.

"With all I've done so far, I think today's journey was the best thing of all," Ian said, with a smile that made Hannah sit back and sigh with relief.

Their bargain was what had brought them together, but he could make her forget that with just a smile. She raised her glass and hoped that one day he could make her forget it entirely. After all, she thought, it was Christmas, a time for miracles.

"I can't stay long," Ian went on. "When the roads are clear, we'll go again."

Hannah's smile slipped.

"But at least, I'm here now," Ian said. "Lord, I'm *very* glad I braved the weather to get here."

So was everyone in the house. Hannah was delighted. Tonight she saw a new Marquis Sutcombe.

He seemed younger and happier than she'd ever seen him. This was a humorous fellow; a man she could laugh with.

There was no height to his manner. In fact, after dinner, he asked their permission to invite Mr. Baker to come join them after he'd enjoyed his own holiday meal with the other upper servants. It wasn't usually done to introduce a servant, but as Ian explained, Mr. Baker was much more than that.

His manservant took some sherry with the gentlemen and then, standing back to the fireplace in the main salon, entertained them all with his highly exaggerated story of the mad journey to London. Ian laughed at any fun made of him.

The time flew by. Hannah never wanted the night to end.

"But we're being selfish," her father suddenly blurted. "Look at the time! My lord, you must be exhausted, and you too, Mr. Baker."

Though Ian protested, Hannah had noticed her fiancé's eyes growing heavier, and felt guilty about not saying the same thing earlier. She hadn't wanted him to leave her, even to go to his chamber. But it was late; her sisters were already glassy-eyed with the effort of staying awake.

"True," Hannah said. "I suggest we all call it a night: a very jolly, wonderful Christmas night."

Ian agreed, and rose somewhat wearily. He bade them all good night, and made his way to the room he'd been shown.

Hannah hurried to her own bed. She wanted to hold the hours she'd just passed in her mind, reviewing them and delighting in them once again. She was also eager for morning so she could experience a repeat of tonight's success. With luck, Ian would be marooned here with her for days. She was much too keyed up with excitement and anticipation to sleep.

But when her head touched the pillow and she opened her eyes again, it was morning—a sad one, for her, at least.

The sun was shining brightly. The wind had turned in the night. A warm breeze had set the eaves dripping. She gazed out the window and watched the last of the glassy surface on the street being churned to mere mud by all the horses and coaches that were moving again.

She dressed and went down to breakfast. Ian was already at the table in the morning dining parlor. He rose to greet her. "Good morning, a fine morning," he said cheerfully.

"Good morning," she echoed. She realized, with sinking heart, what he was going to say before he said it.

"Mr. Baker's already been out, scouting. The roads are free," Ian announced. "That means we can go. I thought to set out after breakfast." He noted her expression. "I hate to leave, especially after the good times we all shared last night. But the sooner I leave, the sooner the work will be done," he explained more gently. "If the weather holds, I can be back home before it can change again. Hopewell Hall must be completed by the time I bring you there as mistress of it. It's arrogant of me, I know, to think no one can do the thing right if I'm not there. But I confess I don't trust anyone else to oversee what's to be done.

"I know what the Hall used to be, after all," he said, "and I want it looking even finer, if possible. As I said, you can choose new furniture and the like when you arrive. But the structure must be made sound and the Hall restored to its former glory before then." He looked at her hesitantly. "You do understand, Hannah, don't you?"

She took a seat at the table. "Of course," she said levelly, not meeting his eyes.

He sat again, but didn't pick up his knife or fork. "Trust me," he said simply. "Please trust that I don't relish another long cold ride today, even if the snow is gone. I don't like leaving you so quickly. But the Hall is both my obligation to myself and to your father, as well as a gift to you. It's the only one that money can't buy, in spite of the fact that your money is restoring it. That's a contradiction, I know. But that's how I see it."

He looked at her expectantly.

She knew what she had to say. "I'll look forward to the Hall's completion," she said.

"I don't doubt you've been subjected to gossip," he added. "And so I'm glad we chose to marry at St. George's here in London. That way everyone will see, and it will end all rumor."

She agreed, but then her sisters came to say their good-byes, and Hannah knew any attempt at quiet conversation was gone.

Her fiancé bade her a private good-bye at the door, after they had breakfasted.

"I'll hurry, and if the weather holds, I'll be back with the first days of spring," he told her, holding her hands, his eyes searching hers.

"Thank you," was all she could say as she lowered her gaze. After all, she didn't know him well enough to tell him how much she'd miss him.

Ian wrote to Hannah and to her father regularly. There were many letters. The weeks passed quickly for Hannah, but the hours went slowly. She didn't like going out on the streets of London anymore. She and her sisters had to go to salons and fabric shops because Hannah was getting her bridal wardrobe fitted out, and the girls needed new gowns too. They liked to go to the bookstores as well, and sometimes ventured to the markets. But increasingly, there was too much talk about Hannah and her arranged marriage. It wasn't simply a fantasy on her part. Hannah saw heads turning her way and whispers blooming in her wake whenever she and her sisters did go.

Since they'd come to Town people had been gossiping about the "Leeds Legacy." Hannah guessed that the amount of her fortune grew larger with every week, along with the rumors of her fiancé's desperation for funds. Unfortunately, since Ian had gone into the countryside to repair his home and left her here alone in London, what was also now being whispered was how strange it was that he had given up on her, considering the size of the ever-growing "Leeds Legacy."

Winter weather returned. Then the cold finally lessened to mere chill. Snow gave way to sleet, then freezing rain, and then dull damp mizzling days and foggy nights. And still, no sign of her fiancé. Sometimes, in the night, Hannah awoke from bad dreams to entertain distressing thoughts. Had he finished his beloved Hall and then decided to bring in a more beloved bride into it? It was possible he guessed her family would never bring any financial matter with him to the courts. The shame of it would certainly ruin her reputation and do irremediable damage to her sisters' as well.

Not that such a lawsuit would bring her father's money back to him, Hannah realized. Noble persons were known for running up huge bills with their tailors and dressmakers. Their grocers, boot makers, butchers, even candlemakers and servants were accustomed to it as well. So certainly, a nobleman wouldn't be expected to stoop to pay a debt to a common man.

Hannah tried not to even entertain those notions. She'd think of the merry, laughing man she'd passed that one glorious Christmas evening with; the man who'd risked life and limb to see her. Or had he done it just because it was such a foolish, daring trick?

His letters were filled with information: he'd had a hod full of bricks dropped on his foot. In spite of the boots he'd worn he'd had to soak that foot and wrap it in bandages. But they'd finished work on all the salons. They'd repaired all the roofs and were now clearing out chimneys. The kitchens were next. The orangerie would soon be able to support pineapples as well as oranges and more common plants.

The letters to Hannah were always signed, "Respectfully." Never, of course, "With love."

Hannah just wanted to be sure she was still going to be married to him in the spring. Because winter was slowly disappearing. Buds were getting fat on all the trees. Mild breezes and pale sunlight coaxed up snowdrops, primroses and then daffodils in the parks and in front of the neat houses on their street.

But nothing brought Lord Ian Sutcliff, Marquis Sutcombe, to Town.

Hannah waited. And worried.

Chapter 9

Hannah didn't recognize him at first. Ian was transformed.

Where he'd been elegant and attractive he was now astonishingly virile and arresting. It was as though everything he had been was magnified.

A gentleman should be pale. So he had been. But now his face was lightly bronzed, and his dark gold hair had bright lights in it. It made his gray-blue eyes silvery, luminous. The planes of his cheeks were gilded, his form was still lean, but now he looked taut and hard edged. His tightly fitted blue jacket showed how wide his shoulders were, how long his torso, and his buff breeches showed the hard muscle in his thighs and legs. Even the cleft in his chin seemed deeper, giving him a determined look. His face glowed above his spotless white neckcloth and pristine linen. He was now, Hannah thought, a dazzling masculine male as well as an elegant gentleman.

And so while she was registering his stunning

appearance, she could say nothing beyond a startled, "Welcome, my lord."

"Forgive me for being so tardy," he said, grinning. "It took longer than I thought it would. But I made it. Spring is here and the Hall is done." He smiled down at her. "Am I forgiven?"

"Of course," she said. She could hardly say more. Because she realized that the words that sprang to her lips had been, *"Why me? A man who looks as you do, speaks as you do, and has your presence, why do you still want me?"*

She forgot the words. One thing erased all her protests. He was returned. He'd come back to her.

She was glad she wore a new rose-colored gown today; it went well with her fresh complexion. It fit well too. She'd had her hair cut and styled so that her curls shone and danced when she moved her head. She'd do. But she knew she wasn't a patch on him. She couldn't drag her eyes away from him.

"Three weeks," he said, taking her hand in his gloved ones and looking down into her eyes. His smile was crooked. "We'll be married in three weeks time. How odd you must find it. You still don't really know me."

"Nor you, me," she said breathlessly. "And you don't find it odd?"

"How many couples really know each other before marriage?" he asked. "Gentlemen aren't trusted alone with the ladies. And young women in the *ton* are so closely watched and chaperoned that sometimes a couple hasn't had above a half hour alone together before they wed. We've had more than that, at least."

"You think my father hasn't watched me closely enough?"

"No, of course not. I forgot how sensitive you are on the subject of breeding," he said with a slight smile. "Forgive me. I didn't mean that."

Hannah heard her sisters approaching. "That will be Jessica and Anthea," she told him. "They'll be delighted to see you. But later, can we find someplace where we may speak privately?"

A shadow crossed his face. He recovered his composure quickly. "Of course," he said smoothly. "It's a fine day. I'll take you riding in an open carriage."

She nodded and stepped back as her sisters surrounded him. Anthea squealed with happiness, Jessica smiled with relief. They'd been worried, wondering if he ever would return. Hannah hoped he thought they were just glad to see him. Her father was all smiles as well; and she hoped Ian wouldn't detect the vast relief in his expression.

After they'd exchanged welcomes and greetings, Ian spoke to Wallace Leeds. "The sun is still out and it's a fine spring day. I came here in a Phaeton. I haven't used one all winter. Such a light carriage is only of use here in London, so I rented one when I arrived. I noted clouds coming in from the west. May I take Hannah out for a ride before the sun goes in? I thought we'd go through the park."

"Certainly," her father said, sounding relieved. "You will take dinner with us tonight, though, will you?"

"I'd be happy to," Ian said as he offered his hand to Hannah.

Hannah hastily threw a rosy Oriental patterned shawl over her shoulders, and tied on a straw bonnet. That was all she needed on such a fine afternoon. She knew she looked as well as she could, but she couldn't summon an interesting word to say as Ian drove through the city streets to the nearby park. He was silent too, and she thought he looked a little grim about the mouth now. She knew what she had to say to him. She could only worry about what he was going to say to her. But in all fairness, it was time to say it, and to hear it, no matter what she felt after it was done.

"It must be important," he finally said as he pulled the Phaeton to a stand and into the dappled shade under some budding trees in the park. They were just off the main road that circled the lake. "You haven't breathed a word since we left, and that concentrated expression makes you look as though you're rehearsing for a Christmas pageant. Whatever it is, don't worry. If you get it the wrong way round, I'll wait until you sort it out. What is it? You can say it now. No one's around to hear but me."

That was true. Other carriages circled the path, horsemen rode by, and passersby walked on it. They were in clear sight, but for all purposes, alone.

She turned to him. "It's more in the nature of a question," she said with stark sincerity. Her gloved hands knotted together in her lap. "I mean, a question for you."

His eyes opened wider. He took in a steadying breath. "All right. Ask away, then."

"Do you still want to go ahead with our bargain?" she blurted. "That is to say, I know you've spent money, but my father's a decent man, and be sure, he won't ask for any back. Well, at least not right away. I'm sure you two can work out a fair repayment plan."

She sat up straighter, and swallowed hard as she awaited his answer.

A frown line appeared on his high forehead. "You want to end our bargain?" he asked. "You've met someone?" He knew that if she canceled the agreement, he kept the funds he'd gotten, and so was surprised at his keen feeling of personal loss.

"Not fair!" she cried. "I asked you first."

He thought a moment. "I don't see any reason to change anything between us," he said carefully.

"I know I was gone all winter, and that wasn't in our plan, but I hoped you'd see it was unavoidable. There was work to do, and more to be overseen. I wrote to you regularly to explain. But no, I have no reason to back out of the arrangement. Do you?"

"No," she said, shaking her head. And then she looked him in the eyes. There was entreaty in her own. "But the way things have transpired, maybe we ought to delay the wedding a bit."

"And cause more gossip? I think not," he said, sitting back, still watching her. "But Miss Leeds, I thought you knew and accepted the situation. Again, has your interest been caught by someone else?"

"No," she said.

"Oh," he said with a quirked smile. "So you were harboring thoughts of a test period before our wedding? I'm shocked."

She scowled at him.

"So it's only that you want more time to make sure you like me well enough to wed? That's no longer possible. I'll spend as much time with you as I can in the next three weeks. But I was under the impression that ours was never to be a romantic match. Again, I must ask, has something or someone changed your mind?"

"No," she said, looking down at her gloves. "It's just that when we became engaged it seemed reasonable, intelligent, and unexceptional."

"And now?" he asked, watching closely.

"And now," she said, and smiled. "And now, I suspect my feet are growing a little cold."

He let out his breath. She wasn't renouncing him.

"We haven't seen each other in a while," she went on, "and you have changed so much."

"How?" he asked, one tawny eyebrow rising in curiosity.

"You seem more . . . sure of yourself," she said, seeking a way to let him know she now saw the vast disparity in their conditions. "More in command. More 'lordly,' I suppose."

"Ah. That may be true. When we met, I suppose I was more desperate." He nodded. "True. No doubt about it, I felt more like a beggar and so I imagine I acted more humbly. You're right. Has this new confidence of mine changed your opinion of me? It hasn't changed who I am. I can never forget that I *was* a bankrupt."

She winced.

"Mind," he said more gently. "I know I was a lucky bankrupt. You're intelligent and sensible. Your family is delightful. I still think we'll deal well together. Just because I'm more sure of myself doesn't mean that I've forgotten anything I promised, or that I'll ever forget your place in my life; indeed, your influence in restoring me to my place. I owe it all to you. That, I will never forget."

"Oh," she said flatly. It was the right answer,

but the wrong one, and the only one he could have honestly given her. She didn't know what she'd been thinking. Perhaps she did, she realized, but didn't want to remember just now. "Then forgive me," she said. "I suspect the reality of our situation, the nearness of our wedding coming so suddenly after your long absence, overwhelmed me."

His smile was gentled. "We'll deal well together, Hannah, don't worry. I don't. I haven't changed, though my state in life already has. That's because of you. You have my promise that I'll always remember and earnestly try to please you."

Her smile was faint.

He touched the reins, and they rode on through the fine spring afternoon.

The social scene in London was winding down. But it was doing so by ratchetting up. Now there were so many fetes, musicales, parties, soirees, and balls to close the Season that the Marquis Sutcombe's appearance again in Town with his fiancée was scarcely noted. There was newer gossip: all manner of broken engagements, foolish marital choices, adulterous doings, and stunning liaisons to talk about.

Hannah was vastly relieved. For his part, Ian made sure to keep her company as much as was possible. But what with all the wedding arrangements to be made: Hannah's fittings for her gowns,

Ian's with his tailor, invitations to sort through to see who was coming, and early wedding gifts to unwrap, there was little enough time for the couple to spend alone together.

Their daytime excursions were taken with Hannah's sisters in tow. The couple was, after all, not yet wed, and there was always, even in this busy season, the threat of gossip to avoid. But their outings were always fascinating to Hannah.

"This is extraordinary," Hannah told Ian one sunny morning a week before their wedding. She stood staring at all the artworks hung on the high walls surrounding them. There wasn't room enough for a mousehole between the dozens of paintings, from the floor up to the glass dome high above them. She goggled at the many works of art of all sizes: portraits of great men and famous women, Greek and Roman gods and goddesses, biblical scenes and characters, rustics tending cows, likenesses of horses, sporting dogs, and landscapes, all clamoring for her attention. Giant gilded frames filled with huge nudes were hung next to four or five smaller framed pictures squeezed together to their left and right. Not an inch of wall space was vacant. All shapes and sizes of art competed for her attention.

The room was equally thronged with visitors. Some sat on the long low chaises in the middle of the room; other visitors stood and lifted quizzing glasses to stare at the art as well as the other visitors. The grand exhibition room at Somerset House was packed with art and humanity. But it was proper art and elevated humanity. There were few commoners to be seen depicted on the walls or standing on the floor of the great room.

"The Royal Academy of Art is a shrine for British art," Ian told Hannah and her sisters as they craned their necks, trying to get a better view, "as well as one to the fortitude of the British public. Because the crowding in front of us is as bad as that on the walls."

"There must be a hundred pictures here," Hannah said in awe.

"One hundred fifty three, so far," Anthea reported. "I've been counting."

"With so many crammed in together, how can anyone evaluate the good from the bad?" Hannah murmured.

"There is no such thing," a tall, heavyset gentleman to her right said on a gruff laugh.

"Mr. Rowlandson," Ian said, greeting the fellow. "Here to view the competition, are you?"

The man snorted. "I have no competition, my lord. I did when my work was displayed here. But now I draw for the public and so will never again hang on these hallowed walls."

"I'll wager you don't mind at all, sir," Ian replied.

"A man doesn't have to starve for his art, my lord," the gentleman said. "Though I'll grant that a full stomach breeds laughter more easily than more earnest art. Give you good day, my lord. I have a commission to fulfill."

"What a curious fellow," Hannah said after the man had left them. Then she added in a lower voice, "Why didn't you introduce us?"

"Still looking for insult where none was intended?" Ian asked. "Because he didn't wait to be introduced, Hannah, nor did he expect it. He's no gentleman; he's a caricaturist. And if you don't mind your manners, you'll find yourself in one of his creations for sale in a store window on the Strand. He was a serious artist and is still a good one. But he's right, there's more money in malicious gossip here in London than there is in classical beauty. At least there is for those who don't want their deeds portrayed in paint or ink."

She laughed. "You mean Venus there, cavorting with all those cupids, can't stop artists from painting when she carries on with Mars. But my lady can, if she pays enough?"

"Exactly," Ian said, giving her an admiring look. She was bright and amusing. Each day he found himself liking her more. He'd chosen well. Mr. Rowlandson had been right. Both art and love were more amusing when a man had money.

Hannah tried to see more, but she began to feel dizzied by the crowd and the assortment of art.

Ian, looking down at her, suggested they take a stroll by the Thames while the weather lasted.

"Oh yes," Hannah said gratefully. She didn't know what made her dizzier, the crowd, the art, or the fact that Ian stood by her side. "Girls," she asked her sisters, "is it all right with you?"

It wasn't for Anthea; it was for Jessica. But Ian was already moving them toward the door.

They went out the door at the back of Somerset House. The great house sat on the banks of the Thames. As they stepped out onto the terrace, Hannah could feel the cool air and sharp scents from the great river reviving her.

"A remarkable place," she commented after a few deep breaths. There was a scent of fish and coal smoke, but the breeze quickened her senses. "But not a place I'd hurry back to see. It's not that I don't enjoy seeing great artworks. But there was just too much to see."

"You mean, to try to see," Anthea complained.

"Is it ever less crowded?" Jessica asked.

"I can't say," Ian said. "Perhaps at private viewings. If you like, I'll try to get invitations to the next one. There must be at least one or two more before summer comes."

"You'll be married by then," Anthea said glumly.

"Married doesn't mean dead," Ian laughed.

"No, but things will have changed," Anthea insisted.

"So they will, but we'll be the same," Hannah said, and wished that were true, even as she wished it weren't.

"You look pale," Ian told her. "Do you want to go home?"

"No," she said, "I just need some more time . . . to recover," she hastily added.

He took her hand in his. He could feel how cold it was even through his glove. "We'll have time after the wedding too," he assured her.

"I know," she said, and said no more. Because the wedding was approaching, and it wasn't only her hand that was cold when she thought of it. Nor was it only that his nearness made her feel overheated. It was that between one emotion and the other, she was confused. And she knew she had set a profound thing in motion that wouldn't stop until she or Ian were indeed dead, as he had jested.

"By God, the girl *is* handsome!" a male voice said in a booming attempt at a whisper. It came from the groom's side of the cathedral.

"Shh," the embarrassed female sitting beside the old gentleman hissed.

"Thought she'd look like a crow," he went on, undaunted, "but she's easy on the eye. Money *and* looks. Always said Sutcombe was a clever lad."

His wife gave those seated around them an agonized smile, cupped her ear and pointed to her oblivious spouse, trying to show that he was hard of hearing.

"Of course she's good-looking," another masculine voice from the other side of the aisle was saying with loud grievance. "All of Leeds's girls are. Everyone knows that. The groom's lucky, in all respects. Let's hope she is."

"Shhh," implored that man's spouse, as she grew red with embarrassment.

Hannah continued down the aisle with Ian. She pretended she hadn't heard a thing, and a glance at her soon-to-be husband seemed to show that he actually hadn't. He looked as calm and composed as he had when he'd met her at the church door.

"You are very lovely today," he'd said then, as he'd offered his arm.

She'd thought she looked as well as she could, but nothing in his expression showed he meant more than politeness. For once, it didn't matter. Today, her wedding day, she wore a cream-colored gown that her mother had worn on her wedding day. It was in the old style, having a cinched-in waist, a wide bell of a skirt, a tight bodice with a low neckline that proved Hannah's skin was just as smooth and creamy-looking as that of her gown. The antique gown also showed off Hannah's generous figure to perfection as the current style of high waists and long lean skirts could not. A strand of luminous pearls circled her neck, and she wore a crown of camellias in her high-dressed hair. Today, she felt beautiful. Even if she hadn't, her sisters' sighs and the look in her father's eyes when he'd seen her had been worth the effort, whatever she looked like.

Ian looked fine. But then, he always did. Today he wore formal clothing, muted colors, the brightest thing about him were his luminescent eyes and the glow of his hair. His expression was sober.

She walked, head high, as guests on either side of the aisle of the great and famous London cathedral began whispering as she passed them, sounding like the murmurs of a freshening wind as it blew through a wheat field. Ian pressed her hand where it lay on his arm. *So he heard them too*, she thought.

Their guests were composed of his lordship's distant relatives and old friends of the family sitting on one side of the aisle, and her father's business acquaintances and family friends on the other. They were all in their finest, but if anything, Hannah noted, her guests were dressed even more richly than his were. But then, everyone knew new money was freely spent, and old money clung to the hands of those that had held it a long time.

The time at the altar was blessedly brief. Hannah scarcely heard the words, or what she herself said. She only knew that after a time, she and the cool, composed man at her side were pronounced man and wife. He bent his head and pressed a quick, cool kiss on her lips. And it was done.

So it was strange that her lips felt so sensitive as she stood in the back of the great cathedral and took the good wishes of the assembled guests. When she was dizzy with introductions, and her smile pained her because of how long it had stayed on her face, Ian bent his head to hers.

"You know everyone's been invited back to your house for a celebration," he said in her ear. "I think it's time we left, so that they can go to it."

Her smile was real. "Yes, please, let's go."

He took her hand and they went to the great stairs in the front of the cathedral. Hannah gasped.

"It's snowing!" she cried. Fat white flakes were settling on her head, and the street was already plated with a coat of white.

"Spring in England is filled with surprises," her new husband said.

"Hannah, move!" her sister Anthea said in a loud whisper. "Happy is the bride the sun shines on, and it isn't raining. I think snow isn't the same as rain at all. You know what it is? It's an omen of what an unusual life lies ahead of you."

An omen of how cold this marriage is, Hannah thought. She picked up the hem of her skirt, ducked her head, and hand in hand with her new husband, ran through a blizzard of flowers, coins, rice, and snowflakes. Ian helped her hastily compress her skirts so she could fit into the coach and then tumbled in and sat opposite her.

He shook the rice, flowers, and snow from his hair. "How did our parents ever get anywhere when the poor ladies had to wear such things?" he asked, laughing as he saw Hannah's head vanish behind the tousled wall of folded silk and crinolines that had risen as she'd sat down.

She poked her head up, and joined him in laugher.

"Well, Lady Sutcombe," he said, sitting back on his side of the coach. "It's done."

She assembled herself and sat with her hands pressed tightly down on her crinolines, glad that the only thing that had been exposed were her own underskirts.

They fell silent and looked out the windows at the fast falling snow. They didn't even chat about the weather. They were thinking about more important things. But what was there to say? It was done.

Hannah didn't know what her new husband was brooding about. She was remembering the night before. As she was readying herself for sleep, her sisters had come into her chamber and perched on her bed.

"Hannah?" Jessica had said bravely. "We just want you to know that if for any reason, any silly, nonsensical reason whatsoever, you decided to end this even now, we would support you."

"And though I said I'd have him if you didn't," Anthea said with unaccustomed seriousness, "I wouldn't. The marquis is too impressive for me. That's the wrong word," she said, shaking her head. "He's too serious. No, he does enjoy a good jest," she said thoughtfully. "He's too grown up! That's it. At least for me, he is. So if you decided to not go through with this even now, I'd stand up with you, not him."

"The point is," Jessica said, frowning at Anthea, "you could marry anyone you wanted, Nan. And you could yet marry for love, and romance. We just want the best for you."

Hannah had felt tears in her eyes. "How do you know I don't love him?"

They were suddenly silent.

"I hadn't thought of that," Anthea said in wonder.

Neither had Hannah. She bit her lip. It was too late to take back what she'd said. And whatever she'd said, she would go through with what she'd promised. The last thing she needed was pity and doubt. And however she felt, she couldn't let Ian down, not now.

"I'm just fretting, my dears," she told her sisters. "I understand it's natural, bride nerves. They'll be gone after a night's sleep."

And so she'd married him and now she sat opposite her new husband, who was still a stranger to her, and hoped with all her heart that she'd soon come to know him. She knew his good qualities: his willingness to work hard, his devotion to his family, and his sense of honor. And trivial as she knew it to be, there was no question that he was as handsome as he could stare, and becoming more so every day.

Whatever he thought of her, she realized she was attracted to him. Not in the way she'd burned for Timothy, but in a new way. Timothy had been moon and starlight; he'd brought her thrills and a new hunger and yearning. His kisses had made her crazed.

She didn't feel that way about Ian. She stole a glance at him, and shivered. She was drawn to him the way she felt when she stood in a high place and felt the ground below urging her to leap. It was folly, and yet, there was that pull, that magnetic attraction. She wanted Ian's attention. She needed his approval. She wanted his touch.

That was likely only natural. She wasn't an ingénue, and he was a madly attractive male. But she didn't know him. And so he couldn't break her heart, as Timothy had. That was a relief.

And . . . Lord! she thought, but he was good to look at.

As though he felt her gaze like a perceptible touch on his cheek, he turned his head to look at her. That crooked smile she'd already grown to expect appeared on his lips. "Too late, poor lady," he said. "Now it's done. We have sealed our bargain before God and man, and no one can put it asunder. Speaking of which . . . I wondered if it would be all right with you if we made a stop at my rooms before we joined the company? We're leaving your father's house to go straight on to my estate. I thought I'd packed everything I needed, but I just remembered there are a few things I forgot."

"Why, certainly," she said.

He grinned. "It won't take but a minute. I have them all ready."

She looked at him quizzically.

"My whips," he said serenely, "my tongs, and ropes, chains, belts, and lashes. My cat of nine tails and . . ." But he couldn't go on because he was laughing too hard.

"Oh, Hannah," he breathed, when he stopped. "Your face! That look of slowly dawning horror is delicious. You're adorable when you're terrified."

She smiled at last. That was the nicest personal thing he'd ever said to her. "Thank you," she said. "Erm . . . You *are* joking?"

"Of course," he said, in perfectly serious tones. "I'd never bring those things where anyone in your family might accidentally see them."

Now she laughed along with him. But she wondered if there were metaphorical whips and chains a man might have, and if she'd ever see them. Again, she remembered that she'd married a clever, wildly attractive gentleman of mystery, at

least to her. And not for the first time wondered if
that mightn't be the way it would always be.

Ian sat back and stretched out his long legs as
much as he could, considering the way Hannah's
huge skirts dominated the small space. He smiled.
Done. He'd actually done it. *And well done at that*,
he thought. He glanced at his bride. Luck had
been with him. She was well-looking, very bright,
had a lively sense of humor. She was also oblig-
ing. He was a lucky man. Some rich commoners
had more airs and conceits than wellborn ladies.
But she was humble. She was well bred, even if
not nobly born.

He'd heard the whispers in the cathedral. He'd
shocked some of his class by this marriage. Let
them be shocked. How many men could marry
where their hearts led? Interfering parents, family
obligations, and matters of similar titles and property made many a match. He wasn't the first to
marry for money and doubtless wouldn't be the
last.

He had his estate and his place in the world
again. He'd weather it. His bride wouldn't have
to. They would respect her at the Hall, and there
she'd stay. So would he. At least, as Mr. Baker had
said, he would stay until all was set right there,
good and tightly.

And then when the whispers had died to
echoes, when another several seven-day wonders
had eclipsed his marriage in the general gossip,

he'd return to London. He'd enjoy gentleman's clubs, activities and other sport he'd had to forgo in his efforts to mend his fortunes. That had been, he realized, for his entire adult life. He'd have a belated time of sowing wild oats then. It would be interesting. Oh, he'd occasionally leave London, travel to see his brother, and maybe elsewhere. He would, to the best of his ability, live well and do right.

As for his bride? He gazed at Hannah's profile as she looked out the window. She'd get her rightful share out of this union. She'd have the title and live at the estate, her family could share the honors; it was all they wanted. He'd help in presenting her sisters, when it was time to, as promised. He'd be kind to her in all things, and try to keep her life easy.

So it was done and settled. He saw Hannah's lovely breast rise and fall in a deep sigh. It made him feel tender toward her. He'd have to make love to her eventually. It wouldn't be an onerous task when he did. But the thing was that it was finally done. He was, at last, free.

Chapter 10

By the time their coach had left the outskirts of London, the snow had stopped and the sun came out again. Now the bridegroom could ride horseback alongside the bridal coach. Whenever he came abreast of the window where his bride was staring out, he'd wave to her. *She must be lonely*, he thought. But there wasn't enough room for him, the gown, and her inside the coach, not for a long trip, at least. And she said she couldn't change her clothes because her maid was in another coach, traveling on ahead with Mr. Baker and the other servants. So she sat in solitary splendor. He'd have felt worse except for the delicious feeling of freedom he enjoyed as he rode with the soft spring breeze against his face. He was a married man, but a free man; free of debts, and since he'd got himself such a sweet, compliant bride, free of added obligations beyond the strictly polite as well.

The coach finally slowed for a change of horses,

and he dismounted at the wayside inn, waiting for her. He helped his bride from the coach, watching her try to stifle her groans as she moved on stiffened legs. It had been miles since they'd left London.

"Would you like a cup of tea?" Ian asked as she leaned on his arm. "Ale? Lemonade? Some sort of refreshment? This will take a while."

"I'd like to find the lady's convenience first," she murmured, eyes downcast.

An ostler overheard her. "Out'n back, Mum," he said, gesturing over his shoulder. "Foller the path to the bottom of the garden. There be the Jericho."

"Do you want me to accompany you?" Ian asked when she hesitated.

"No, thank you," she said, "I'm a country bred girl, after all."

But she hadn't been bred to walk down a narrow weedy path while dressed in full ballroom regalia from another century. By the time she reached the outhouse, she was sure not only mud from the melting snow, but also thistles and mites, ants, and all the sundry things that clung to her trailing skirts were sharing her gown. The act of arranging her skirts in the little wooden outhouse so she could relieve herself was something she earnestly prayed she'd never have to do again. She was red-faced when she met Ian waiting for her by the inn.

"I don't know how our ancestors did it," was all she could say to him.

"They used a chamber pot in the coach," he said calmly. "Or, if the weather was fine, a convenient field."

"How do you know?" she asked.

"I've seen caricatures," he said blandly. "Now, for some refreshment. Or do you want to change your gown first?"

But she didn't want to ask a stranger, either her husband or a serving wench at the inn, to help her undress and redress. And too, she harbored a dream of exiting the coach in her bridal gown to the awe and admiration of her future servants at her new husband's Hall.

Though a chilly wind began to blow and thick clouds rolled over the sky again, the second half of their journey was spent as the way there had been. It was clear Ian was enjoying himself as his horse trotted beside the coach. *Just as well*, she thought. How did you carry on a polite chat with a stranger you'd just married? Lovers would pass the time embracing and cooing nonsense. Old friends would laugh about the amusing things they'd seen old friends do at their wedding. She and the marquis were neither lovers nor old friends. They were just beginning to be friends. Or so she hoped.

When shadows began to grow thicker, and darkened the landscape, her coach slowed and

Ian rode up to her window. "I don't mind traveling through the night," he told Hannah. "But not only is there no hurry now, it's also no way to treat a bride. The driver thinks the snow is coming this way now. So I suggest we stop. We've had a trying day. And we have another whole day, maybe two if the snow falls hard, to go."

Her heart sank. What a fool she'd been. She'd suffered in her wedding gown until she was sure it would become her shroud, and all for nothing. She'd loved wearing the ancient gown, but reality had set in. Now she couldn't wait to tear it off. She wasn't used to corsets and cinching. Her body felt squeezed and constricted, where she could feel anything at all.

He misinterpreted her sudden expression of misery, and his voice softened. "Yes, it is best that we stop for the night now, have dinner, rest, and get some sleep. We'll continue to take the journey in easy stages."

"Easier than this one, at least," she muttered. The coach slowed more as it steered into the yard at the *Angel's Arms*, proudly declared by the weather-beaten sign.

Ian rode ahead to prepare the innkeeper for their arrival.

Hannah sighed, and tried again, to no avail, to scratch the awful itch that came and went on the bottom of her left breast beneath her corset strings, without actually lowering her bodice to get at it. At least she could feel it, she thought. No matter how well sprung the coach, riding on the highways for a day had left her bottom numb as a corpse's.

She looked forward to stopping until she saw the ancient lopsided, sway-topped inn by the side of the road that the coach pulled up to. It was her wedding night. She'd expected something more than this.

Ian apologized as he offered her his hand. "There's nothing better for miles, and I thought you'd had enough riding."

"Yes, you're right, I have," she said, wishing she could say something clever or bright. But she was weary, itchy, and aching.

"I've ordered a tub of hot water to be brought up to you," he said.

Her eyes brightened. "Oh, yes, please," she said with gratitude.

It wasn't the worst place, Hannah decided as they went into the inn. It was ancient, but clean. The landlord and his wife were gracious and respectful. A fire blazed in the front-room hearth against the chill of the spring evening and the inn smelled of some savory roast. Ian signed the guest register, and led his bride up a creaking stair, down a tilted hallway, to a bedchamber. He opened the door for her, and Hannah was overjoyed to see a maidservant awaiting her inside.

"I'll wash up at the pump and then I'll be downstairs, waiting for you," Ian said. "They have a private parlor for us to dine in. Take your time. There's no hurry now."

The maidservant, hastily recruited from serving at the tap, was happy to take on her new duties. She helped all the buttons on Hannah's beautiful gown and peel it off her, and then unlace, unhook, and drag off all the underpinnings. They both gasped in dismay when they saw the deep marks that the stays and laces, fabric folds and creases had left imprinted on her skin.

"Hot water will soak 'em out," the maid said as Hannah stepped into the tin bath that had been brought to the bedchamber and set up near the blazing hearth. She was cramped, knees to nose, in the small bath, but she was still ecstatic. She passed a half hour crouched in the tin bath, feeling the aches in her body flow away as the maid kept pouring in new pitchers filled with steaming water.

At last, refreshed, smelling of scented soap, dressed in a warm soft gown of pretty pink muslin, her clean damp hair combed free of rice and petals, Hannah descended the stairs, truly comfortable for the first time that day.

The landlord showed her to a private dining parlor, behind the front room, and apart from the common room. It wasn't much: a small chamber with a sagging ceiling, and bottle-thick, time-warped glass windowpanes. It was furnished with a worn red settee, carpet whose patterns had been erased by generations of shoes and boots, and heavy red draperies. But her groom stood up when Hannah arrived, and took her hand. In the flickering fire and lamplight, she could have sworn his welcoming smile was tender. This was more like the wedding night of her girlhood dreams, even here in the modest old inn.

Hannah took a seat at a small table, accepted a glass of champagne, and smiled at her husband. *Her husband*, she thought looking at him. She felt a warm glow that had little to do with the champagne. The marquis, *her husband*, wore casual attire too. For the first time she saw him without a well-fitted jacket. He had left it off. Now she could see that he had needed no padding in his shoulders, because they actually did wing out impressively above his tall, straight frame. He wore a white shirt, open at the neck, and a colorful waistcoat, tight breeches, and high boots. In the fiery shadowy light, he looked rakish, dangerous, like a highwayman or a pirate, only one from out of a Minerva Press novel: not a real villain, out for rapine and jewels, but a fellow fit to fulfill all a female's sleepy midnight fancies.

He smiled at her. "Done," he said, "and well done. If the weather clears we'll start early in the morning, and try to get to Hopewell Hall as soon as we can. That is, if you're willing to ride for that long a time?"

"Now that I'm out of that iron maiden of a wedding gown," she said, "I could ride on to the ends of the earth."

He chuckled. *She has a nice sense of humor*, he thought. And she looked much better to him now than she had in that glorious gown. He knew he might insult her if he told her that. But she wasn't made for elegant gowns and high fashion, antique or modern. Her high-breasted, generous figure showed off to her best advantage dressed as she was now. Her curling hair was scented, her simple gown was in a color that brought out the natural pink in her complexion. She was definitely appealing. She couldn't compete with the sensuous sirens of the courtesan class, or the brittle beauties of the upper class. But she was perfect for what she was. Hannah was like a pretty milkmaid, a charming, uncomplicated country bred miss, seldom seen in London's highest realms.

Which was good, he thought comfortably, because she'd be content staying at Hopewell Hall, and he felt she'd be a fine mistress over it. He wouldn't torment her, or himself, by making her trot around London with him again, unless they absolutely had to do it. He'd be free there. She'd be free at his estate. Their bargain was turning out to be all he could have hoped.

Now they dined, drank, and rested, and easier in mind, they both chatted about their wedding. They commented on the guests, the reception, the cathedral itself. Hannah smiled as she remarked about how proud her father had been as he'd watched the ceremony, how lovely her sisters had looked. He agreed. She grinned when he mentioned her numerous cousins.

"I have dozens," she admitted. "And as you saw, all thrilled to be there. Papa has four sisters and three brothers, and Mama had two brothers and five sisters. But not even Noah had as many who called themselves 'cousin' as we do. Many of them are only long-term friends of the family or my father's business acquaintances. Still, I've come to think of them as family."

"The ancient parties there were all that's left of my family that I cared to invite," Ian said. "Apart from my brother, Simon, who is still not well enough to travel in these dangerous times. We had more family, but they cut themselves off when my father married my stepmother. Those that didn't then quickly did as well when they saw my father's rapidly worsening financial state. I think he tried to borrow from them too. Nothing turns distant relatives more distant than being asked for money. Those old ladies and gentlemen who attended had trouble walking, seeing, hearing, and remembering who I was.

"But they did know the name, and so they came. And so would the others had I asked them. Hopewell Hall is the family seat, after all, and I, the senior ranking member of our clan. I wish my brother had been able to come. You would like him."

"I'm sorry he couldn't be there," she said.

He shrugged. "He wrote to say that so was he. And that one day, maybe, he will return to England. That's my dream."

She sat upright, her cheeks flushed, her eyes sparkling. "Or maybe we could visit him? That's mine. What a wonderful opportunity that would be for me. Not only to meet him, but I've never traveled out of the country."

He looked startled. "Perhaps," he said, slowly. "When the work on the Hall is entirely done, and we've restored the London town house too. Still, the crowd was dizzying enough as it was. I did invite old friends and companions in arms. They all came to get a glimpse of you. You did very well."

"Do you think my sisters made a good impression?" she asked, putting down her fork and looking at him eagerly.

He smiled. "Your mission was accomplished. They were charming and prettily behaved, and, by now, I'm sure everyone there had verified your father's fortune."

She frowned. "Is that all you *gentlemen* think about?"

He stiffened. "Hannah, my dear," he said, "the plain harsh truth is that even now, titled gentlemen who have funds would not court your sisters. Those who don't, however, now see that they may without fear or shame. That is, if they insist on marrying for a title. There are plenty of other decent fellows of good birth and fortune who don't care about such things."

She blinked. Then she fell silent and paid close attention to the strawberry she was cutting into small bits with the side of her spoon.

"Hannah? Did I insult you?" he asked. "I never meant it."

"I think," she said, looking up and straight into his eyes, "that if you consider it, you did insult me. Because what you're saying is that if you had the funds you wouldn't have married me either."

He sat and looked at her for a long moment, his eyes bland. "No lies between us, Hannah," he finally said. "I never would have even been introduced to you. But I didn't mean to hurt . . . Blast! Maybe I did. I'm still tender on that score. There were comments made that I did my best to ignore. Whether we like it or not, I am seen as a fortune hunter."

"And I," she said softly, "as a social-climbing mushroom."

"Time will change that," he said. "You'll see."

They finished their dinner in silence.

Their bedchamber at the *Angels' Arms* had a slanted floor and a huge lumpy featherbed with a canopy that sagged even more than the fat mattress did. A fire grumbling in the hearth kept the little room snug. Hannah's impromptu maid had helped her into her night shift, a gauzy thing that was, Hannah privately thought, too thin for a cool spring night. But it was her wedding night, after all, and she didn't want to disappoint her maid, who giggled and blushed through the process of dressing the fine newlywed bride.

Hannah had no idea of what her husband would think, so she got into bed, propped herself up on pillows so she wouldn't drown in a sea of eiderdown, pulled the coverlet up to her chin, and tried to pretend she was reading whatever book she'd plucked up out of her luggage.

She read until her eyes blurred. Then she put down the book and waited. She knew what the marital act would be. She'd almost committed it with Timothy that last evening they'd been together. She remembered how hot she'd felt, how rapid Timothy's breathing had been, how she'd squirmed under his hands on her body. But she could only wonder about how tender or rough her new husband might be with her. She was more curious than frightened, and yet titillated just thinking about that tall, cool, gentleman holding her, wanting her, whispering to her, caressing her with passion, and giving her pleasure. It was hard to imagine him impassioned, but fascinating too. She felt her body prickling just thinking about it.

It left her with an itch and aches in places she could, but wouldn't, name. She hoped her body would please him. But she knew she couldn't daydream all night until he came. She'd be in a rare state when he joined her if she did. So she picked up her book again, trying to make sense of the words and restore her reasoning.

She'd fallen asleep by the time the bedchamber door opened and Ian came into the room. She woke with a start, and looked wildly around the room. The fire had crumbled to gray ashes long before and the only illumination came from the lamp Ian carried. She saw him outlined by the blaze of lamplight, and realizing where she was, pulled herself up and tried to focus her bleary eyes on him. He put the lamp down carefully on the only table in the room. The flickering glow showed her that he was still dressed as he had been at dinner.

She wondered why he hadn't dressed for bed. But she was suddenly stricken with shyness. Was it appropriate to ask him that? Did the nobility make love with their clothing on? Timothy had been low born, and desperate to get her clothes off. He, she remembered, hadn't taken anything off at all; he'd just fumbled with his trousers, until he'd suddenly stopped and drawn away. But maybe that was how it went with all classes; men kept their garments on. The forbidden drawings a girl-friend had showed her all those years ago might only be fancies of some perverse artist's mind, as her friend's mother had said when she'd caught them giggling and goggling over the pictures and snatched them away.

"Ah, you're awake," Ian said in a soft steady voice. "Or did I cause that? I'm sorry for it if I did. It's very late. Go back to sleep."

"Are you coming to bed . . . sleep?" she asked, correcting herself.

He smiled as he sat on the one chair and began to tug off a boot. "Yes, I'm coming to bed . . . but not necessarily sleep. Although this is a charming inn, and our landlord seems an honest fellow, I want to be in condition to make sure my judgment of him and this inn is correct. It isn't clever to be unprepared in strange places. And I'm a suspicious fellow. You go to sleep. I'll stay here to be sure all is well. In fact, I'll join you in bed, and sleep with an eye open, and with my clothes on."

"Oh," she said.

"Don't worry," he said as he tugged off the other boot. "I don't doubt you'll have an exceeding boring wedding night to remember. I'm just trying to ensure it."

When he was in stocking feet he padded over to the bed and sat. He laughed as he sank into the mattress. "It's like sitting in a pile of feathers! How do you stay up? Well, you're lighter than I am, and you've cleverly braced yourself with pillows."

She tried to scramble to a sitting position, and whip some of the pillows out from behind her. "Here! Take some," she said, thrusting one at him.

"Never mind," he said. He sat and looked at her. She couldn't see his expression because the lamplight was behind him. Nor could she know that her thin shift had slipped, and so the light flickered over her, illuminating most of her full and shapely breasts.

He stared. Then he broke from his immobility and suddenly bent over her. He loomed there, propped on two straight arms, looking at her. She caught her breath. She could scent faint bay rum on his cheeks, rich red wine on his breath. Then he reached for her, and slid one strong arm beneath her shoulders to raise her up. She held her breath, closed her eyes, and parted her lips.

He stuffed the pillow she'd given him back behind her head.

"Rest easy," he said, before he drew away.

Then he laid full length beside her, atop the

coverlet, and turned his broad back to her. "Good night, Hannah," he said.

She lay back again, feeling wounded and forlorn, relieved and very confused. She closed her eyes.

In the morning he was gone.

Chapter 11

The newlywed couple took the rest of the journey in easy stages. So Hannah was surprised when her coach suddenly turned off the main road, drove down a long and winding drive, and then stopped.

"Hopewell Hall," Ian said with quiet pride.

Hannah gasped, "I never expected such a place!" She turned from the coach window and showed a glowing face to Ian. "I never *knew* there were such places! Your home is magnificent!"

"Your home is too," he answered with a smile, watching her radiant expression.

She laughed. But then she sobered. "It's enormous. How shall I ever feel at home here? It's fit for a king."

"You will," he said simply. "Because it is your home. And here you will reign as queen. Or at least," he added, as the coach finally slowed to a stop in the great circular front drive at the Hall, "as my lady."

But it seemed that it was the same thing, Hannah thought after she stepped from the coach. It had snowed here too, but now the setting sun shone on the lawns and paths, looking like diamonds sparkling at the base of a great sugar wedding cake—because her new home was huge, sparkling with windows and wings, rising gray and white out of the snow.

She placed her hand on Ian's arm and they walked toward the great front doors. They had to stop midway because hordes of liveried servants came out of the door, while others ran from the sides of the Hall. They stopped and stood to greet them on the steps and in the drive. There were maids and footmen, bakers, potboys and scullery maids, gardeners, stablemen, dairymaids, and more. Though they looked at Hannah with curiosity, they didn't look for long. Their greetings were for their lord, and they were too busy bowing, scraping, and curtsying to Ian to pay more attention to her. It was, she thought, as though he was indeed their sovereign. And she, Hannah thought with a swell of pride, had given this back to him.

After she'd been introduced to the crowd, and then separately to the housekeeper, the butler, and the cook, that triad that made any great house function, Ian took her on a brief tour of her new home.

"You told me so much, but never this," she said,

pausing on the staircase. A huge dome of glass was high above them, illuminating the interior of the Hall. The setting sun now lighted snow that had fallen on the glass and the interior of the house was shown in stunning rosy golden detail.

"I've been to some estates," she said. "On tour day, of course. Most were built so that if you started walking on the left side you'd eventually end up on the right, where you came in. The rooms seemed to melt into each other. This is like a real house, only so much more."

"What I didn't like, I changed," Ian said as they went up the great stair. "I finished repairs on our wing first so that our bedchambers and sitting rooms would be perfect by the time I brought you here. Once we started, I didn't want to stop. Some of the artisans came from abroad, and I refused to send them home and then bring them back again. Apart from some work still to be done on the outbuildings, most of it is done. This is the Hall as it used to be."

They were in the hallway at the top of the stair now. He stood tall and proud and smiled down at her. "If you don't like something, it will be changed again. It will be your job to choose the colors, fabrics, and any new furniture you wish. It's your home now, and where you'll pass most of your life."

She should have been pleased, but Hannah felt a shiver when he said that. "Certainly not all my life?" she said. "Unless you intend to lock me in the attics like a mad great aunt?"

"Of course you'll be locked up," he said lightly. "Only not in the attics. In the cellars. The spiders are more congenial there."

She laughed. "Thank you. But surely, we'll travel?"

"Surely," he said, "in time. For now, here are your quarters."

He threw open the door to the first chamber they came to.

It was a huge room, with a set of windows that went from floor to ceiling. The room was bright even in the approaching evening light. The walls were covered with stretched patterned ivory silk. The great bed was covered with high white puffy coverlets. There was a graceful lady's desk and a chair that matched its slender design. A charming dressing table with a gilt-framed mirror matched it. There were two chairs, both white, with tiny yellow roses woven into their fabric. A wardrobe covered one wall; another was taken up by a lady's bureau, with a great mirror hung over it that reflected the light from the many windows.

Hannah went to the long windows and looked out.

"Oh," she said with pleasure, "a Juliet balcony! With room for a secret lover or two to visit me by moonlight! And a view of the gardens, although I can't see more than snow now."

She turned around and smiled. "There are arbors, so there must be roses. This is beautiful, so much brighter and lighter than I expected."

"What did you expect?" he asked, leaning a shoulder against a wall, watching her with a slight smile.

"You kept saying 'Hall.' It sounded dark and dangerous. This is beautiful."

He levered himself from the wall. "I hope you think it all is. Now, I'm going to my bedchamber to wash. Then I have some business to see to before I dress before dinner. I suggest you do the same. You might even want to take a nap. You've time. We dine at seven."

"Your bedchamber?" she asked. Husbands and wives shared quarters in her world. When she saw his eyebrow raised she realized again that they came from different worlds. Of course, noble couples had separate chambers. She'd heard about it.

"Yes," he said. "It's next door. We have connecting rooms. This door," he said, strolling to a door at the far end of her room, "leads to my precincts. The door on the opposite wall leads to your dressing room. The bath chamber is there as well. Yes," he said with obvious pleasure, "we have indoor plumbing. The latest thing in one of the oldest homes in England. Amenities in the finest homes in London made me consider it. It was possible, and it's been done. Your dowry went to good use."

It was good of him to put it that way, Hannah thought. Dowries came from the bride's family, and were given after a marriage ceremony. They weren't fortunes paid to a man to get him to marry a woman.

Ian bowed, and left her. Hannah stood in the middle of her new bright, light, very white bed-chamber. If she'd had the making of it, the walls wouldn't be white. Ian had said he'd restored this room. Now she realized that its former occupant must have been his mother or stepmother. One of them had to be blond. She pictured them as fair, slender, and aristocratic. Everything she was not. The spotless patterned fabrics made her nervous. White showed stains. It made her feel like a child with jammy fingers. She glanced at herself in the mirror over her new dressing table. White dulled her own color too. Still, she didn't look like a rosy milkmaid any longer. But she didn't look like a grand lady either. She looked out of place. Something would have to be done.

She stood alone and indecisive until she heard a small scratching sound at the connecting door Ian said led to her dressing room. She went to open it, and found her own maid standing there, beaming.

"Was there ever such a place, Miss? I mean Missus," Millie said eagerly. "No, I mean, 'my lady'," she corrected herself, ducking a curtsy. "Baths and water in the house, and rooms the size of houses. Even the servants' quarters are warm and snug with fire in the hearths too. Leastways, mine is! And my chamber's my own, I don't have to share with no one. Should you like a bath now?"

Poor Millie, Hannah thought. Her speech was worse than ever. It wasn't country, nor was it proper. It was a weird new combination that fell heavily on the ear. The girl had been brought up in the countryside and always worked as maid to a rich gent's daughter. Now she was maid to a real ladyship, and trying hard to fit into her new position. She was attempting to speak like a lady's maid, but she'd never been one.

"A bath please," Hannah, said. "And then, a nap, I think. And then if you'd wake me so I can dress for dinner?"

"I can. I will. Just you see, my lady."

That should be my motto, Hannah thought, as she followed her maid to her dressing room and promised bath. *I can. I will. Just you see.*

Hannah let a footman pull out a chair for her, and looked around the great dining room. She wore a soft-peach colored gown, and had her hair done up in a coronet, looking very sleek and sophisticated, she thought. A strand of pearls lay at her breast. But she still felt as though she didn't belong. It was a magnificent room. Huge framed paintings of the hunt hung high on the gold brocaded silk walls. The dark gold draperies were pulled closed against the night, and two fireplaces, one near the head of the table and the other by the foot, blazed a welcome.

She was grateful that the table hadn't been lengthened to accommodate the crowd it obviously could. And grateful too, that she'd been seated on her husband's right-hand side, rather than all the way down the table, like the caricature she'd seen of a noble host and hostess dining in solitary splendor and shouting to each other in order to be heard.

Still, she didn't feel comfortable. This was far too elegant for her tastes. Her new husband fit in as though the room had been crafted around him. He was every inch the master of the Hall in his formal evening dress. He looked as a nobleman should: humorless, bitterly handsome, and utterly at his elegant ease.

Hannah sighed as the footmen served them steaming soup. She had much preferred the ease she and Ian had shared dining at little inns along the road. They'd chatted and laughed then. Now she could actually hear herself swallowing.

"My lord?" she said after she'd tasted the soup.

She'd said it so low he had to incline his head to hear her.

"What?" he whispered back, smiling, so she could see he was teasing her.

"This is much more of a formal dinner than

I'm used to," she said, low again, so the footmen couldn't hear. "Please, tell me: don't you talk at dinner here?"

"Yes," he whispered again. "But we don't whisper. Why are you doing it?"

"If we speak any louder," she said in a tiny voice, "the footmen will hear us and I didn't want to be caught asking a stupid question."

His laughter was hearty. Her face grew pink as the prawns the footmen were bringing in.

"We can speak in any tone we choose," he said, bending toward her again. "If there's a private matter, we can discuss it in private, later. The staff lives off gossip in a place like this, and I'm afraid we do provide most of it. I apologize. You're right. We don't want them thinking we're not speaking—and so soon."

He grinned, sat back, and spoke in normal tones again. "I was quiet because I was so content, sitting in my own dining room again, at last. And it returned to its former glory. Then I began thinking about what's to be done next in this great pile. I want to keep it up, but anything I do from now on requires planning, and your consent, of course. Tell me, do you like your bedchamber?"

"Well, actually," she said, sitting up, "I could like it more than I do. White is a lovely color for a lady's room, but it makes me feel . . . grubby. That's the word for it. I can't help it. I feel like putting my hands behind my back each time I look at it. I'd prefer a pastel. Or any other color, except of course, no black or brown."

She'd put him in a good humor; she could see that. He smiled and urged her to try each dish that was brought to them. And so they discussed color schemes through the fish course, as the fowl was served, and only decided, once the roast was carved, that maybe pink would suit her best.

She looked doubtful. "I'll look so *rosy*," she said. "My color is high. Like a country girl's."

"But that's what is delightful about you," he said. "You are fresh and blooming. It is your style."

Flattered, she ducked her head. But not before she saw the footmen nod to each other.

"Tomorrow," Ian bent to whisper in her ear. "They'll speak of nothing else around here but the color of your bedchamber."

She shivered with startled pleasure at the feeling of his breath against her ear.

He noticed, and trailed a fingertip along her neck. "And this is how to convince them that we are, after all, newlyweds." He breathed; drew back and saw her expression. "Isn't that what you want?"

"Yes," of course," she said, but once she realized that he was playing to his audience, all the pleasure of the moment vanished.

* * *

They sat in the library after dinner. Ian poured himself some port. Hannah took a small cup of dark coffee, and nibbled at tiny cakes that had been placed on the table before her.

"All alone at last," Ian said as he settled into one of the two huge leather chairs placed by the hearth. "Now, what is the private thing you wanted to say to me?"

The room, for all its size, was snug. Hannah thought it might be because of the atmosphere. It was so civilized, scaled to human comforts. It might have been the walls of books that reached to the high ceilings that gave it that aura. It could have been the cozy feeling of the fire in the hearth, or the lamps that lent a softened glow to every corner of the room. The rich Oriental carpets lent a comfortable air as well. All it needed was a friendly dog or three lying before the fire on their backs with their paws in the air, waiting for their stomachs to be scratched by an idle toe, Hannah thought. Then she'd have felt right at home.

"Do we have to dine like that every evening?" she asked.

He coughed. "Swallowed wrong," he explained, and then smiled a crooked smile at her. "Didn't you like it?"

"Actually, no," she said. "It was just the two of us, and yet it was so formal. It was like there was a phantom group of noble ancestors dining with us. Ah, I'm saying it wrong. It was not something

I'm accustomed to. It was too formal for my tastes. But if it must be done, if you want it, I can grow to accept it, I imagine." She lowered her gaze. "I don't come from such grand beginnings, so it's new to me."

He gazed at her. "Actually, neither do I. My step-mother took my father to London, and there they stayed most of the time. Dinners were taken in the nursery until I was old enough to be sent away to school. My only company was my brother, and our nurses, governesses and tutors. By the time my father was gone, so was most of the money. I left His Majesty's service and spent the rest of my earnings and inheritance to send my brother away to heal, and live in some comfort. By then, all the money was gone and the Hall on its way to ruin. Tonight was a dream I'd entertained for too many years to resist."

"Then we'll dine like that every night," she said with a trace of anger at the way he'd had to live.

He shook his head. "A house must be lived in to keep it whole. Dreams tend to shatter easily. In truth, tonight's dinner was a bit much even for me. There's a smaller dining room we could both be more comfortable in." He smiled at her. "You cast your lot in with me. That doesn't mean you have to cede your life to me too."

A real wife would do both, she thought, and said, instead, "As you wish. But I could get used to it."

"Why bother? When we have company we'll

dine like royalty. When it's just the two of us, the smaller parlor will suit perfectly. Now," he said, putting his empty glass down, "as for tomorrow. I thought I could take you on a tour of the Hall and its grounds. And then after luncheon we could visit the tenants. It's the tenants that bring in funds. We have farms, and there's timber here."

He frowned. "Of course, these aren't the old days. Without your money, that didn't amount to enough to restore the Hall, much less keep it going. Now, thanks to you, I have investments. They're not so colorful or pleasant to chat with as tenants, but they pay much more and more regularly." He paused and then said, more brightly, "And then, if you aren't too weary, I thought to take you into the village to meet the folk there. Everyone must be eager to meet the new lady of the Hall. What do you say?"

"I say it sounds very good," she said.

But she didn't think so later that evening, as she lay in her vast bed, alone and waiting. He hadn't come in after he'd said good night to her at her door. She'd been listening to every creak in every floorboard of the Hall, but he never came to her. They weren't in an inn tonight. He had no excuse, she reasoned, except for indifference.

She gave up waiting, but couldn't sleep now, thinking about his other offenses.

Never once, she noted, had he said the word "wife." She was "the lady of the Hall." So how was she to present herself to all those people she would meet tomorrow? She wasn't really his wife yet. Tonight, as every night since they'd been married, he'd taken her hand, smiled down at her, and whispered, "Good night, my lady." In the inn they'd stopped at, he'd then turned on his side away from her and gone to sleep. Tonight, he'd let go of her hand, bowed, and gone to his own chamber. The walls were thick in this old Hall, but she'd heard him murmuring to his valet, and then, she'd heard nothing but silence.

She was not the lady of the Hall. Hannah lay in a magnificent bed in a great Hall, and considered the fact that she was still a virgin bride.

She reviewed her situation from every angle. She'd a lot of time to do it. She'd gone to bed at nine in the night. The dainty white-and-gold ormolu clock on a far wall now read only eleven. London was just hitting its stride of nightly revels. Even at home with her family a good game of piquet could keep her up until midnight. Her sisters often invaded her bed and sat up to gossip with her until after that witching hour. Only true milkmaids went to bed with the sun and rose with it. She mightn't be nobly born, but she was of a higher class.

Hannah sat up straight. She *was* noble now. That's what this whole farce of a marriage was all about. And the pity of it, she realized, was that she found her new husband increasingly desirable. She concentrated on things about him as never before: the cleft in his determined chin. The changeable color of his watchful eyes. The tall straight figure of the man. His dignity and grace. She wondered how he would look in the grip of desire, and the throes of passion.

She wanted him. But she had no idea if he desired her. She guessed not, or he would have made some attempt by now. She wasn't afraid of sexual relations. Her experiences with Timothy had been thrilling. It couldn't be the same with her new husband, of course, because she didn't love him as she had Timothy. But there was no question she desired him.

Ian's breath on her ear this very night had weakened her knees. Was he unaffected? Was she only to be a source of funds to him? That, Hannah considered, was unfair. That hadn't been part of the bargain. In fact, he'd agreed to give her a child. How long could she wait for him to pay attention to his duty toward her?

She lay back down, pulled a pillow over her head, and groaned. That was awful, thinking of herself as a duty to be done. She dashed the pillow away. They'd been married for four days. The suspense was making her say foolish things and be anxious beyond her capacity to endure. Was he ever going to attempt to make love to her? She had to find out how, exactly, he felt about her, physically. If a marriage wasn't consummated it could be declared annulled. Which while not as socially horrific as divorce, was also shameful.

Hannah's eyes opened wide. Could he want her money to repair his fortunes, make his investments, and then be able to keep his money and discard her by claiming non-consummation? No. He was far too noble. Or so she hoped.

But he wasn't remotely interested in making love to her. She'd seen admiration and humor but never desire gleaming in his eyes when he gazed at her. Had he another love, after all? Was this whole marriage a fiction?

Hannah rose from bed, wrapped a night robe around herself, and went to the window to stare out into the dark. How could she know? How could she ask him? Indeed, could she ask him? It was embarrassing. It was upsetting. Should she ask him at breakfast? How could she? While they were touring his grounds? When they were greeting his tenants? Lunching at his local inn? Tomorrow night, when he took her hand and gave her a polite good night again?

It was growing late, and she was getting tired, but dread grows in the darkness, and solitude magnifies everything. Even courage.

Hannah went softly to the connecting door to Ian's rooms. She put her ear to the heavy door, and heard nothing in his room. She tapped on the door, and almost fled back into her own bed after she did it. But there was no answer to her summons. She tapped harder, and then impatient, she knocked on the door, so that if he was in there, he would hear unless he was dead . . . unless, of course, she thought, he was out somewhere, and in the bed of another female?

"Come in," she heard him say. Ian's voice repeated the words, with a bit more worry. "Come in!"

Hannah edged the door open. The room was dark, but light from her own chamber showed that Ian was half out of his bed, a coverlet wrapped around his body.

"Hannah!" he said as he pulled himself out of his bed. "What is it?"

"Why don't you make love to me?" she blurted.

Chapter 12

Ian was glad she couldn't see him clearly. He was half awake and beyond surprised. He ran a hand over his face and felt the slight scratch of night whiskers. So this wasn't a dream. He'd been sleeping and suddenly there was a noise, and he'd said "come in," expecting his valet, though he didn't know why Baker would want to see him at this hour of the night. And there she was. Hannah Leeds, his bride and benefactress, stood in the doorway between their rooms, her figure in her night shift outlined by faint lamplight behind her. He sat in his bed, in the dark, in many ways.

"What?" he said, though he'd heard her, but didn't believe it. "That's an inspired thing to say," he grumbled to himself. He reached for his robe by the foot of the bed, flung it on, and belted it tightly before he faced his bride. She didn't move from where she stood. "Now, again," he said as he approached her. "Say again, I was asleep."

But she wouldn't say anything. She just stared up at him.

He ran a hand through his hair. "If I'm actually awake now," he said carefully, "and given that you said anything, I could swear you asked me why I don't make love to you."

She didn't move.

"So," he said, "since you haven't transformed into a sea serpent, and the scene hasn't changed, I must assume I'm awake, you are too, and you did ask me that."

She nodded. Her voice, when she spoke, sounded painfully compressed. "I didn't know you were sleeping," she said. "I wouldn't have woken you. But it was on my mind, and I didn't know when else to ask when no one was around to hear, so I came straight to you. It was a stupid thing to do, I see it now. Maybe I am half asleep at that."

He took a deep breath. She looked woebegone, and hung her head.

"No," he said gently. "Not a bad time or a stupid question. But why didn't you ask sooner? For that matter, why haven't you shown any interest in the subject before this?"

But of course, he thought with a pang of pity. She was afraid. They were married, and he hadn't touched her yet. He should have had this out with her days ago. He winced, picturing her lying awake for hours, afraid to sleep, wondering, and maybe dreading his coming to her.

"We don't know each other yet," he said. "I didn't think you'd be eager for lovemaking. We've only been married for what . . . ? He closed his eyes. "Four days. Counting this as another day. So you can go to sleep and don't worry. I won't disturb you. In fact, I promise to give you plenty of notice if the idea occurs to me." He turned back to his bed.

"What if it doesn't?" she said.

He checked.

"That is to say, do you intend to do it?" she asked. "Or are you waiting for some other reason?"

"Other reason?" He shook his head. "I don't understand. What other reason would I have?" He stayed still a moment, thinking, gathering his wits. "But may I ask you what your hurry is?" He took a step closer to her. "I was away for a long time before our wedding, we were only together for three weeks before we tied the knot. It takes about four, I understand, before a female begins knitting little garments. May I ask you if there's a reason why you want this done now? I'm not accusing you of anything, Hannah. But your sudden interest in the carnal nature of our marriage surprises me and I'd like to know what fostered it."

He heard her quick intake of breath.

"I know what you are insinuating, and I tell you I am *not* with child," she said coldly. "I didn't even go near another male while you were gone."

He nodded. "Good to know. Is that what spurs this desire then? Are you so used to masculine attentions that a few weeks without is giving you some discomfort?"

Ian ran a hand over his face again. He didn't know why he said that. It sounded much worse than he intended. But her tension had communicated itself to him. She was accusing him of something and he was tired, and she wasn't making any sense to him.

"Is that what you think of me?" she asked. "Just because I wondered why you had no interest in me? Did it occur to you that the thought came to me that if you didn't consummate this marriage, you could eventually say I denied you? Then you could petition for an annulment, which isn't as bad as divorce, socially at least, and my father could do nothing about it. And," she added bitterly, "you could keep my dowry because I'd be judged the one who defaulted on the bargain."

He straightened. "Is that what you think of me?" he asked incredulously.

"I've had a lot of time to think about it," she said, backing a step, because even in the dark she could see that he was very angry.

"Four days," he said flatly. "And because I didn't immediately take you to bed, you accuse me of trying to steal your damned money?"

"No!" she answered angrily. "But we don't know each other and this is a strange marriage, and you did say you'd give me a child. And yet you're only polite with me. What am I to think?"

"That I want to cheat you?" he asked.

"I'm sorry," she said. "I think I just got nervous, waiting."

Nervous because she was a maiden waiting? he wondered. Or because she had experience with men before and now that she was married she wanted more from him? Or if she was a maiden, perhaps she thought that once she'd had sex with him, she'd be free to see some other man without him knowing? There was so much he didn't know about her. It was too much to ponder, here in the middle of the night, with her standing still as a post before him. She was his wife. More than that, he was her debtor. There was only one way to know what to do.

"Do you want me to make love to you now?" he asked.

She closed her eyes. "Yes," she murmured. "Then it will be done and there won't be any possibility of annulment."

He felt the fury rise in him. How dared she question his honesty? *But,* he silently answered himself with bitter clarity, *maybe she thinks an honest man doesn't sell himself like a whore.*

"Well," he said curtly, "a bargain's a bargain. Go to your bed, Hannah. I'll join you there."

She turned as though sleepwalking, and went back to her bedchamber. He stood impassive for a moment. He'd never made love without desire. He'd never made love in anger either, and he knew he had to quell his rage at once. But whatever he did, he had to perform. She deserved her pound of flesh. His lips turned up in a cynical smile. If she were expecting a pound, she'd be disappointed. He wondered if he could even raise an ounce, beset as he was with internal conflict. But he had to placate her. The fact was plain. He'd given himself in wedlock, and as the daughter of a businessman she expected a fair bargain. But it would be unpleasant and difficult, and he wished it all were a bad dream. He wondered if she could yet be talked out of it.

She was waiting in her bed. Her draperies were partially drawn open and the subtle silvery moonlight streaming in served him better than unforgiving yellow lamplight tonight. So he bent and turned down her lamp. Then he walked to her bed and joined her there. He didn't remove his night robe. The thought of stripping naked before her while he was doing her bidding and giving her his body was too painful. He thought he wasn't a proud man, but that thought shriveled him, body and soul.

He didn't know how a man could have sex with a woman and not desire her. At least, he thought, he'd never done it, not even in his youth, when he was being entertained by a light lady he'd purchased for the evening. Then it had been laughter and wine and what appeared to be mutual enjoyment that spurred him. Now he had nothing but the cold reality of a debt owed.

He lay beside his wife, and touched her hair. It was silky and cold. He tried once more to end it now.

"Hannah," he said. "It's late, and we're both tired. Don't you think it would be best to wait until more time has passed?"

"I won't insist," she said. She lay immobile. "That would be embarrassing. Good night then."

She turned her head from him.

"I didn't say that," he said, because there wasn't anything else he could say. "Hannah, here I am. I only wanted to be sure of your feelings."

He checked. He thought that, perhaps, if he didn't commit the act, *she'd* sue for annulment, and then where would he be? His investments hadn't borne fruit yet. In all honor, he'd have to work hard and for years to give her father the money back. He'd be poor again, only this time he'd also be mocked behind his back, and called a capon.

But he felt no rising of his flesh as he brought his lips to her cool cheek. She made no move to assist him. She just lay there, her eyes half closed. He stroked the smooth flesh at her neck, and then, slowly, brought his hand down to caress one of her high breasts.

She gasped.

"Damme!" he said, drawing back. "I'd forgot. My hands are rough from work. A gentleman shouldn't touch a female with hands like emery paper. Forgive me."

But the feeling of her round, firm breast in his hand had stirred something in him.

"I don't mind," she said.

That was, he thought, both better and worse for him. She might be used to hard hands. That led to doubt and doubt would lead to impotence. He was thinking too much. And so he blocked his wayward thoughts and stifled his conscience, and held her breast again, feeling its sweet weight, kneading it. Its nipple dimpled to a hard knot in the center of his palm. That was better. He forced himself to think of nothing but sensation, nothing but pleasure, and there was nothing in the world so good as the feeling of a soft female body against his own.

He brought his mouth to the peak of that breast, and ran his hand under her thin night shift, over the rest of her voluptuous body. Her body was very fine. Her breasts were well-shaped, tart as apples, her waist nipped inward tidily, only to flare out to round, firm hips and bottom. Her skin was smooth; her scent like water lilies on a hot summer's day.

If he forgot who she was, and who he was, and simply let his body show him the way, he thought he could accomplish it. She didn't speak, and he was glad of it. That way, he could forget with whom he was.

He thought of all the lovely women he had accommodated. He closed his eyes and thought of the curves and shapes he was stroking and nuzzling, until he felt her flesh warming, and his own rising. She was, at last, damp, when he finally touched her intimately. It was not enough preparation for him, and it was too much for him too. But it was time. He could do it at last.

He raised himself and leaned over her, balanced on his elbows. Her eyes were closed. He couldn't afford to close his own. He had to look down to see her body in order to stop thinking. He nudged her legs apart. She allowed it and then he moved them wider apart, so he could settle between them. He felt her pliancy become strained. In a quick convulsive movement, she became rigid and tried to close her legs.

He stopped. Then he quickly pulled away and fell to the bed beside her.

"I'm sorry," she whispered. "I was just surprised. I couldn't help it. You can start again."

He said nothing. He only lay there, and then flung his arm across his eyes.

She sat up and looked down at him. "Is anything the matter?" she asked in a small voice.

"Everything," he muttered. "It shouldn't be like this, Hannah. Lovemaking is too fine a thing to ruin with anger, and I must tell you that I'm very angry now. Yes," he said before she could speak. "And whatever you think, you wouldn't want me like that. *I* don't want me like that. But that's what happens if you come into a man's room in the night and demand that he make love to you. *Especially* if he feels obligated to you. And certainly not if you want pleasure." He moved his arm away from his eyes. "And absolutely not if you wish to continue to like him. And without doubt not, in my case, if you want him to continue to like you."

He sat up in one swift movement. He took her icy hands in his. "Hannah," he said. "It was difficult for me to stop, but it would have been much worse if I went on. I'm only glad that I realized it in time. But it was a close-run thing. That was a wretched experience for both of us. Do you understand?"

"You don't want me," she said flatly.

"I wouldn't have married you if that were true. But I want you when you want me. And not just for stud service."

He could see her wince, even in the shadowy light.

"And I don't like the thought of having to make love to prove myself. That's performing," he said. He ran a hand over his mouth again. He thought a moment. "You wouldn't like it if I treated you like that, would you?" he asked. "If I wakened you in the night and demanded that you service me?"

She hung her head.

"There was no real desire in that request, was there?" he asked. "You just wanted me to prove something to you?"

She nodded.

"What?"

"That it wasn't just my funds that thrill you," she said in a small voice.

Now he grimaced. "Oh lord. Of course, I should have thought of that. Hannah, there is no way I can demonstrate that to you. Making love to you tonight wouldn't have done it. There are men who regularly have sex with women for money. Some do it for a living. And not just abjectly poor men, but those who want to live well and not work hard. But in my estimation making love when it isn't in your heart is working far too hard. Most of the names for such fellows are unpleasant. They have to be all smiles and flattery and in readiness for their mistresses or wives whenever asked. Believe me, the *ton* is filled with such men. So had I accommodated you, it would still prove nothing. But I couldn't do it."

She went still, realizing she hadn't considered that. She knew of such men, and hadn't put him in that category. He was right.

"You do attract me," he said, touching her cheek gently. "I have no intention of letting you remain a virgin bride. But for both our sakes, it must be mutual desire and shared pleasure. Only lovers with long experience with each other should try to mate after a fight. That can be delightful. This was not that time. Can you see what I mean?"

She nodded.

"As for the other," he said, "I was too angry to answer you properly before. I have too much pride; I know that. But I do have a proud name. Do you think I'd muddy it with an annulment?"

She bit her lip, and then shook her head. "I don't know what I was thinking," she admitted. "I was feeling alone and getting worried. Ours is an unusual situation, you must admit. I don't know how to behave or what you want of me."

"I want us to live in peace and contentment," he said honestly. He said no more, because he began to think her idea of achieving that state differed from his. "I didn't want us starting out on the wrong foot."

He leaned forward and placed a light kiss on her lips. It was unexpectedly sweet for both of them. He took her in his arms and kissed her again. When they stopped, she clung to him. He could feel the hardening tips of her breasts against his chest.

He drew away with difficulty. "There. You see? Our time will come soon. I just want to be sure it's the right time. That would have to be with no assumptions of supremacy on either side."

"Yes, that, I understand now. Are you still angry with me?" she asked quietly.

"No," he said. "But let's let it be for a while, shall we?"

He rose from the bed. She looked up into his face.

He pressed a kiss on her hands and left her to go to his own chamber. Then he got into bed, and lay silently for a long while, staring into the darkness.

He heard the door to his room slowly opening, and saw a slice of flickering lamplight fork into his chamber. He sat up abruptly. Had she changed her mind? He was still aroused. If she was ready, he was, no matter what he'd said before. There was a time for thinking and one for action, and there was only so much he could take.

"My lord?" a deep voice said softly. "You all right? Need anything?"

Ian sank back down to the mattress. "You know damned well what I need, Mr. Baker, and you can't supply it. I've no doubt you had your ear to the door. Don't perjure yourself by denying it. Go to sleep. That's what I'm going to do."

"You're a true gentleman, you are," Baker said. "And that's a damned shame. Good night." He closed the door quietly behind him.

Was he a true gentleman? Ian wondered. Or a coward for leaving as fast as he decently could? There was more he might have said to Hannah. He knew there wasn't any more he could have done. There was only so much control he had. The body could abduct the mind. If he'd continued stroking her lush form much longer, his body would have responded beyond any stopping point. They would have made love; only it wouldn't have been love. It might or might not have conceived a child. It would have definitely sowed disaster for any chance they had for anything like love in the future. Marriage was a deal more than he'd expected. But what had he expected? His mother was long gone; his father had been a fool for his second wife. His brother had never married, of course. And he himself had been working too hard to reverse his fortunes to socialize and so notice any married couples and their situations.

It might have all been a dream, he thought as he started to drift off. If it were real, he thought sleepily, she wouldn't soon ask him for sex again. Nor would he seek it from her. He wasn't sure if that were a good or bad thing. He only knew that if he'd started off their relations with anger on his part, and disappointment on hers, they'd never reach any decent kind of accommodation with each other.

And then, exhausted and weary of himself, he closed his eyes and obliterated thought and fell asleep instantly.

Chapter 13

Lord Sutcombe didn't see his bride the next morning. He woke before the dawn, washed and dressed. The weather, as so often in the early spring, had been mild and clear. The snow was entirely melted, so he went thundering out on his horse before he breakfasted, and rode hard and long before he returned to his Hall.

His wife didn't come down to have luncheon with him. Her maid said she was feeling unwell. He grimaced, gave his best wishes for a speedy recovery to be conveyed to her, got on his horse again, and rode off for the rest of the day.

At six in the evening, he came back into his Hall, went up the stairs and to the door of his wife's bedchamber. Her maid cracked the door open and her eyes opened wide too. The master of the Hall was disheveled, his boots a disgrace, his hair windblown, and his face set in hard lines. He asked for admission. He looked more like a high-wayman than a marquis, but would command obedience in either guise. The maid quailed, looked back over her shoulder for an answer, and then quickly curtsied, let him in, and scurried from the room, leaving the master alone with her mistress.

Hannah sat curled up in her bed, backed by cushions, an opened book on her knees, a plate filled with fruit and small cakes at her bedside. She wasn't in bedclothes. Rather, she looked peaceful and calm, young and charming, in a lovely blue gown, with her hair neatly arranged. She looked up at him with sudden, deep suspicion, and perhaps a little fear.

"You don't look at all sick," he said curtly.

"No, because I'm not," she said, closing her book.

"You said you were."

She shrugged.

"And you didn't come down all day," he said with accusation.

"I didn't have anything to do," she answered.

He paced a step. She'd never seen him so carelessly dressed. He looked hard driven, she thought, watching him with faint pleasure. It wasn't fair that she should be the only one embarrassed and contrite about last night.

"I'm sorry," he said, without looking at her. He held his head high, looking, she thought, aristocratic even in his disarray. "It's last night, isn't it? The truth is that I've seldom felt so confused. You made a demand of me and I felt too much in your debt to refuse you. I thought I did the right thing, but there's no right thing to do in such a case, is there?"

She ducked her head. "No," she said quietly. Then she raised her eyes and looked at him steadily. "But why didn't you just say you were tired? That would have ended it right there."

He sat on the edge of her bed and looked at her steadily. "Or that I had an aching head?" he asked, shooting a sardonic look at her. "That's for disconsolate wives, not bridegrooms."

She colored faintly. Then she tilted her head to the side, considering what he'd said. "You thought it was a demand? I didn't mean it that way. In fact, I don't think I've really demanded anything of anyone since I was an infant. You needn't worry," she went on. "I'll never demand anything of you, because it's not in my nature. Well, of course, if you're strangling someone I might demand you stop it." Her smile was sudden, unexpected, charming. "If they didn't deserve it, that is."

The merest smile appeared on his hard mouth.

"But last night?" she asked. She looked up at him, her face pink with embarrassment, her expression forlorn. "I merely asked. Insistently, to be sure," she added thoughtfully. Then she sighed. "My lord, the truth is that I'd been alone so much since we married that I was beside myself. I'm not used to solitude, especially at night. I was far from my home and my two sisters, who chatter to me all the time. I'm not used to having no one to talk with. I was lonely and I wanted to feel, if not desired, then needed. No, *necessary*.

"Now I see you were right. It would have been disastrous," she went on. "One thing I must tell you, though, if we are ever to deal well together. It may have seemed to you as though you were bought, and I'm sorry for it, though in a way it's true. But no more true than it is that my father was desperate to buy a husband for me. Purchasing a husband is thought to be just as bad for a woman as being bought is for a man, I think. Until we both manage to forget that, I don't know how we'll deal well at all."

He nodded. "True. A truce then? A mutual pact of polite dealing and nothing more for now? And let it stand until we both agree it's time to end it? Or begin our lives together?"

She sighed. "Isn't that what you wanted in the first place? You wanted no relations with me at all before I insisted on a child."

He paused. "I wasn't thinking then. I was feeling pushed and desperate; my obligations had the upper hand. I was at my wit's end, Hannah, too eager to accept a simple solution even if it was a degrading one for me. But it was a foolish assumption on my part. Why should a vital young woman like yourself agree to a celibate life?"

"Maybe you didn't want to disbelieve it, because you didn't intend to have one for yourself," she said simply.

He looked uneasy. "Gentlemen are known to have their diversions."

She looked at him steadily. "Do you?"

"Not now I don't."

"And will you in future?"

"Will you?" he countered.

They looked at each other.

"We don't know each other yet, do we?" he asked. "But I humbly suggest we get started on it. Again, are you agreed?"

She nodded.

"Hannah," he said quietly, "the woman I am slowly coming to know is nothing like the one I agreed to marry. You're changing before my eyes. Miss Leeds, the dutiful daughter, would never demand anything of her noble husband, even in jest. Miss Leeds, the shy young female I courted, would never deny her noble husband anything, nor argue, nor let him know she was angry at anything he did, however vile."

She tilted her head. "Why would you want to marry such a gutless milksop?"

"Why would you pretend to be one?" he asked.

It silenced her.

He looked at her ruefully. "I had to marry money. You knew that. There was no other course open to me. Believe me, I tried. I thought you were simply a good, sweet young woman who followed her father's plans without question. I could make such a woman happy. Now I see you were never that. More to the point now, for me at least, is why did you agree to marry me?"

He waved a hand as though brushing away mist from between them. "And please don't tell me about providing opportunities for your sisters. They can do very well for themselves. And your father isn't an autocrat. He is, in fact, putty in your hands. Do you trust me enough to tell me why you—the you I am coming to know—would agree to marry a stranger, titled or not?"

She lowered her gaze.

He remained still, watching her. "You'd been deeply disappointed in love," he said flatly.

She nodded.

"And just before we met?"

She nodded once more.

"I knew you'd had some attachment, but not such an intense one," he said. "You were feeling squashed, were you? So that's why you were so subdued and agreed to such a foolish thing? And what a clever fellow I am. I simply accepted it. What a fine pair of noodles we are."

She smiled at him. He looked very handsome and commanding, even in his careless dress. She doubted he could ever look bad. But suddenly he sounded better to her than he ever had. If this was the real Lord Sutcombe, she was glad of it, and eager to meet the rest of the man she didn't know.

"The next time you have a doubt about my motives for wanting something of you, *please* tell me what you're thinking," she said sincerely. "And please ask me why I want it, will you? Oh!" she added. "And if ever you think I'm demanding, let me know. Be sure I'll let you know if I think you are."

"Your father brought up hard-headed young women," he said, smiling.

"Oh no. Anthea and Jessica are far more amiable than I am. Well, maybe not Jessica."

"Why didn't I see that before?"

"Because I wasn't myself when I agreed to marry. I am slowly remembering who I was."

"I, on the other hand," he said, "have always been what I am. Honest, fair to a fault, and reasonable beyond all patience."

She giggled. It seemed to please him very much.

He suddenly turned serious. "So we can work together on this?"

"Surely," she said. "We may try."

They smiled at each other with a certain knowing affection, looking for the first time, if they could see it, like a newlywed couple.

"So," he said, rising from her bedside, "we start all over, anew. Good morning, Lady Sutcombe.

What is your pleasure this afternoon? A stroll in the gardens, perhaps? A tour of the rest of the grounds? Do you think you will move your ever so sensitive bottom out of bed before nightfall?"

She giggled, and he laughed, and she thought there might be hope for them, after all.

But he was in a foul mood at dinner.

Hannah took her seat at a smaller table in the smaller dining parlor, and looked at Ian. He had risen automatically when she came in the door, and then sat again, still reading a much-read letter, and scowling at it.

"Something else I did?" she asked.

He raised his head. "What?"

"Your lively mood," she said.

"Oh, no," he said. "Not you. Forgive me, I brought my troubles to dinner, when the thing to do with them is to lock them out."

"Do you . . ." she hesitated. "Can you share them? That often helps me when I'm troubled."

"But you're a totally socialized creature," he murmured, "and I've been on my own for a long time." He folded the letter, and looked up. His expression cleared. "You look lovely tonight. What an oaf I am not to have noticed."

She preened. It was a cool spring evening, and since she felt as though she were beginning a new life with her new husband, she'd felt the need to liven it up. She wore a light green gown with yellow stripes and long sleeves, and a single gold locket on a black ribbon shone at her breast.

He was dressed neatly, and well, but not in formal garb. He wore buff breeches, a white shirt, and beneath his exquisitely fitted brown jacket, she caught a glimpse of a gold waistcoat. The smaller room, his casual attire, and his smile made her feel more comfortable.

"I have a letter from my stepmother," he explained. "And yes, you may envision all the wicked ones from your fairy stories at will. She's not so beautiful as those witch queens, merely passable for a woman her age, but she is decidedly evil. In my eyes, at least, and those of my brother. She had little to do with us after she married my father, thank God, so we didn't suffer from her machinations. Not directly. But she was fifteen years my father's junior, and money hungry. She bled the estate dry. He, poor fellow, was trying to please her, and always had a weak grip on economics. And he was growing older than he cared to admit, in mind and body. He had already frittered away a great deal of money, and begun to beggar the estate. She didn't attempt to put things right. All she wanted was to have things lavish and amusing.

"They traveled where they could with a war on, they gambled everywhere, she wore the latest fashions, and they gave extravagant parties, I hear.

When he died, there was little left to the estate, and that which she could she sold or took away with her.

"Now," he said with a black look at the letter again, "she seeks money from me. She congratulates me on my marriage, and makes special mention of how lucrative a union she heard it was for me. She congratulates me on my wisdom. And she tells me that as her coffers are empty, she knows it would be my father's dearest wish that I help her financially." His hands closed to fists on the table, even though he held the letter in one of them, and crumpled it.

"Not in this world, I don't think," he said. "Let her receive generosity from a greater lord than I. Though I doubt he has anything in store for her but flames, as I wish I did." He looked up. "Oh good Gads!" he said bleakly. "I'm only showing myself to be an angry brute in your eyes, aren't I? Do you want to meet her and judge for yourself?"

"Well, not after that introduction," she said. "But if you don't mind, when we go to London again, I think I should. I expect there will be no way to avoid it, actually."

"True," he said. "If she had any sensitivity, she wouldn't write to me at all. She must be in bad condition. Perhaps not," he mused. "She never had enough money."

"Well, it would be interesting to meet her," Hannah said. "I don't doubt you're right about her.

But she's not the one I'm interested in getting to know. I want to know more about you, my lord."

"Then know I want you to call me by name," he said. " 'Ian' will do fine, unless, of course, you want to be called 'My Lady' all the time. She did."

Hannah didn't have to ask who "she" was. "No," she said. "No, thank you, Ian. 'Hannah' will do, or, when you come to know me better, perhaps 'Nan.' Have you no pet name?"

"It's difficult to shorten Ian," he said. "But you may try, or call me anything you wish."

"Are you certain?" she asked with a twinkle. "I have a vivid imagination."

"Yes," he said, "I imagine you do, but you're hindered by propriety."

She laughed.

They dined, and talked as they did, and slowly Ian's thunderous expression lightened and fled as darkness always does before laughter.

After dinner they sat in adjoining chairs in his study and chatted about the townsfolk he would take her to meet the next day. But that, he insisted, only after he made sure she thought she felt well enough for the excursion.

She grinned. "I will. I usually don't have many ailments, only excuses."

He grinned in appreciation.

"Even when I was a girl, I mended quickly," she mused. "Maybe if I were born to the purple, my skin would be more tender, but as I am, I enjoy robust good health. That is one advantage to marrying a commoner."

His pleasant expression fled. He leaned forward and took one of her hands in his. "Hannah. That isn't amusing. Or true. You are a most uncommon woman."

When it grew late, he walked her to her bed-chamber, and stood with her at the door like a bashful suitor saying good night before a frowning chaperone. He leaned down and kissed her cheek.

She caught a faint scent of sandalwood. Last night, she remembered, she hadn't been able to smell anything of him, but then she had been suffused with shame, her senses blocked by her own humiliation.

He stepped back. "I mean no more than to give you a good night, my wife," he said, showing both his hands in a protest of innocence. "You have my word on it. Lud! Now here we have a new problem," he said in a whisper. "If I attempt to make love to you, I'm afraid you'll think I'm doing it in apology for last night. I feel inhibited, and I don't want you getting the wrong idea. How do we deal with this?"

She paused, and looked up at him. "I don't know. But maybe I will when the right time comes. That's it, I think. Time is the answer."

He smiled. "That's a good idea. And I promise I will make sure you're well aware, and very willing. So sleep well, and undisturbed . . . unless," he added, his gray eyes glinting in the dimmed light, "you demand otherwise."

"I do not!" she said. "And good night to you too, my lord husband. Ian. Sleep well. You will be undisturbed by me, at least."

"So you think," he said enigmatically. "I'll see you in the morning."

She went to her bed, bemused. No one disturbed her. But he'd been right; his memory didn't leave her. She didn't sleep well at all. She kept getting the scent of sandalwood, and looking up to see if he might be standing in the doorway between their rooms.

He wasn't.

Chapter 14

Spring had finally returned, to stay. The weather was fine enough for the lord of the Hall and his lady to ride out and meet their neighbors.

The tenants of the great Hall bowed and curtsied. Their children smiled shyly at their new lady when they were introduced. Then after a tour of their cottages, Ian and his bride drove into the little village that served the great Hall. It was an old one, with a duck pond, a village green, and a perfectly preserved simple Romanesque Church that the Normans had built soon after they'd landed here, centuries past.

The vicar and his wife were gracious, and seemed sincere. The shopkeepers came out of their shops to greet the couple. In fact, everyone who raised a toast to Hannah at the local inn when they stopped in there, and who met her while she and Ian were walking through the village, was kind and welcoming to her. She was pleased but even more so when she realized that although they seemed to accept her completely, they all worshiped her husband.

Ian stood out from his people because of his height, his posture, his elegant casual clothing, and his impeccable manners. And yet he stood among them with grace and charm and a touch of condescension, like an ancient lord visiting his serfs. He was, Hannah thought, perhaps a bit too stiff, a trace too formal for her taste. But they seemed to expect and admire it. He employed many of the people for miles around, and was the latest in a long line of noblemen who had owned the largest estate in the district. The Hall was listed in the guidebooks, and was on every map. Best of all, the new marquis had restored it from ruin. In so doing, he had reclaimed the local folks' pride, as well as their village. They purely loved him.

And he seemed to love the adulation, Hannah thought. He didn't act surprised or delighted, or as though he was humbled. He behaved as though he was only getting his due. No wonder the man had such immense pride. He was treated like royalty. And no wonder, she thought sadly, and not for the first time that day, that he'd responded to what he'd perceived as her orders in the way he had done. In fact, she thought her new husband was more sensitive than she'd have thought possible for a man who had been raised like a prince, and now ruled like a king. No wonder her demand and the terms of his marriage had stung him so much.

She questioned if he'd ever accept her as his wife. She couldn't help wondering what sort of woman he would have married, if he'd had a choice. She really didn't want to find out. And so when he bent to whisper to her that it was time they moved on because there were other estates in the neighborhood where they were expected to pay a call, Hannah became anxious again.

"The Morrisons have been here since the year dot," he said casually as he tooled their light carriage out of the village and on down the road. "An ancient baronetcy," he added, "and a matching manor, though they've always run the place like a farm."

Was that disdain she heard in his voice? For a baron?

"You must have been in dire straits . . ." she began, and then closed her lips. She'd been going to blurt, "to even have considered marrying me, given the way you feel about lesser titles, considering I had none at all." Belatedly she realized the danger in starting that up again, and bit her tongue.

He turned his head to look at her. She couldn't judge his expression because it was so purposely bland. "In dire straits?" he asked with too much interest.

"Yes," she said in a quick recover, "when you saw how your stepmother was looting the Hall. Everyone loves it so much. How did they feel about her?"

She'd guessed right. Talking about the woman diverted him.

"They didn't like her," he said. "Or so they say now. I don't know. I was away at school half the time, and then in the service of His Majesty. I heard about the excess, not the deterioration. My father died when I was three and twenty, when I was away. I made my way back here, and sold whatever little was left so that I could send my brother to physicians. They recommended that he move to a warmer climate where there was decent medical care. It took me over a year, what with seeing him set to rights. I went with him to see that his travel evaded the war all along the way. When I returned, I inspected the Hall again, and found ruin. Real ruin. Deserted rooms, holes in the roofs, the place stripped to its bare peeling walls. She had returned and took anything that might be sold. I imagine vagrants and local children did the rest. A house must have a beating heart living in it or it deteriorates, whether it's a cottage or a manor."

He cocked his head to the side. "Hannah, you're blushing. *Now* what have I said?"

"I just realized," she said carefully, "I don't know how old you are."

His sudden bark of laughter made the horses put back their ears. "Lord, girl, didn't you study the marriage contract?"

"I never saw it. Well, I did, actually, when I signed it. But I didn't notice much then."

"Did you love him that much?" he asked quietly. "That you went through all of it in a daze?"

She studied her gloved fingers, and tilted her head down. She wore a straw poke bonnet, so all he could see was the crown of it when she did that. That suited her. "A daze? I suppose so. I had been very full of myself until then. So it came as a shock."

"It?"

"Our ending the connection." That wasn't true. Timothy had ended it. But she didn't want to go into that. Ian probably felt her lack of worth enough already. No need to add fuel to the fire. She lifted her face to his. "Can we please not discuss it?"

"Fine," he said, looking out to his horses. "But odd. You want to know everything about me, but you tell me little about yourself."

"Oh, come," she said with a tilted smile. "You know you're so much more interesting than I am, my lord."

This time his laughter made the horses' ears flatten.

"Gad, what you think of me," he said. "Seven and twenty. That's how many years I have. Eight and twenty come August, if I have the luck to achieve such antiquity. And you are four to five years my junior, depending on the time of year."

She nodded. "I'm not a fool. It's just that I acted like one in so many ways, I see it now."

"We all see so clearly in hindsight," he said. "But what I want to know now, question for question, is what about going to visit our neighbors the Morrisons has put you in such an anxious mood? They're dull, but not murderously so, I promise."

She laughed and settled back on the seat beside him. It was a glorious day, the late spring trying to fulfill all its belated promise at once. The untimely snow hadn't lingered long enough to blight the new growth it had covered. Fruit trees blushed pink and white as fat buds opened to the sun. Hannah took off her bonnet, and though she knew the warm sunlight might brush her nose and cheeks with freckles, she didn't care. She couldn't bear to lock out the long promised, unexpectedly glorious day.

A warm breeze stirred the newly cultivated fields, riffling their rows of ankle-high green promise. The meadows were already studded with half-opened poppies and daisies, fenced in by newly flowering bramble hedges. The edge of the wood showed the ancient trees budding green, and the forest floors, dappled with sunlight, showed opening bluebells on the carpet of green beneath.

It was fragrant and warm, perfect for riding in an open carriage. If it weren't for the fact that every time Hannah looked down she could see her new husband's well-developed thigh, so clearly delineated by his snug breeches, positioned right next to her own, and his long muscular legs stretched out against the floorboards as he drove, she'd be comfortable and easy as the day itself.

As it was, she was acutely aware of his body, and the sensations she felt when she considered it. He was so handsome, and the daylight became him. Although he wore a high beaver hat, glimpses of his dark gold hair glinted in the sunlight. The current fashion of tightly fitting clothing showed his trim body to perfection. He seemed to be a perfect model of a man. But she'd never seen him naked; she mused, and wondered if she ever would, even if they tried lovemaking. Timothy had never removed so much as the kerchief around his neck. Ian's body might always be a mystery to her too. She'd certainly never ask him to remove so much as a handkerchief. She was done with asking him to do anything that related to lovemaking.

And yet she couldn't stop thinking about it, especially when he was so near. She wondered if she was in some way damaged, a secret lustful sinner, like Lilith, the evil female the preachers warned men against. Because she'd yearned for Timothy, and now she found she wanted this strange new

husband of hers as much, or maybe more. Whatever caused it, Hannah was more aware of the
physical side of her bargain now than she'd ever
been.

The Morrison manor was as Ian had said. It
looked more like a working farm than a manor
house. They drove in under an ancient arch
and arrived in a courtyard studded with parad-
ing geese and dotted with muddy puddles. The
house itself was long and sprawling. The stables
were close by, and one didn't need eyes to find it.
As they pulled to a stop, an assortment of spotted
dogs rushed out to bark at them, a few farm workers looked up from their chores to doff their caps.
It was like arriving in another century, Hannah
thought.

Ian gave her a hand down, and she lifted the
hems of her skirt so as to avoid splattering her
legs with mud. She'd worn her best new walking dress, a confection of mint color, and a pair of
stylish walking slippers. But the muck in the yard
was everywhere.

"The boards, tread the boards!" a woman's
voice called.

Hannah looked around.

"Good wife wasn't asking you to emote, my
dear," said a hearty older gentleman as he appeared in the doorway. He looked like a caricature
of a country squire, complete to his round belly.

That was when Hannah saw a rough board-walk lying atop the mud, leading to a door in the sprawling house. She quickly stepped on the boards. They shifted as she did. She held Ian's hand tightly.

"Wife has got to learn to say, 'step aboard!' " the squire said.

"Then they'll think we're starting up a new Puffing Billy. And we have no railroad tracks here," laughed his female counterpart, appearing beside him. "Welcome, my lord, my lady." She did a creditable bow for all her girth. And then the doorway seemed to fill with young women of all sizes, all peering out at the company.

Even after Hannah had been admitted to the house, she never guessed how many daughters the Morrisons had. The family had gotten word of their coming and their girls had sent word to their friends, and so there were a bevy of local fe-males: sisters, mothers, aunties, and other females suddenly pressed into service as chaperones. All were there to see the marquis. And, it seemed to Hannah, to slyly eye his new bride, and then pro-ceed to exchange covert whispers about her with each other.

The baron, two of his sons, and a near neigh-bor were the only men among the company apart from Ian. Hannah gladly took a seat in the front salon, and tried to disappear. She found it very simple to do. No one seemed to want to talk to her anyway. They were all surrounding her new husband. He stood, towering above them, looking amused and pleased with their company.

They all knew each other. Hannah knew none of them even after she'd finally been properly introduced. Some of the young women were lovely and some were not; some close-mouthed and some wickedly clever. They came in all shapes and sizes. Many were obviously wealthy or well to do, and not a few were titled or related to someone who was, and if they were, they made sure Ian didn't forget it. And every single one of them—and most of them were single—ignored her after they met her.

They each in turn came to make their bows to her. Hannah couldn't remember their names afterward, but unfortunately, she never forgot their faces: especially the looks they gave her. They looked at her with either hostility or cold evaluation, or wonderment, which was somehow even more insulting. Some were far too chirpy and artificially friendly to be taken seriously. After they'd been introduced, the young women drifted back to Ian, obviously their star attraction.

Hannah was glad of that. She eventually ended up spending all her time chatting with the baron, who was a nice enough fellow even if he was obsessed with breeding foxhounds with pointers, to get a hunting dog that would do double duty; pointing out vermin and chasing them too.

She was served little cakes and sweet watered wine, and took a nibble of one and a sip of the other until finally the visiting hour was over. Then, with many a promise to see each other soon again ringing in their ears, Ian and Hannah took their leave of the Morrisons and their neighbors.

Hannah picked her way back down the tilting boardwalk over the mud to the carriage, and let Ian help her up into her seat. Once seated, they waved back to everyone clustered in the Morrison doorway, and took to the road at a trot.

Hannah didn't say a word at first. And then she chanced to look up at Ian. He was watching her with a tilted smile on his lips.

"Come, say it, or you'll burst," he said.

"Say what?"

"What you're perishing to say. Don't worry. You won't get me angry. Good God, I don't think you *could* after a visit like the one we just paid."

"Why didn't you marry one of them?" she blurted. "Any one of them would have had you with a silver spoon."

He laughed. "Wrong, my clever lady. In the first place, many of them wouldn't have had me with an iron trowel. I had no money. And in the second place, those who would have had me would have done it for the title and the Hall."

She was still for a moment, and then said quietly, "Isn't that why my father wanted you?"

"Yes. But he wasn't a local luminary whose family had an eye on the place for generations. These people have known me since I was in short coats. Marrying one of those young women would have meant my family-in-law would come to share the Hall with me, and believe me, they'd have taken equal ownership. They would have taken over my life and my home and my heritage as well as myself. That I could not, would not tolerate."

His expression grew bleak as he stared at the road ahead. "Hannah, you and I know what our bargain was, as doubtless most of London guesses as well. But they can never be sure. Had I wed one of those women you just met, there would have been no doubt, and I never would have lived it down. Can you understand?"

She nodded, but said nothing.

"And in the third place," he said, "I wouldn't have considered one of those females for the space of two minutes. In fact, I didn't. I knew they were there, and I never even entertained a thought of courting one. Now I see I was right. They put on false smiles, those who tried even a little, and yet they didn't have the breeding or manners to be really gracious to you. And that too, I can't forgive."

He looked up at the dimming sky. "Rain clouds streaming in from the west. I knew it was too glorious a day. Well, at least it isn't snow." He picked up the reins and gave them a shake. "Hang on tight, my lady, we're going to make a run for it before we get drenched."

They made it to the Hall as the rain came pelting down. A stableboy took the reins and rushed the horses to the stable as Ian took one of Hannah's hands and ran with her. As they raced over the crushed shell drive toward the Hall, he laughed. "At least we don't need a boardwalk here," he said. "I think the Morrisons' guests will need rowboats to get home."

"Now," he said as a footman opened the door to let them in the Hall, "get you up the stairs, my lady. You're soggy. We'll meet again in my study and dry out thoroughly before a fire and a hot drink. You were a trooper today. It can't have been easy for you. But you carried yourself like a lady."

Hannah nearly floated up the stair to her bedchamber.

"The fire is delicious," Hannah said as she curled up in the chair close to the hearth, "but the astonishing thing about this Hall of yours is that it's warm in every room, even when it's chilly outside. How did you do that?"

She'd seldom seen the Marquis of Sutcombe beam. But he turned from poking the fire in the hearth to actually radiate his smile toward her.

"It took an engineer to show us how to do it," he said, dropping down into the chair opposite her. "It would have been foolish to do so much renovating if the Hall was intact, but since it was far from it . . ."

He started explaining and launched into a dissertation on connecting flues and reinforced northern walls, and hot water streaming through underground pipes. Hannah soon lost both interest and comprehension in what he was saying. But she was so pleased at how happy the subject made him that she kept smiling and nodding, encouraging him.

"You don't follow," he said suddenly, stopping his flow of information.

"Not entirely," she admitted. "But if I'd been here to see it being done, I think I would have. No matter how you achieved it, I imagine that you now have the newest ancient home in all of Britain."

He threw back his head and laughed. "Well said. I think we do. And now, let's go in to dinner. You will notice that the food is always served hot too. Want to know why?"

She rose from her chair, took his arm, and went into the dining parlor with him, glowing with happiness as he explained. He had said: "*we* do."

It was long after dinner, far beyond the time when Ian and Hannah had had an amusing time of playing a few hands of cards. Mr. Baker came in to ask Ian something, and his smile was almost avuncular as he gazed at the pair of them. Hannah went to her bedchamber feeling content and hopeful for the future for the first time since she had agreed to marry.

Her bed was soft; her pillows downy, she lay down and stretched, and sighed. She lay there, listening to the exquisite quiet; the only sounds that of rain tapping at her window. She should have been asleep an hour ago. She changed position yet again, and again, the new position she found was finally comfortable. The temperature in the room was just right. There was a hint of light at her windows because the sky outside was thick with cloud and so was gray and not velvet black. Hannah closed her eyes, and found herself bored, not sleepy.

And then she sat bolt upright. There was a noise at her connecting door.

She scrambled out of bed, into a night robe, and ran barefoot to the door. "Yes?" she asked softly. Her heart was pounding so loudly in her ears she didn't know if she'd hear an answer.

"My lady?" Ian said in his deep carrying whisper. "May I speak with you?"

She flung the door open.

Ian was respectably dressed, covered from the collar of his long blue night robe to his slippered toes.

"I just wondered if you were sleeping," he said.

She shook her head.

"Why not?" he asked suddenly.

She raised her shoulders. "I don't know. It's comfortable here, and quiet." She quickly raised her eyes to his. "But I just couldn't sleep. I suppose I'm still not used to being so alone in the night."

The way she said it made them both fall still. The rain hissed against the windows.

"I thought so," he said. "I swear I could hear you being awake."

She grinned.

"It kept me awake," he said. "How about this? You lie down again. I'll sit next to you, and we'll chat." It sounded odd, even to his own ears, because no sooner had he said it than he frowned. "That is to say," he went on, "I never really told you about our house's relationship with the Morrisons'. Nor did I say a thing about my neighbors to the east, the Blenfields and the Rogers, both of whom I hope you'll visit with me tomorrow. That is, if you haven't had enough of the petty snobbery hereabouts."

She opened the door wider. "I'd like to hear about them," she said. "Why don't you come in?"

It was such a formal invitation that she frowned after she said it. But he entered her chamber, and she closed the door behind him. There was an awkward moment when she looked down to her bare feet, and he didn't seem to know where to perch.

"I'll wager you'll be asleep before I tell you Mrs. Blenfield's first name," he said. "But where shall I sit?"

She laughed and made a sweeping bow, indicating her bed. Then she went to it, hopped up and pulled up her covers so she was covered to the neck. He came and sat at her side.

"Now," he said. "Better?"

She smiled, touched and flattered by his attention.

"Now," he said, sitting back against her pillows. "The Blenfields. They live to the left of the Hall. Several miles on down the road, toward the village of Nutley on Marsh. They've been here since the Conqueror, they say, and get very annoyed when the Morrisons say their ancestors were here to greet them when they came."

He spoke in a deep low voice, and went on and on about people Hannah didn't know. She cuddled into her bedcovers, smiling as she listened to that calm, slow, deep voice. He saw her eyelids opening and closing as she sank into sleep.

He didn't stop talking until he could see she was sleeping soundly. Then he stopped and looked down at her. She was young, defenseless in sleep, he thought, and very charming. Not beautiful, but very pretty, indeed. And he thought with a strange sense of pride, she was a brave woman. She was also a very lost and lonely one who was doing her best to fit into his life and please him. He hadn't done that for her. That was why he was here tonight.

For a moment, just for a moment, he was tempted to lie down alongside her and rest, feeling her warm breath on his shoulder. But it was later, very late, and he realized he wasn't thinking clearly. He tried to rise slowly, so the lifting of his weight from the bed wouldn't betray his leaving by so much as a sound. He'd comforted her; that had been his errand. He'd have done the same for a young pup he'd taken into his house. Anyone who knew social animals knew how lonely it was for one who'd been taken from the familiar comfort of all the other warm bodies in its litter to lie alone. But he didn't trust himself to sleep beside that warm shapely body.

He was about to stand up when he heard her murmur sleepily, "Don't go."

He turned to her.

"Oh!" she cried, sitting straight up, coming completely awake in sudden dismay. "Please don't think I'm commanding you to stay. I'm not. Honestly. It was just that it was so pleasant to have you here, and I wasn't sleeping yet. Do you want to tell me some more about our neighbors?"

He smiled. "Fascinating stuff, wasn't it? I think I'd rather just sit beside you, thank you. And no," he added as he sat and settled himself again, "I know it wasn't a command. Hannah?" he asked, turning to face her, "Can we forget that incident? And the reason we married? And all the nonsense that's been coming between us?"

She nodded.

He did too, and then, to congratulate her for the right answer, he bent and kissed her lips. Her drowsiness had made her toasty warm to the touch. He raised his head and put his hand against her flushed cheek. "So warm," he whispered, and bent his head to hers again.

She sat still, only her lips silently responding to his rising desire. He drew her into his arms. Then he moved back to try to see her expression. "Yes?" he asked. "Or would you rather I tell you some more stories?"

"What?" she asked, blinking, confused.

"I kiss you, and though you don't seem to mind, you don't embrace me?" he said softly, stroking her cheek with one finger. "Is it that you'd rather not?"

"Oh no," she said. "I just didn't want to appear too eager. I don't want to make another mistake."

"Then let me try," he said against her ear as he took her into his arms. "Be sure to let me know if I go too far for you."

She put both arms around his neck in answer, and pressed herself to him. They kissed again. He discovered that his breath in her ear made her shiver. He found that her mouth was warm and sweet and responsive. They kissed yet again, and then he pulled away and looked down at her, wishing he had more than the moonlight to see her in, yet not wanting to get up and turn on a light, and risk breaking this soft, sweet dream that had enveloped them.

"Now I'm too warm," he whispered. "Do you mind if I take off my robe?"

She shook her head, and he shrugged his night robe off, and tossed it aside.

"Do you think you might take yours off too," he asked, "so I don't feel odd?"

He heard her giggle. "So formal," she whispered back. "So formal doing such informal things. Is that the nobility's way?"

"It's my way when I don't want you to stop," he said, his throat getting dry as she slipped out of her robe. She wore a thin night robe beneath, and even in the scant light he could see the darker centers of her high white breasts as they rose and fell with her rapid breathing.

She shivered when she saw that he wore nothing beneath his night robe. His strong chest was bared; it was as tanned and muscular as any workman's that she'd ever seen in the fields.

"We must see that you don't take cold," he said as he drew her back in his arms.

She shivered again.

The pointed peaks of her warm breasts seemed

to bore into his chest, making him shiver with heat as he lowered her to her back into the nest of pillows. He remembered that he hadn't meant to begin this so soon. He tried to remember that he was a gentleman too. He knew he must have her, and slowly so as to make her happy as he did. Not because she was in command, because she wasn't anymore. She hadn't insisted on anything. His own body had.

He lowered her gown and ran his lips over the smooth skin at her neck. Then he dragged the neckline of her gown down more impatiently so he could put his mouth to those impudent breasts, one and then the other. She sighed, moving under him, stroking his back as she kissed the side of his cheek.

He sat up again. "Let us be rid of this," he said in a hoarse voice, tugging her thin nightshift upward.

She raised her arms, and her bottom, so he could free her from the lacy gown.

He sat looking at her for a moment. Then he drew her close once more. "Skin to skin," he whispered, "heart to heart and nothing between us now, Hannah. But I want there to be. I want to be one with you. Are you willing?"

She burrowed her nose into his neck and held him tightly. "Yes," she whispered, taking deep breaths of him, his scent, male and spicy.

He kissed her as much as he could, wherever he

could, for as long as he could bear it. She was restless and hot, and soon moist everywhere under his hands and lips. When he touched her intimately, she gasped and her body jerked upward.

"No?" he managed to say as he moved back.

"Yes," she sighed. "Only it was a surprise."

"Let's have more of those," he said as he came to her again.

He finally put his knee between her legs. After a heartbeat, she relaxed, and opened to him. He remained still, holding himself back with sheer will and great effort.

And then he had no more will power, and his only effort was to go as slowly as he could. But she had bewitched him. He felt like a callow youth in his lack of control, and then he couldn't say how he felt at all, only that he had to be one with her, no matter the cost. He heard her quick intake of breath, and felt her give as he pressed forward. He moved within her and lost all sight and sound except for the great rising ecstasy that soon, too soon, utterly consumed him.

He was the first to speak after he'd drawn away from her and lay at her side. "Did I hurt you?"

She tugged a bedcover over herself. "A little. I think it's customary," she said.

"So formal?" he asked, rising to an elbow, and looking down at her.

She reached up to stroke his damp hair. "Well, I don't know what I'm supposed to say now."

He took her into his arms again. "Let me think," he said as he held her. "Ah, yes. You could say, 'Oh that was wonderful!' or 'You were so good!' or 'Encore!' But you'd be lying. One day, I promise, I'll get you to say all those things and mean it. But Nature isn't that kind with first times."

"Is it that way for men too?" she asked curiously.

He let her go, rolled to his back, and laughed. "Original in all things, aren't you? But it's an interesting question. I'd say yes and no. It doesn't hurt us physically. Actually, now I think on, I believe first times aren't wonderful for us either. There's so much fear of failure and . . ." He paused. "Enough of that. This is definitely not a proper subject between a gentleman and a lady, even in their marriage bed."

"But I'm a commoner," she said softly.

"You're enough of a lady for me," he said seriously. "And I don't want to remember anyone else or any other experiences when I'm with you. Not now or ever."

"Thank you," she said. Then she moved again. "I must go wash up," she said.

"Love is a rapturous but sticky business," he said sympathetically as she arose, stepped out of bed, and went into her dressing room.

He heard a sleepy, murmurous voice asking her a question. Her maidservant, he guessed.

When Hannah came back, he was half asleep. She slipped in beside him, and lay close, but was as wakeful as she'd been before he'd come to her. She'd rejoiced in their lovemaking, even though it hadn't been entirely successful for her. But she'd had faith in the future.

And then he'd gone and said he didn't want to discuss other women he'd been with, "Not now, or ever." It was the "ever" that disturbed her. He mightn't have meant it that way, but it made her think of the future. He'd never said he'd be faithful.

In time, she slept, from sheer exhaustion. And in time, he woke, and carefully rose, and walked silently back to their connecting door, quietly opened and closed it behind him. He went to his dressing room and used the pitcher of water and basin that was there. Then he got into his own bed. He didn't want to wake Baker. He didn't feel like conversation now. Baker had known his master and his wife shared nothing between the sheets of either of their beds but a warming pan. Ian had been getting disapproving looks from him. The old fox knew everything. He'd be grinning in the morning, Ian thought, smiling himself. But still, Baker wouldn't be entirely happy. He disapproved of separate bedchambers for husbands and wives.

Ian lay there, unable to sleep. He realized that his bed and his chamber suddenly felt vast and empty. Astonishing how quickly one grows accustomed, he thought on a yawn. But their nightly separation was for the best. There was the future to think of. For now, he was trying hard to befriend his bride, for her sake, and make love to her, for his. And of course, he thought before sleep overtook him, for the future tranquility of this odd and difficult union of theirs.

Chapter 15

"**B**ored?" Ian asked, looking up from his daily post a week later.

Hannah's face flushed. He knew her too well. He, on the other hand, was just as opaque to her as he'd been from the first, even if they'd made love together. Now she knew his body and exulted in his strength and kindness. But she didn't know if his desire or acts of kindness toward her were offered out of pity or the desire to see her happy. But in all, she had to admit; they were getting on very well. Still, that didn't mean much. There were few others for them to get on with, after all.

"We could have a party for our neighbors," he said as though guessing her thoughts. "But I'd like to get all the finishing touches on the estate finished before we do that. And I didn't think you were that taken with any of them."

"Ah well," she said a little sadly, "I know how it is in small towns. These people have built up friendships and even enemies over the generations. I'm a recent addition. And one, I think, that they aren't too thrilled with. They know too much and too little about me. I think only time will cure that." Time, she thought, or a child. The one asset she had, the other, she wondered if she could provide.

"It would be easier," he said shrewdly, "if you could have your sisters and your father present when we entertained." He saw her eyes lighten, and nodded. "So I thought you'd like to have them come when we do throw the place open at last. It can't be for a while yet, there's still work to be done."

"I thank you for the thought. That would be grand. I wouldn't care a snap about your neighbors' attitudes if I weren't alone." She put a hand over her mouth and looked at him with widened eyes. "I mean," she said carefully, taking her hand away, "I can take on the world if I have my family with me."

He wore such a serious expression that she went on quickly, "The problem is, I think, my own attitude. I'm bone-idle. I know as a noblewoman I'm supposed to sit on a cushion and sew a fine seam, but I don't like sewing. I don't find great joy in embroidery, or painting, or playing the harp either. I'm used to helping to run a house for my father with my sisters, but this place seems to run on invisible greased wheels. There is, literally, nothing for me to do. I find riding pleasant, but not when

I'm alone. I do read, though. Your library is a delight, by the way.

"You ride out to see your tenants every day," she told him. "You're busy working on the Hall, and the tenants' cottages. I've seen you strip down to your sleeves and dig in with them. From afar," she added hastily as he gave her a bemused look. "You enjoy hard work. I love gardening, but the gardens here are magnificent. I actually dared to start one of my own. I thought a little bit of space out back, beyond the kitchen gardens, something for modest, seasonal flowers. But it gave your gardeners the pip to see me digging in the earth. I think they're still talking about it. So I do nothing but lounge around the place, and it doesn't add that much to the Hall because I'm not even that ornamental!"

"Fishing for compliments, are we?" he laughed. "You are ornamental."

She ignored that. She never trusted compliments. "But I'd like to be occupied with something I can be proud of. I'd like to pass the time being useful." She sighed, thinking that if they were a young couple in love, time would be flying.

She looked up and could swear she saw the same thought in his eyes.

"Would you like to go to London?" he asked. "I don't mean forever. Just for a space of time."

"Without you?" she said without thinking.

"Would you rather?"

"No, I just wondered if you'd be glad to be shut of me for a while."

She saw real warmth in his smile. "Hardly," he said. "You're never in my way. In fact, we barely see each other these days, do we?"

"At meals," she said slowly. And then, looking up into his eyes, she added, "And when we say good night, of course."

He hadn't made love to her again. At first, he said, because he was sure she was still sore. He was right, though she'd never had denied him. Being so close to him was worth any pains. But then she'd gotten her courses. Even if he didn't want to disturb her when she wasn't well, he'd made a habit of coming to her chamber at night before he went to sleep. He'd sit on the side of her bed and chat with her, telling her how his day had gone, and asking her about hers, even though they had spoken at dinner. After dinner he'd usually go to his study and take care of accounts.

But at bedtime, he came to her chamber and stayed with her until she was obviously sleepy, and then he'd bid her good night. He'd plant a soft kiss on her lips or brush a careless finger across her cheek too. He never slept in her room again, or even waited for her to fall asleep.

She was, she thought, becoming a habit with him. She was part of his routine, like saying good night to an old mother or a small child. She was a marker of the day's end for him, a touchstone, she thought with sad irony, but perhaps not one to be touched again. And the worst irony was that he daily became more attractive to her.

He'd always had an elegant, stern appearance, but now she saw it as a great silent masculine beauty. His hands were long and well shaped, his carriage was erect, his stride athletic, and his eyes fascinated her. Those gray eyes seldom showed emotion but she could see flashes of his thoughts race by in them, if she tried hard enough. His voice alone sent tremors up the back of her neck. And his body was, she now knew, in superb condition: long and lean and supple.

She was, she knew, growing too fond. She was letting herself in for disappointment, and maybe even real sorrow.

But the more she saw him, the more she liked him. She supposed it was easy when there was no one else around to compare him to. And she feared it was easy to fall in love with a distant ideal. Husband or not, he had become just that.

"I can understand your boredom here," he said. "But there are things for you to do in London. You still have to choose colors, wallpapers, paints, carpets, and the like for your bedchamber, and some of the other rooms here. Actually, whichever rooms you wish to change. I have more papers to sign in London, that's why I must go. If you like, you can come with me. There may be more extensive changes you'd like to make, and if so, there'll be more artisans to hire on as well. I think I can leave the work I'm doing here in about a week's time. Should you like to come to London with me?

"In fact," he said pensively, before she could answer, "we can entertain there. Yes," he said, looking up with a smile. "I've been thinking. I was disappointed in your reception here, and embarrassed for my neighbors. But it takes generations for these folk to warm up to someone new unless they feel they have a compelling reason to. They all have sons and daughters whose careers they would like to further, whether it's in wedlock or career. I've come to think that once you're really introduced to London society you'll prosper. And once you're established there, they'll be falling all over themselves to please you here. We can have an impromptu soiree at my town house."

She quirked an eyebrow at him.

"*Our* town house," he corrected himself. "You haven't seen all our treasures. I wanted to surprise you. I've had workers fixing it up again, to my specifications. They sent word that their work is almost done. Our wedding guests would come to us, and dozens of others as well. They'd *pay* to come," he said, laughing. "It would be a gossip's delight. If you can face anything with your family at your side, why don't we try to launch a maiden voyage for the Family Leeds in the wild wastes of London Society while we're there?"

"Oh yes!" she cried, and actually clapped her hands in glee.

"Do you think they'll leave their home in the country to journey back to London again?" he asked.

"I think my sisters would slay my father if he didn't. Oh, that would be wonderful!"

He grinned. "And that way too, I can fulfill another promise to your father, by providing your sisters' entrée to the *ton*."

Her smile fled. "Continue to earn your wages, you mean?" she asked quietly.

He stared at her across the table. His expression was suddenly cool, his eyes unreadable. "Yes, I suppose," he said.

She winced. "I shouldn't have said that, I know I'm being too prickly," she admitted. "I think it's because the thought of meeting London Society again is terrifying."

"So you don't wish to do it?" he asked.

She shook her head. "I'll become accustomed," she murmured.

They didn't speak again until they met again, at dinner that evening, when they both pretended to have forgotten what had been said.

And he did not come to her bedside that night.

"I know it marks me forever as a country squab," Hannah exclaimed as their coach drove in under the arch and entered London. "But every time I come here I feel I'm entering a new, exciting, dangerous, and delightful world."

"I thought you didn't care for London Society," Ian commented.

"I mean all of London Society, from the beggars in their rags to the soldiers in their red coats to the ladies of Fashion and the gentlemen of business," she said. "It's colorful and fascinating; such activity at all hours! So many different kinds of people in one place, all going about their own business. I wouldn't like to stay on here forever, and I really can't see how anyone could. Well, I suppose if you're born and bred to the city the countryside must seem awfully dull. But to be able to come in every so often and just see this place! It never ceases to thrill me. Does that sink me forever in your estimation?" she asked looking at her husband from under her eyelashes.

They were sitting in the coach with his crest on the side, driving to his town house. He'd been idly gazing out the window. She could see no excitement in his expression.

"I may not seem excited, but believe me, I am too," he said slowly. "It's just that gentlemen aren't supposed to show boyish glee. And yet I think I feel exactly the same way you do. I enjoy the theater, I remember the clubs, the gaming—don't worry, I only played for small stakes once in a while, just to keep my friends company. Of course, later on, when my fortune dwindled I couldn't do even that anymore. Now I think I'd like to play just to show myself that I can. That's a luxury. London isn't quite so delightful for a fellow with empty pockets. But I remember I enjoyed . . ." He paused. ". . . a great many of the pleasures London provides. I heard about other places that were equally fascinating, but I had neither the time nor the money to enjoy the city to its limits. There's always more to discover," he mused, as if to himself. "That's the thrill of London."

He seemed to hear what he was saying and sat up. "So, we're here. After we arrive and unpack, do you want to pay a call on your family?"

"Oh yes," she said rapturously. "I'd love to."

"Not tired?" he asked teasingly.

"Not when I'm going to see my family," she said.

He looked, in that moment, a little sad, a trifle disturbed. And then the coach went down a street where the traffic was stopping because there was a shouting match going on between an iceman on his wagon and a pushcart vendor in front of him. They were vying for right of way.

"Ah yes, London," he said, laughing. "Where a simple matter of giving way to another becomes major warfare."

Hannah giggled. Again, he was amazed at the transformation in her. He didn't know whether it was because he'd become used to her nuances of expression, but he could read her easily now. Even more interesting, he thought, was that he found her growing prettier by the day. She could never be a great beauty. She was too short for that. And her features were more kittenish than majestic. The great Society beauties were tall and impressive, with imposing noses and chests, along with swanlike necks and great round eyes. Hannah was adorable, down to the sprinkling of freckles on her little nose that nothing could seem to prevent, and the faint outline of them on her sweet breast. She was very pretty, indeed, but it was a comfortable sort of charm, not the eye-watering, demanding kind of beauty that was lauded in all the broadsheets, fashion plates, and magazines.

Hannah reminded her husband of illustrations he'd seen of the Merry Monarch King Charles's mistress Nell Gwynne. She was said to have been cheeky, adorable, and decidedly lower class. That was exactly what they said Charles had found so refreshing and charming. She'd been his favorite mistress. So too did Ian find Hannah refreshing. Sometimes, though, he wondered if he would, in time, accept that kind of beauty as fitting for his marchioness.

It bothered him that he even wondered about it.

He also wondered, watching her, if he'd ever attempt her again. Lovemaking with her had been delicious, but disturbing. It had been strangely emotional, almost soul shatteringly so, and so it was treacherous, at least for him. It wasn't what he'd expected. He recalled the trap his father had fallen in. He never thought his convenient bride would threaten him in such a way. But if they continued making love, it would lead to a different kind of marriage than he'd planned. He might end up in thrall.

He realized he was being foolish. He liked her. But he hadn't seen another woman in weeks. That would account for some of this fascination he felt for her. That would soon change. They were in London now. He also knew, as certainly as he knew his own name, that she'd never ask lovemaking of him again. That gave him wondrous freedom. Who could blame a man for straying when he wasn't exactly roaming, since his presence in his marriage bed wasn't requested? It would be a fine excuse to do what he wished with whomever he wanted.

And it also gave him a perfectly magnificent way to destroy any chance he had to make this marriage work. She would not understand adultery. She would come to, of course, eventually. Most people of his class did. Certainly it was common among the upper classes, when one partner tired of the other. He wondered if such an understanding was worth it. Because with that acceptance usually came utter rejection on one party's part or another's.

"Is something the matter?" Hannah asked him.

She watched his expressions the way a novice sea-farer watched the changing tides, as though she feared terrible misfortune if she guessed wrong.

"No, no," he said. "The opposite, in fact. You've never seen my—*our*—town house, have you?"

She shook her head in the negative.

"I couldn't show it off before. It was an abandoned shell of a place. My family has owned land here in London since the inhabitants threw up a wall against the night and the pagans. The town house has been restored to its former glory, or so my workers have promised me. Your whole family can move in with us and we can all be merry as grigs. It's huge. I doubt we'd run into each other for months, except by prearrangement, if you wished. We have a ballroom, a famous one. An invitation to a famous ruinous duel was once issued there, a century ago. There have been balls, musicales, and frolics, dating back to when we had to stick tarry torches in the walls to get enough light for a feast. I've modernized it, of course. Just wait until you see."

She laughed. "Are you waiting until I see it, or my father does?"

He inclined his head to the side. "When your father sees it, it will help, I hope, prove my value as an investment. And when you see it, it will make you blink, I hope. I want to see that. You're very hard to impress, you know."

No!" she said. "I'm terribly impressed by all your . . . *marquisly* things." She looked at him, her eyes brimming with mirth, and giggled. "Well, your personal *things*, yes. But your noble title? I suppose I'm not. Would you rather I were?"

"You know," he said with perfect honesty. "No. I prefer you as you are."

"That is the nicest thing you've ever said to me I think," she said.

"Then I'm a poor piece of work," he said. He leaned forward, and tapped on the glass separating him from the driver. "Here," he said.

He turned to Hannah. "Here," he said, more gently. "Our house. Mine. Yours. Ours. Come see."

She took his arm and walked to a tall gray town house in the middle of the street. There was a short front stair, and as they climbed it, the front door swung open and a footman in livery bowed them inside.

"Our house in London," Ian said proudly. "Too big, of course. It always was. But it is on a quiet street, near the park and backing on a meadow, I can't think there's a better spot in all London for a lady who loves the countryside."

"Oh my," Hannah said as she entered the house and looked around. The hall was suffused with afternoon light. The floors were made of checkered marble; the ceilings high, she saw painted landscapes of cherubs and clouds high above her.

The colors were typical of Adams: celestial blue, dawn pink, gold and new leaf green. "This place is . . . why, it's just magnificent, Ian."

He bowed. "Tell me more," he said with a pleased smile.

She laughed, and he joined in.

"This place," he said seriously, standing at the bottom of the great stair, "always had the potential to be the most beautiful of all our holdings. But my father never refurbished it. And after he died my stepmother emptied it. I've filled it again. And you are to fill it with whatever you please. This is our house now."

She saw the growing warm look in his eyes as he looked down at her. She didn't know whether it was because he was grateful for her part in the restoration of his fortunes, or whether it was because he was so genuinely happy he could share the moment with her, or maybe, perhaps even because he genuinely wanted to kiss her, here and now. She didn't care. She leaned toward him and raised her face to his.

She closed her eyes. And then snapped them open.

"Ah! The newlyweds," a softly mocking voice said. "Pray do not let me interfere."

Hannah looked up to see a woman on the stair. She was of middle age, slender, not especially handsome because her features were too sharp, as were her eyes. But she had a certain elegance and dignity about her. Her hair was soft brown, her eyes were also brown, there was nothing remark-able about her at all, and that in itself made the slight hint of amusement in her voice jarring.

"Stepmother," Ian said, straightening. "I did not expect to find you here."

"Obviously," the woman said. "Am I barred from this residence?"

"I hadn't thought to make that a rule, but now that you remind me, yes, I am afraid you are. But while you are here, Hannah, let me present my late father's still-present wife, the Dowager Mar-chioness of Sutcombe. Unless you have moved on to another happy union, madam?"

"How can I forget your dear father so soon?" Lady Sutcombe answered with a thin smile.

"I'd think, with ease," Ian said. "There's noth-ing left for you to sell or barter here. Everything in the place now was bought with my money."

"Your wife's," Lady Sutcombe corrected him. "But I did think, if only for the look of things, that you would allow me some sort of dower rights here."

"I don't care how it looks," Ian said. "There is a dower house that I refurbished. It's three miles from the Hall. If you want to take up residence there, you may. Nowhere else. And nothing may be taken or sold from out of it."

"Do you see anything in my hands?" the lady asked, raising one gloved hand. "I'm just passing through. You've done a marvelous piece of work here, Ian. I couldn't attend the wedding, my dear," she told Hannah. "Someone seemed to have misplaced my invitation. Well, soonest said, soonest mended. My dear Lady," she said, coming down the rest of the stair and bowing, "I am your husband's stepmama. But you can call me Lady Sutcombe, which I still am, by right of marriage. I may not have the money or the influence, but by God, I still do have the title. I am the Dowager Marchioness." She shot a bright look at Ian. "Try wresting that from me, Ian."

"I wouldn't think of it. But I suspect the only reason you still have it is that you couldn't think how to sell it."

"I sold some trifles, true. There was no money left in the estate. How was I to live?" the lady asked.

"And why am I to care?" Ian said. "That's the way of it. You had a good, long ride of it, Madam. You profited aplenty. And now, you may go."

"And profit no more?" she asked.

"Exactly," he said.

"He's a hard man, your husband," the lady told Hannah. "Not to you of course. He was never a fool. You hold his fortune, if not his heart. I never had either. I was merely trying to survive. I'll go now," she said. "I just may take up residence in the Dower House. I find myself lacking funds at the moment."

"As you will," Ian said in a bored tone.

The lady lifted her head, and gripping the head of her parasol, went out the door.

Only then did Ian's expression change. "Good God," he said bleakly, slumping against the stair rail. "I'd hoped to never see her again."

"You probably won't," Hannah said. "She can't be that thick skinned."

"She is because she wants, Hannah. She wants, endlessly. I think we will see her again. Please remember, you owe her nothing. *We* owe her nothing. She, in fact, still owes my brother and myself much."

"Don't worry," Hannah said. "I won't forget. Now, will you show me our home?"

He hesitated. "I was sure you'd argue on her behalf. I was afraid you'd think me some sort of a monster for denying her."

She grinned. "You were actually afraid I'd disapprove? Now, that's something wonderful."

"I'm that sorry," a gruff voice said, and they looked at the stair to see Mr. Baker standing there. "She come in and I couldn't toss her out, milord. But I watched her close. Not so much as a spoon went up her sleeve, that I promise you."

Ian laughed. "I knew I could count on you, Baker."

His man laughed. "Aye, so you can. I got the place humming like it must of done years ago."

"So soon?" Ian asked.

"Aye. The old servants that come from the Hall went straight to work. The new ones look good too, but I'll keep an eye on them. The place is ready to live in, my lord, any time you want."

"Like tonight?" Ian asked.

"Of course," Baker said.

Ian turned to Hannah. "Should you like that?"

"Oh yes!" she said.

"You're a gem, Baker," Ian said. "I'm lucky the dowager didn't snabble you up before I got here."

"Likely," Baker scoffed. "Well, if there's nothing else, I'll see to dinner," he said, then bowed and went down the hall to harry the new kitchen servants.

Ian took Hannah's arm and led her through their town house, both of them trying very hard to achieve a moment of easy peace, and to recapture that moment of easy intimacy they'd shared.

The Dowager Lady Sutcombe paused on the outer doorstep after she left the house. She wasn't smiling now. She looked chagrined, so angry that she hardly noticed the young man standing at the bottom of the stair.

There was no reason she should have noticed him. He was dressed well, but not wonderfully. He looked like a young law clerk, or some other chap from the countryside trying to make it in the big city. He had a fresh complexion, wide blue eyes, and a shock of freshly barbered inky black hair.

"Pardon me, my lady," he said respectfully, bowing to her, "but may I ask? Can you tell me? Are the master and mistress of the house finally at home? I mean, the marquis and his new lady."

"They are, indeed," she snapped.

"Ah, I see," he said and, nodding, turned to leave.

Her eyes narrowed. "Aren't you going up to see them?"

"No," he said. "I just wanted to know if they were here. I'd like to see the mistress of the house but I think it's too soon."

"For what?" she asked.

"I'm an old friend," he said quickly.

"Indeed?" she said with a hint of interest. "Isn't it always the right time for old friends to visit?"

"You'd think so," he said. "But she's a bride."

"Are you a friend of his, or hers?"

He put his head to the side and studied her. Then he smiled. It was a wonderfully winning, utterly insincere smile. "I was a friend of the lady's," he said, "from her country home. We knew each other . . . well."

The dowager's eyes narrowed.

"My name is Timothy Adkins. And you, my lady, if I may make so bold?"

"I am the Dowager Lady Sutcombe," she said, "widow of the late marquis. I think it is the right time for us to have a talk, perhaps also for the poor bride's sake."

Instead of looking surprised or sad, he looked more eager, if possible, when he heard her say 'poor.'

She noticed it. "We may discover we have things in common, Mr. Adkins. Things to talk about for our common good."

He looked at her quizzically.

"Our affection for the bride," she said coolly, "and our interest, if nothing else, in the groom."

His smile grew wider, and he nodded. "I'm certain of it," he said.

Chapter 16

They walked through the town house like children who had slipped in the back door and were marveling at what the grown-ups had done. Hannah was both amused and touched by the way that Ian tried to hide his great pride in the place. He'd been trained as a gentleman, which meant he knew he shouldn't openly show such emotions, but there was no question that he was as thrilled as his new bride at what her money had wrought. This was a great house. More than that, it was now a beautiful home.

"Red rooms and green rooms and ballrooms. Asian carpets and French furniture. Windows everywhere, and bright hangings. Oh, Ian, I've never seen the like. I know that's not saying a lot," Hannah added, "because I am, after all, not a staple of London's *ton,* but surely this must be the grandest house in London?"

He laughed. They stood in the saffron-colored morning salon. "I can't say either," he told her.

"Being penniless is a certain way to curtail one's social life around here. I didn't get invited to the best homes, no matter what my title was. I suspect I will be now. But it doesn't matter. What I want to know is if you really like it? I had the painters refresh the original colors in some rooms, and told the decorators your favorite colors too. I told them what you liked. This is what they created."

"For me?" she asked, diverted.

"Of course."

"Nice attempt," she said laughing. "But how would you know my favorite colors?"

"I asked you once. I didn't forget. 'Springtime shades of yellow, pink, gold, and green. And the blue of the sky,' you said."

She stared at him.

"But the most important thing, they said," he went on, "was for me to describe what you were like."

Suddenly, that was the most important thing in the world for Hannah to hear. "And you told them?" she asked breathlessly.

He smiled down at her. "I said that while many Society women here in London reminded me of tropical orchids or other rare and exotic succession house prizes, and very lovely they were too, you reminded me of a meadow in the spring. Lush, green, filled with colorful surprises. Your scent, I said, was like first spring clover. The pink and white kind. Not elegant, perhaps. Nor suitable for corsages, bouquets, and arrangements on a grand dining table. But pure and true, fresh and sweet. Clover, I said, with hints of red poppy and dashes of meadowsweet, bluebells, and violets. All the flowers of the field. Common yet all too commonly overlooked."

She cocked her head to the side. "And they said?"

"They said I was a lucky man."

She ducked her head. "No one said that a grand marquis ought to have married an orchid?"

"No," he said gently. "No one. Now. Did I do the right thing? The colors are all spring hues. The house is filled with light. Does it suit you?"

"Down to the ground!" she said. "I want to go round the house one more time with you. And then can we invite my family to see it?"

"We can, and we shall, of course," he said.

Anthea went into raptures. Her older sister, Jessica, was quietly astonished, and couldn't stop smiling. And their father beamed so much that Hannah was afraid his face would begin to hurt.

"This is the grandest place!" Anthea said for the fourth time.

"So it is," Ian said. "And so, will you ladies, and you, sir, do me the honor of moving in here with us? It will leave us only six spare bedchambers, but I think we can somehow soldier on, no matter how cramped the facilities."

"Now, now, my lord," Hannah's father said. "It's a good impulse, and comes from sheer generosity, I know. But are you sure you want your in-laws living with you? That was never part of the bargain."

Hannah's breath halted in her chest. That word again. She summoned a smile, and said, "I'm sure the marquis knows to the letter what the bargain entails, Papa."

Ian shot her a look. "So I do. I think, sir, that the days of our bargain are coming to a close. A successful one. Your infusion of money helped me get my accounts in tune again. I have property free and clearly owned, and wise investments to bank on now, literally. Hopewell Hall is already beginning to pay back some of the funds we put into it. Happy tenants produce better crops. As for the invitation to come live with us here in London, I asked you as a favor to me, actually. I'll be dashing around, getting things in order again, and I don't like the thought of Hannah being alone. London can be a harsh climate for shy country blossoms. And she did say she could face anything with her family by her side."

"Shy? Hannah? Ha!" Anthea said. "She's just taking the measure of the place. They had better watch out for her when she has it."

"We can't present either Jessica or Anthea until next Season," Ian went on. "First, Society must accept me and my bride. But after that, all can go according to our plans."

"My dear boy," Hannah's father said, "we'd be honored to stay here with you, for whatever reason."

Ian bowed. "And I'd be honored to have you. So, move in at your leisure. This very weekend there's a ball that I want to take Hannah to. It's time to introduce her to my world. No one knows you're here yet, so you haven't been invited. But I know Hannah will feel better for having you here, at her home, as her security against such a new and different social world."

"And in time, why, we can go with her everywhere, and so she'll never be alone, and you'll be free to do as you will," Anthea chirped. "Then everyone will be happy."

Hannah looked startled. Ian looked thoughtful. And that startled her even more.

"Why do we always end up in bed?" Hannah asked sleepily.

Ian laughed. He wore a night robe and had no shirt beneath, so she could clearly see the long strong line of his neck when he threw back his head. It made her shiver. The man was so intensely masculine, so very vital and virile. The problem is that she still didn't know if his visit would lead to pleasure or sleep for her. They hadn't made love since she'd had her courses, and she'd gotten over them before they'd left for London.

"We don't always end up in bed, in the usual sense," he said gently, touching the tip of her nose. "We end up talking, and gossiping, and going over all the events of the day together in the most comfortable place we can find. Even here, in our new town house, it seems, that place is bed. Mind, my new study is a joy to me, but it has a very official feel to it. The salon is formal. I'd sit in the kitchens with you but the staff would wake and come scurrying to see we were fed and happy. So we come here. It's become habit, and a good one too.

"I come in to bid you good night, you offer me bed room, I settle down, and we end up telling each other things we might not be able to anywhere else. Ask any gentleman who went to public school. Ask any lady who went to sleep over at her friend's house. Ask your sisters. Bed chat transcends the genders. No question but that a bed is the best place to trade thoughts between friends. And other things, between lovers."

She nodded, but said nothing.

He sat up against the pillow he'd put behind his back.

She sat up, wrapped in a primrose-colored robe.

He was diverted. "That robe suits you," he said with admiration.

She'd been busily trying to form what she

wanted to say into very proper English, so it didn't sound like a command or like pleading, or pitiful in the least. And here he'd gone and confused her with a compliment. "Thank you," she said tartly. "I take it that I now remind you of a clover again?"

He laughed. "That stung, did it? I could see it when I told you, but I still don't know why it would be considered anything but a compliment."

"Clover is for rabbits and cows, sheep, and bees," she said patiently. "A woman who reminds men of roses and orchids, lilies and such, is a female of rare beauty. But common clover? If it's anything, it's simply tasty and, at that, only to creatures of the fields and forests."

"I'd rather be tasty than merely decorative," he mused. "But you may have a point. Forget it for now. Instead please tell me what you've been trying so hard to think of how to say. Don't look so surprised. Your face gives you away every time."

"Then we should talk in the dark," she grumbled.

"Where there's a good chance I might fall asleep?" he countered. "Oh, no. Out with it."

She hesitated, looking uneasy. Then she lowered her gaze and her voice. "If a person wanted to ask another person to make love . . ." she said slowly, looking at the coverlets. She raised her eyes and blurted, "How could they say it so that it won't be taken as a command? I mean, say it so that a refusal won't seem like a killing blow, because it wouldn't be. Oh, blast it. How can it be said simply and conversationally?"

His eyebrow rose. "Conversationally? Never. Before I strain my brain with this, may I guess that it's what you might want to ask me, without insulting me or humiliating you?"

She nodded.

He laughed. "The answer is that I don't know."

She bit her lip.

"In fact," he went on, edging closer to her, "the truth is that you don't have to say it at all. I was trying to think of how to get around to saying it myself."

Her eyes widened.

"Only I was going to do it as men do," he said. "By bypassing words so that if I were refused it would be tacit, not verbal. Words are so hard to think up and yet sometimes impossible to forget. Rejection hurts less when it's something that a fellow can convince himself he misunderstood. So I was going to try a casual contact," he said as he put his arm around her. "And if you edged away," he whispered, "I could pretend it was because you were so tired you only were thinking of sleeping."

"If you didn't, I was then going to try a light kiss there," he said as he nuzzled her ear. "And if you shivered away I could imagine it was because you were chilly. Then maybe I'd try a touch there," he added as he brushed a light kiss across her lips. "And if you didn't stir I'd check to see if you were asleep. If you weren't, I'd wait, and hope I communicated the idea to you."

She cocked her head to the side. "I think I have a notion. But I'm not entirely sure of what you mean. Do you think you could try again?"

He laughed. "Pardon me. I have such trouble making myself clear. Do you think you could take that lovely night robe off, so I can try harder?"

She giggled and slipped off her robe.

He sighed. "And lovely though it may be," he said, "I think I can commune with you more easily if you'd discard that night shift too."

"Really?" she said pertly. "How could that be? Because you're dressed almost to your nose."

He pretended he was startled. "Too true. It is getting warm in here. Do you mind if I disrobe?"

She lay back and looked at him. "I'd not mind in the least," she said.

She watched him take off his robe, and sighed herself when she saw he wore nothing beneath it.

He bent to her, kissed her neck, and breathed in the scent of her. "Bluebells," he whispered. She felt his smile against her breast. "I didn't know your favorite scent so I asked your maid."

"Clever," she said on a caught breath as he moved his mouth to her breasts.

"Ah, but now, this is clover," he said as he tasted

the tip of one breast. "Not bluebell at all, but pink and white, fresh and sweet budding clover."

She stroked his back, feeling the subtle shift of his smooth muscles as he bent to her other breast.

"Note that I do not favor one above the other," he said as he kept one hand covering the breast he had savored and moved his lips to the other. And then he raised his head and kissed her lips.

She tasted the warm dark liquor of his mouth, and touched her tongue to his. She didn't know which one of them shuddered as he moved over her; she only knew she had to move with him.

His body slipped over hers, and she felt his arousal against her belly, even as she could feel the rhythmic probing of his hand, caressing, gentling, making her feel all her need as well as his own.

"Yes," he whispered, "relax. Let me; let go."

She held on to his wide shoulders, and closed her eyes. Then she felt the sudden shock of rapture and gave a muted gasp of pleasure as she rose against his hand. She shook and throbbed, and shivered again, and only then did he join with her body to share the ecstasy she was feeling.

It took a while for her to recover. He was so still by her side she thought he might be sleeping. She'd heard men slept after sexual bliss and felt amused and annoyed that he'd left her in any way.

"That," he said, breaking the silence, "was delicious. I'm so glad you didn't ask me to make love to you any more than I asked you."

She laughed. "Ian," she said, "shall I always have to ask you first? Because although it turned out wonderfully well, you know that I did."

He remained still for a moment. "It did. And certainly, you need ask. I don't want to impose on you any more than you want to command me. It's a difficult balance, this marriage of ours."

"You mean," she said, "that lovers don't have to ask. And that we are not lovers."

"That isn't to say we can't be one day," he said.

He was drifting off to sleep in her bed, a thing he never did, when she spoke again.

"Ian? If we did become lovers, in time, would you nevertheless stray one day?"

His eyes opened. He came entirely awake. "Did you want to make love to me only to ensure that I don't?"

After a moment she answered him. "If I say 'no,' I put myself in an awkward position, don't I? If I say 'yes,' though, I'd be lying. You're right; this is a delicate business, this union of ours. But yours is no answer at all."

He sat up, and took her in his arms. "Hannah. Infidelity is a thing I don't think most newlyweds trouble their heads about, at least, not unless it might arise. What can I say? My father, for all his sins of gullibility and fecklessness with his heritage, was a faithful husband. My mother deserved it. My stepmama did not."

"My father was faithful," she said softly. "I'm certain my mother was too."

"You see?" he asked. "We come from good, faithful stock. But our marriage wasn't made out of friendship, or trust, desire or love, as theirs were. It was arranged for expedience. It's up to us to see it through as we wish. Let's see what time brings us, shall we?"

"That's not an answer," she said, drawing back from his embrace.

"It's a difficult question," he said.

She didn't say anything.

"Don't worry about what may be," he said. "We have enough difficulty with what is right now, don't we? We dance around questions we hesitate to ask, and answer carefully every time. Yet our marriage progresses. It's already far different from what I envisioned. Let's deal with *now*, and let it shape *then*. Agreed?"

"Agreed," she said.

He dropped a kiss on her forehead and rose from the bed. "Sleep now," he said. "And don't let what 'may be' trouble you. Let's live now."

She lay still and watched him leave. His naked body, she thought, was magnificent. Not bulky and toughly muscled, but instead, slender, firm, all lithe strength. His chest was filmed with golden hair so soft she hadn't noticed it until it caught the moonlight's faint glow. Though he stood tall he looked like a picture she'd seen of a recumbent Adam receiving the touch of God. But Ian, she thought, had more need of a fig leaf than that drowsy Adam ever had. She grinned, lay back, and fell into an easy exhausted sleep, thinking all the while that their marriage had indeed progressed, and smiling at how far it had yet to go.

"You here again, milord?" Baker asked as Ian came back from Hannah's bedchamber and into his own.

"Waiting up for me like an alert concierge?" Ian asked as he got back into his own bed.

"Just making your room ready," Baker said.

"Well, there's a polite lie," Ian said.

"Give you a polite good night then," Baker said. "But I think a man and wife is happiest in one bed. But what do I know, being a peasant and all?"

Ian threw a pillow at him. "Go to bed. You know too much."

Baker left, with a smile.

Ian didn't sleep at once. He lay abed, thinking. He had to discover just what this new wife meant to him. He knew he desired her, and thought he cared for her. Was it only gratitude? Surprise that a business arrangement had turned up such an intelligent and sensitive female? The pleasure he found in her arms? Or was she only half what he thought she was because he had no comparison to make these days?

These days she seemed delighted with him. Perhaps she was so pleased with what she'd got, she wondered why he was exerting himself to please her. He had to find out what he meant to her. He knew he was a changed man, little like the one who had married her. He no longer felt shamed and at fault, like a failed son and a weak brother. He'd restored his estate and his pride. He couldn't have done it without her. Was that good or bad for their future?

But her body hadn't helped his finances, and neither had the soft scent he associated with her, or the laughter that made him return, again and again, seeking her company. Or her lovely figure, or soft lips . . .

He moved in bed, got the faint scent of bluebells. He raised an arm, sniffed it, and got the scent even more strongly. *She's on my mind and my body,* he thought, smiling. And he slept at last, content.

Chapter 17

"**Y**ou look magnificent," Anthea breathed as Hannah and Ian came down the stair.

"Thank you," Hannah said. "He knows it. Now how do I look?"

They all laughed. There was no question but that it was comforting to have her father and her sisters down in the front hall to see them off, as in old times, Hannah thought. It made her feel accepted and warm. How Ian's friends and acquaintances would react was another thing, but this, at least, made her feel at home again.

Tonight she felt altogether beautiful and loved. She had not yet gotten over Ian's lovemaking of the other night. He hadn't come to her again because he'd had papers to go over far into the next night, and last night, after she'd helped her family settle in, she'd chatted with her sisters until long after their bedtimes. But she knew he'd come to her again, or she to him. She knew she pleased him, and that he cared with infinite tenderness for her well-being. Tonight was a perfect night to debut as his wife in public with him. Perhaps later tonight they would share mutual and triumphant love.

She looked at him with pride. Ian was the perfect gentleman of Society, she thought with a little shiver of pleasure just looking at him. He was freshly barbered, his dark gold hair giving color to his strictly formal garb. He was impressive-looking. And his expression had changed. She didn't know if he even realized it. It wasn't that he looked superior, or at least as though he thought he was superior. But there would be no question in anyone's mind that he was a rich, titled gentleman of means and manners.

She wore a gown designed especially for such a night. He'd said she reminded him of clover; she'd consulted with her dressmaker. She wore a straight, long-sleeved, low-necked gown of blush pink shading to white at the hemline. It was sashed with pink and her skirts were covered by a filmy green overskirt. The silhouette was slender, in the latest fashion. Just thinking about Ian's tribute to her body as clover made her feel warm.

She wished she could wear wildflowers in her hair to bolster the image, but her hairdresser had said it was orchids, roses, or sweet spring violets this Season, and nothing else. He'd talked her into having her hair cut and arranged to curl around her forehead, while the rest was drawn back with a few curls permitted to fall to her bare shoulders. She had a filmy pink shawl to wear over her shoulders when she stepped out of the house in her new pink slippers. A single row of pearls her mother had left her adorned her neck. She would not, she thought proudly, shame Ian.

After her family's many repeated assurances of her grandeur, she smiled up at her husband.

"Now let's go reap some more compliments," he said.

But when they left the house, he stopped before he helped her into the coach. He touched the pearls at her throat. "I will buy you jewels," he said soberly. "I realize I should have done before this. But I want to buy them with my own money, when it starts coming in. Can you understand that?"

She nodded, too touched to speak, took his arm, and climbed the stair to the coach. When she had settled herself there, she sat on the edge of her seat as they drove to the ball, afraid to move lest she muss her hair or her gown. But it wasn't in her nature to remain silent for long.

"Do you have many friends where we're going?" she finally ventured to ask.

"A few," he said. "At least I hope I do."

"A friend wouldn't have deserted you in your time of need," she said reprovingly.

"True. Some didn't. I deserted them. It was my pride. I treated myself like a pariah, and avoided them because my lack of funds was so exquisitely clear in their company. When a fellow doesn't have the price of a good beefsteak dinner, he has a hard time going with his friends as they select even more expensive prime horseflesh to race. I didn't want charity or pity. I hope I can renew old friendships tonight. Some people will be happy to see me. Some will be glad to see my success.

"Hannah," he said suddenly, turning to her. "Just so you know, some will not be as sociable. It's still considered embarrassing to marry for money although nobles and royalty have done it from time out of mind. So if there are any criticisms, believe me, they will be aimed at me, not you."

"That's very kind of you," she said softly. "But the truth is that I know the *ton* considers the merchant class far beneath them. They call us 'mushrooms' because we sprang so suddenly from the dirt. They dislike us more than they do the peasantry: farmers and fishmongers and such, because those people don't attempt to climb higher or to change their places in Society. I've talked about it with my father. You said I remind you of clover, and that's fine. I am from the earth. I have been educated, and as mill owners we've lived well for generations, but there was never so much as a noble breath rustling a leaf on our family tree. I know that will make some people at this ball sneer at me. I don't care if you don't. I am what I am.

"Well," she added, with a frown, "I'm not an angel. Of course, I'd care. But I won't let it bother me if it doesn't bother you. If it does, I'll leave at any moment you ask it of me. Our bargain said you'd introduce my sisters to the *ton*. It doesn't say where or how. So don't worry."

He clasped her hand tightly in his.

"I don't worry," he said. "And for this night, at least, can we please forget that damnable bargain?"

They left their populated section of London, and drove down the city streets as the houses got fewer and farther between. Darkness closed in around them. The shock of sudden light surprised Hannah's eyes as they approached a long curved drive lined with tall flaming torchieres. Light moved toward light as a line of carriages, each lit by lanterns, queued up in the drive to let passengers off at the front door to a gray stone mansion, set far back from the road.

Hannah took a deep breath.

She stepped from the coach in her turn and went up the stair on her husband's arm. She was all but blinded by the sudden brilliance of the many torches, lamps, lantern lights, and blazing flambeaux carried by torch boys. She barely could see the people going into an even more brightly lit entry ahead. They seemed to be swimming in a watery golden nimbus. She went into the house at Ian's side.

A footman took her wrap, and she clung to Ian's side as they waited for the butler to announce them. As Hannah's eyes adjusted to the brilliance of the chandeliers and lamps, they were assaulted by the blinding radiance of the guests she could see within.

The men were all in black and white, as elegant as she had expected. But the women! They wore golden gowns, and scarlet ones; they wore silk and gauze in every color of the rainbow. Their high-dressed hair gleamed with the radiance of the jewels in their tiaras, vying with the shimmering gems at their throats, on their ears, arms, and fingers.

Most of all Hannah was staggered by the very presence of these women. Many were tall and slender and looked as though they'd stepped from the pages of fashion plate books. Even the less shapely ones were magnificently gowned. Their faces glowed, their fluting, musical voices rang out; they seemed to float in a sea of grace and fragrance and glitter.

She looked up at Ian. His expression showed nothing. He was right, she thought. She was exactly as the clover in the field to these females, ready to be trampled by the gentry as they frolicked on pastures she couldn't see from where she stood, rooted to the ground.

She and Ian were announced, and stepped forward. A sudden thunderclap of silence fell over the company as every head in the room turned to look at the marquis as he entered with his bride.

"And this, dear Auntie, is my new lady, Hannah," Ian said to a woman who hurried up to greet them. "Of course, you knew that, having been at our wedding. But as this is her first ball in London, I thought you might like to be the one to introduce her to those you think she'd enjoy meeting."

Hannah's eyes widened. He'd said he had no relatives in London.

The dowager nodded. She was a comfortable-looking stuffed pigeon of a lady: middle aged, small, plump, with a sweet smile that made one forget how many swathes of material it had taken to get her gowned. If her smile didn't achieve that, the amazing variety of diamonds strewn about her little person would.

"I'm not really his aunt," the lady confided to Hannah. "But I was his dear mother's good friend, and as a good friend I always shall stand to her family. Except for that fool of a husband she had. And of course, for that hideous second wife of his. Come, my dear, let this dashing fellow go see old friends. I shall be glad to introduce you to new ones."

Ian bowed, turned and strode into the thick of the crowd in the room.

"Now, my dear," Ian's "aunt" said, tucking her arm into Hannah's, "you mustn't worry. I'm the most comfortable thing in existence. I have few kin left, alas, but am lucky enough to have dozens of friends. Don't worry. I'll keep you away from the jealous flirts and the curious, and the simply evil-minded. I'll find you company you can enjoy. Call me 'Auntie' if you will, everyone does. My name is 'Henrietta,' but I'd rather be your auntie. My husband was a baron, but it was a purchased title, and will not pass on to my son. Nor did most of his estate. Oh, how I wish I'd known you were on the market! Wealthy, pretty, and clever too. Lucky Ian."

Hannah said nothing. Some of what she heard stung, but surely this little squab of a woman hadn't meant to insult her. And yet she hadn't said a thing and had already been called clever.

"Auntie!" a silvery voice called. "So here you are!"

A lovely blond young woman in a startlingly beautiful gown of buttercup yellow rushed up to "Auntie" and bent her willowy form enough to embrace her. She kissed the air around Auntie's cheeks. "I found her!" she trilled as she stood tall again.

Another lovely, fair-haired slender young female joined them. She wasn't so affectionate as the first one. But she was just as beautiful and magnificently gowned.

The two young women looked frankly at Hannah.

"And here is Sutcombe's bride," Auntie said. "His new marchioness. I'm to introduce her round."

"I'm Lady Jergens," one of the ladies said with a tiny dip of a bow. "Here is my dear friend, the honorable Miss Avondale. And here's Lady Phelps. We were just speaking of you. Oh, how lucky you are to have snagged Sutcombe. Just look at him. That face! He belongs on a coin!"

"Or in a museum, on a pedestal, with fig leaves," one of her friends said, with a giggle. "Oh, Gillian, my love," she cried, lifting her head, "we found her! Here's Sutcombe's lady!"

In a few minutes, Hannah found herself surrounded by a group of lovely young women. A dark-haired beauty and a brunette soon joined them. They were all perfectly coifed and gowned, their faces were clear-skinned, their fingers, necks, and ears were covered with gems and their figures were all that Fashion demanded. Their voices were eerily similar, with distinctly upper-class accents. They were smooth, fragrant, and powdered, and flocked around her like splendid, scented moths. They seemed, all at once, as different from Hannah as from any women she'd ever met. But best of all, she thought with embarrassed relief, now that they were assembled, they weren't paying the least attention to her anymore.

That gave her time to judge herself in their eyes. The gown she wore that she'd thought so daringly sophisticated was plain and dull next to the obviously latest French creations they had on. Their discussion, all about people they knew, was as alien to Hannah as their faces. She felt as though she'd suddenly grown invisible and didn't know whether to be relieved by that or not.

"Oh dear, Lady Sutcombe!" one of them suddenly said, holding a gloved hand up to her lips and goggling at Hannah. "How rude of us. We're talking about the Abbots' upcoming *do*, and you obviously aren't going there."

"I don't know them," Hannah said.

"But *everyone* does," the lady said. "Perhaps your handsome husband can still get an invitation for you. It isn't until next week."

"Oh, Hermione," one of the others said, her hand going to her pale breast and resting on the diamonds she wore there, "Now, *that's* a rude thing to say. The Abbots would never ask her!" Her lovely blue eyes grew round. "But I've put my foot into it now, haven't I? My dear," she said, putting her gloved fingertips on Hannah's shoulder, "it's not anything you did. It's what your new husband did. The Abbots are such high sticklers."

"Well, I think they wanted him for Abigail," one of the other young women said.

"Of course," the one called Hermione whispered. "But who didn't want him? So distinguished! Such a form, and such presence, and an ancient title as well. But who could come up to scratch? His price was far too high, and however much Abigail yearned, they expected a decent settlement on her. Fitzhugh isn't anyone's idea of a prince, but his pockets aren't to let. I hear the parents did want Sutcombe, though. Told family friends and such. They just refused to pay the toll."

"Or they couldn't," another young woman put in.

"Bosh," one of the other young women said. "Don't pay them any mind, Lady Sutcombe. There's no question but that you have done more for Sutcombe than any of us could or would. He made a wise choice. The town house is supposed to be completely restored, and I hear the Hall is nothing short of magnificent. Everyone's dying to see them. And everyone was dying to be with him. But alas, my father had three other daughters to pop off, and Hermione here is still recovering from what her parents had to pay for her sisters being settled. We aren't *made* of money."

"We just think we are," another said, to make them all laugh.

"Now, ladies," Auntie said. "You're going to give Lady Sutcombe the impression that all we care about is money!"

"Until we're wed, it is!" one of them said on a laugh. "It must be. After that . . ." She gave Hannah a bright look. "Just wait, my Lady Sutcombe, after marriage comes pleasure. It's when we're finally free to choose exactly who and what we will. Just as you were," she added with a jewel-bright smile that had too many teeth in it.

"And if we had our eyes on him before . . ." another began.

"As of course, we did," another pastel lady interrupted with a burbling laugh.

"Now that he's securely tied," the other young woman went on, "who knows what may happen when we are too!"

"Just teasing," Hermione said to Hannah.

"Just warning," another lady said, wagging a playful finger at Hannah.

Hannah didn't know how to answer. She was too grown-up to run away. She knew she'd never see these women again, not only because they were contemptuous of her and let her know it, but because she now detested them. Still, she had to say something.

She glanced over to a knot of gentlemen to the side of the room, and saw that the center of their attention was her husband, the top of his golden head could just be seen in their midst. Just looking at him gave her courage. She wouldn't shame him. Neither would she shame herself.

She raised her own head. She slowly looked over each young woman surrounding her in turn, and then smiled. "It's lovely to be envied so much," she finally said in a cool, even voice. "Thank you, ladies, for that, if nothing else. It's quite made my evening."

When the ladies turned from her and left without another word, Hannah sagged and looked for a place to sit. She felt drained.

"There you are, my dear," Auntie sang. "Tired? Oh my, not in the family way so soon, are we?"

"No," Hannah said. "But I should like to sit down for a while."

"And I have just the person for you to talk with," Auntie said cheerfully, leading her to a side of the room where there were rows of chairs set up. Old women and their companions, ancient gentlemen with walking sticks, and too obviously unfit dance partners and their chaperones took their seats.

Auntie led Hannah to a pretty young woman who looked up anxiously as they approached. She was what the *ton* called a "pocket Venus," a small, perfectly formed little fairy of a girl, with pale golden hair and huge violet eyes. Her nose was perfect, her complexion fair, she was gowned in a lovely creation the color of a sunrise. And yet she sat alone, although the pinch-faced older woman who sat behind her, industriously knitting, might have been her companion.

"Lady Harkness," Auntie said as the young woman rose from her seat, "here is the new Lady Sutcombe. I'm sure you two will find much in common. Oh, I see my old friend Harriet across the room. I'll be back in no time." She waddled off, leaving Hannah and the lady to stare at each other.

"I hope you don't mind if I sit for a moment," Hannah said. "I feel in need of a bit of rest."

"Oh, please do," Lady Harkness said in a soft voice. "But I'd be wrong to let you think you could stay too long."

Hannah had just seated herself with a sigh. She started to rise. "Why? Am I taking up someone's seat? Do forgive me."

"No," the lady said with a tinkling laugh. "No one wants to sit there. That's what I warned you about. I suppose a few seconds in my company won't ruin you. I'm Helena, by the way. I'm not used to being a lady yet. That's the point," she said sadly. "I am utterly out of my place here. It won't do you any good to be seen with me."

Seeing Hannah's perplexed look, she added, "I've been invited because the baron, my husband, is an old friend of these people. But I don't belong here. I had no station, no *entrée*, nothing but money before I wed him. It was a marriage of convenience," she whispered, looking around to be sure no one else heard her. "That's no secret, everyone knows it. And as I heard yours was too, it certainly won't help you to be accepted if you sit by me. I tell you what. I'll stand, and walk to the left, and you can follow me after a moment. We can perambulate and we won't be as noticeable together."

The lady rose, a moment later, so did Hannah; they joined at the back of the great room, and began walking the huge circle of it.

"How long have you been married?" Hannah asked.

"A year, almost to the day," Helena sighed.

"And they still don't accept you?"

"Oh, they never will. I'm not only common, but I'm a Jewess," Helena said in a small voice. "Well, on one side, which is the only one anyone here ever looks at. There it is. I'm not pure blood. I'm totally not *comme il faut* and never will be. Please don't worry, I won't be angry if you leave. I do understand. You have a great deal of work to do to get them to accept you as it is."

"I'm not going," Hannah said indignantly. "But did you know this would happen when you married?"

"Most of it," Helena sighed.

"Surely then, in time, when you have children, things will change?"

Helena looked away, her huge violet eyes clearly filled with tears. "That won't happen," she whispered. "I shouldn't tell you this, but you have no idea how strange one's thoughts can get when one sits alone for a long time. I tell you because you seem sympathetic, but you must first promise not to tell anyone else. Although," she said sadly, "I don't suppose it would make much difference if they knew. But I'm fond of the baron, and don't want any more difficulties."

"I promise not to tell," Hannah said urgently.

"Well, the truth is that the baron is very fond of me too, I know it. But he doesn't want my child to be his heir. He has three younger brothers, you see, that he hopes will produce sons to fill the position for him when they marry. Don't feel bad for me. I'm treated well."

"Surely," Hannah said, aghast, "you can annul such a marriage!"

Helena smiled mistily. "The baron is far too clever. The wedding was consummated." Her smile was sad. "A few times, actually, until I suppose, he remembered. He does love me, in his fashion, you see. But that love will never be consummated again."

"Oh my dear!" Hannah said, in shock. "Can your family do nothing?"

The lady smiled sadly. "And what in the would could they do? I don't tell them, to spare them pain. Papa would be furious, and our family has enough difficulty as it is. But it was a mistake on everyone's part. Mind, I tell you this only so you understand," Helena went on quickly. "They have dozens of ways to fence us out, those of us who don't belong, who married to better themselves or their families. And so I urge you to leave me now.

If we're coupled in Society's mind, you will be ostracized, perhaps even more than you are now. I thank you for your offer of friendship, but I know too well the cost of it. Please leave. No, wait!

"My Lady," Helena went on after Hannah, confused, had taken a step back. "Don't trust that poisonous Auntie creature. She's no friend of yours."

"I *will* see you again," Hannah said defiantly. "If you don't mind, that is to say."

"Thank you," the little lady said, "but I believe once you think on it, you'll realize it would never do for you. You may have a chance to make your way in their world. I only caution you so that you know how difficult it will be. But now please leave me. Auntie left you with me because she's a meddlesome creature."

Hannah dipped a slight bow, and left her. She looked back once, and thought she saw a faint smile on the lady's lips. She couldn't read the meaning in it, and didn't know whether to trust what she'd heard or not. Was the woman's story a jest, a part of someone's scheming? She had no idea of where to go now.

Hannah saw Ian still in the center of the room, but now lovely young women surrounded him. He threw back his head and laughed at something one of them said. He belonged here, Hannah thought. She did not. She walked to a corner of the room where the hosts had erected a floral display, and stood in the cool shadows of ferns, while the soiree swirled all around her. And then, only then, did she allow herself to think about all that the lady had told her. Had she told Hannah out of kindness, out of plain misery, or from envy or sheer mischief? It didn't matter. It rang too true.

That marriage had been consummated. There was a form of physical love that still went on, obviously. But it would never be the kind that might result in pregnancy. Just like her own had so far been. But how could anyone have known that?

Hannah shuddered. She trusted no one now. The two-faced "Auntie" had first introduced her to enemies who coveted her husband and her fortune, and sneered at her common birth. She'd been shown that she'd never be considered their equal. Then she'd been steered to the unfortunate Lady Helena. Auntie must have known they'd chat. It had opened Hannah's eyes.

But what could she do with what she didn't want to see?

Chapter 18

Hannah stood quietly behind an improvised floral arbor of ferns, wondering what to do next. She'd had enough. She couldn't seek out Ian and ask him to take her home. She wasn't actually ill, and even if she had been, she found she hadn't the courage to approach him when he was with his glittering cohorts. He seemed a different man with them, as urbane and carelessly superior as any nobleperson she'd ever seen. Neither did she want to go back to where Auntie or the other noblewomen could find her and humiliate her again.

If she dared, she'd leave Ian a message and go home by herself. She knew that that would be not only cowardly, but also insulting to Ian. She could wait in the lady's withdrawing room. But that room would be filled with the same women who had scorned her, or their kind. Hannah stood in the shadows wondering how to get through the next hours without incurring further insult or scorn.

She passed some of the time watching her new husband from her hiding place. Now the ladies had discovered him, and so she could see more of him because they weren't as tall as his male friends had been. He stood surrounded by fashionable beauties, laughing and smiling down at them. Hannah was amused to see how the ladies' feather headdresses sometimes made it appear that he was rising from a fantastical, colorful nest, amidst all the bobbing plumes. It would be more amusing if there hadn't been some real beauties among the ladies, and if Ian didn't appear to be enjoying himself quite so much. Hannah watched and wondered, and was glad she was hidden from the crowd, and at the same time sorry she'd been made so insecure that she was glad of it.

"Hannah!" a familiar voice said, waking her from her reverie. "It *is* you. Oh, by God, Hannah, at last!"

She turned. And she froze. It couldn't be. But he was standing next to her. She hadn't seen him in a long while, but she'd never forget that face. She'd seen it in too many dreams and nightmares and daydreams since they'd last met.

"Hello, Hannah," Timothy said more gently. "Or should I say, 'my lady'?"

He was dressed as she had never seen him, in costly fashionable clothing. He wore a high white neckcloth and perfect formal garb. That was what had taken her that moment to recognize him. His face was the same: the charming smile, the lovely sparkling blue eyes. But he was nevertheless entirely different-looking to her. It was more than his clothing. He'd grown older; he'd gained some weight. Now he was a solid-looking fellow. Now, too, his nose seemed too short to her, his hair too dark, his black curls too contrived. No sort of hair had a curl that always fell perfectly on a forehead. She'd tried it herself. Now too, Timothy's face looked too round, and in short, he was nothing like the other man she'd grown used to looking at. But it was he.

"Timothy!" she gasped. "What are you doing here?"

"I was invited," he said smugly.

"The devil you were!" she blurted. "You were never in London. You know no one here."

"I am now. And I obviously do. I didn't sneak in. But that doesn't matter." He looked at her with the same sincerity that used to melt her defenses. "I've been searching for you, Hannah. I was wrong to leave the way I did. I should have told you the truth. But I didn't, to spare you anxiety. I really left to seek my fortune so that I could return to court you in proper style. I did find prosperity! Not a fortune, exactly, but enough for any man, or woman. So, no more secret meetings for us or any more hasty scrambling attempts at lovemaking. You deserved much better and I always knew it.

"But I was a poor lad, and you rich as a princess. I wanted to make you my bride in full view of the world. My mistake was that I thought I could make my way fast enough to come home and surprise you with my success. Imagine how I felt when I came home to find you married to someone else!"

"You told me you'd met someone else," she blurted.

He paused. "So I did say," he went on quickly. "I had an ocean to travel across and new worlds to visit. I reasoned that if I came to harm I didn't want you to linger, a spinster, grieving for me. Better to break cleanly and quickly, and surprise you with my return. Or so I hoped. Things took longer than I thought."

"You never wrote to me," Hannah said, surprising herself at the hurt she still felt at the memory of his betrayal, because she believed it to have been long buried. But the sight of Timothy brought so much pain back to her so fast she couldn't think clearly. She was both angry with him and in some small part of her mind, thrilled to see him. He had, after all, loved her for who she was. And yet, she didn't feel the excitement as she used to experience at first seeing him. The sensation of floating on air, the hollowness in her stomach, the desire, none of that was there either.

Timothy scowled, which made him look not at all like the boy Hannah remembered.

"It was a wrong decision," he admitted. "A stupid gesture of boyish pride because of the pain I felt at having to leave you. But that's done. Now I'm here," he said proudly, "and so are you, and whatever you had to do you can't tell me you stopped loving me. Because I won't believe it."

But she thought, so she had. She didn't yearn for his kisses anymore. In fact, the sudden thought of kissing him, or any man other than her husband, actually made her feel ill. And yet at the same time Timothy brought back so many good memories of home. She welcomed them, at least here where she stood in the midst of so many people who insulted her, reviled her or made mock of her. Never had she felt more of an outsider than she did tonight. Timothy made her remember how sweet it had been to be accepted everywhere she went.

She took in a deep breath and steadied herself. She was at a London ball, with her husband. It didn't matter what Society thought, or even what Timothy did. She'd had enough tonight.

"Timothy," she said. "Believe it. You did make a mistake. I didn't. I finally gave up on you, and in so doing, I grew up. What we had was then. Time has passed. I'm a different person now."

"Yes!" he said eagerly. "Exactly. You're married and so you are your own mistress at last. You can have the ordering of your own life now. And you'll need to, my poor girl. I hear your new husband isn't as in love with you as any sane man should be."

She gasped. "Where did you hear such a thing?"

"It doesn't matter," he said with a shrug. "I know what I know. And so should you. I can fulfill our dreams now, Hannah. We can be together at last."

He took a step toward her and she retreated, holding up one hand to stop him coming closer. "By still meeting in secret?" she asked him incredulously as she began to accept that this was actually happening. "By still hiding from the world and sharing hasty scrambling lovemaking?"

"No, it's not how I dreamed it would be for you and me," he said. "Of course not. It's not how I wanted it. Still, all isn't lost. There will be nothing hasty or scrambled about it. We can have pleasure and time together again. Married women take lovers. Although," he chuckled, "you'll need no other but me. You can do it, because that's how things are done here in Society. It's how people get on in your new world."

She drew herself up. "Timothy," she said, "it's not how I do things, in any world. I have a husband. I have a new life. I think you should find one too."

"Why? When I have at last found you?"

She was still too busy thinking about what

he'd said to hear what he now said. "Who told you that my husband wasn't in love with me?" she demanded. "For that matter, who invited you here?"

"Does it matter? I can see you're too shocked to be thinking straight. Who can blame you? I muddled things, and I know it. But now know this. I've come for you. I must go now, but I'll be back, I *will* see you again. I never stopped loving you, and never shall. Nor can I believe that you stopped loving me. I know you. And you know we were meant for each other."

"That's not true," she said. "Times change, people change."

"I haven't," Timothy said. "You must know that."

"There you are," a deep voice suddenly said as Ian ambled up to them, and stopped to stand beside Hannah.

Timothy looked shocked. Hannah knew she must look guilty. And Ian merely raised an eyebrow as he stared at Timothy.

Hannah recovered quickly. "Ian, this is an old friend from home, Mr. Timothy Adkins. Timothy, this is my husband, the Marquis Sutcombe."

Timothy bowed. Ian lowered his head in a curt semblance of a bow, but when he raised it again, he still looked at Timothy. There was no expression on Ian's face, but he loomed over Timothy, and his silence seemed threatening.

How could she ever have compared them? Hannah saw it wasn't just the height difference, or their starkly different sorts of good looks. Ian's composure was unflappable; a faint sheen of perspiration had appeared on Timothy's wide forehead. Ian looked at home wherever he was. But now, even in his fine clothes, Timothy seemed wildly out of place.

"I must leave now," Timothy said hurriedly. He gazed at Hannah hungrily. "I hope we will meet again, my lady, for old time's sake. Good night, my lord." He bowed, backed away and, in a blink, had disappeared into the crowd.

Hannah said nothing.

Ian looked at her. "An old friend," Ian said, dropping each word slowly, as though they were as heavy on his tongue as they were on her heart.

"Yes," she said, lifting her chin because she hadn't done anything wrong tonight, except perhaps for a second, in her thoughts. "And it was lucky, I think, that we met. I needed someone to bolster my confidence tonight. I was standing here braving myself to face those people out there again, he appeared as out of a dream, and did just that for me. He reminded me of a time when I was considered as good as anyone and better than some."

Then she fell still and lowered her gaze. Because there was no mistaking that in that first moment she'd been glad to see Timothy and almost wished she could go home again and be the girl that he had known.

"A handsome fellow," Ian commented dryly.

"Yes," she said, looking at him again. "Or so all the girls at home thought."

He considered that, his face still expressionless. "Even you?" he asked, and then frowned, as though he was surprised and unhappy that he'd asked it.

"Even me," she said bravely.

He nodded and took a deep breath. "Shall we dance?" he finally asked.

They were playing a waltz. Ian took his wife in his arms. "You're shivering," he said, frowning again as they moved to the center of the dance floor. "You're cold. Of course, you were hiding under the ferns."

"I wasn't hiding!" she exclaimed, and then realized she was protesting too much. "Well, I suppose I was. But Timothy and I met by accident."

She felt his body go rigid, and bit her tongue. She shouldn't have defended herself. It made her look guilty of having had a secret assignation with Timothy. "It wasn't anything secret," she said defiantly. "I expect that Timothy was also ill at ease here, amongst the *ton*. He must have been skulking around the edges of the dance even as I was."

"Indeed," Ian said. "Lucky Mr. Adkins. It took

me the devil of a time to find you." He looked into her eyes, and seemed satisfied with what he saw in them. "We'll let the subject drop. But why were you, as you say, 'skulking around the edges of the dance?'"

She shivered again.

"Not taking ill?" he asked with sudden concern.

She moved with him, unconsciously keeping to his lead and the lovely waltz music. "Ian," she whispered, "I was hiding because they all hate me."

"Surely not," he said. "You're just new to this."

"I'm not new to insult and scorn. The fine ladies made a jest of me. Your 'Auntie' led them to me, and they teased me, and not in a kindly manner. Then she took me to sit next to poor Lady Harkness, another outcast because she was married off to a titled gentleman, for money. We sat together, yet apart from the crowd, like a pair of lepers. Then even she dismissed me. I tell you, Ian, I'm not welcome here."

He frowned. "If you believe it, then it's as real as if it was real. But I find that hard to believe. Still, if you're not comfortable we won't stay. I was going to introduce you to my friends. Are you sure you don't want me to do that? They're anxious to meet you. And I promise they'll be delighted."

She shook her head violently. "Not now, not here, please," she whispered.

He sighed. "Very well. But we don't retreat under fire. We'll finish this dance, and then another. Then we'll sit and chat quietly together, not like lepers, but like lovers. Or we'll stroll in the garden for a while. It's mild out tonight. We'll still be here, but not in the midst of things. Will that please you?"

She glanced out the long windows. The gardens seemed to be lit by pools of fairy lights. She could clearly see the outlines of couples standing on the terrace, looking out at the other guests promenading there.

She shuddered, and looked up at him. "I don't like to disappoint you. You seemed to be having a wonderful time. But I can't meet your friends just now. I can stay as long as you wish, so long as you don't leave me."

"I won't. I want you to be comfortable. I tell you what we'll do. We'll stay for another dance together, and see what happens."

The next dance was a country set, and so Hannah went from partner to partner, whirling up and down the line of partygoers, meeting up with a new partner every time, seeing Ian only periodically as the dance reeled on and on. She pasted a smile on her lips as she danced, and saw that Ian held his head high and was smiling too. When the music stopped, she dipped a curtsy to her partner, and Ian came to collect her. They retired to the sidelines and accepted cups of punch from a footman.

They stood cooling down from the lively dance. It was only then that Hannah saw that Ian was frowning again.

"I *have* upset you," she said.

"No," he answered slowly. "But suddenly I see I'm no longer surrounded by well wishers. It's as though I'd already left, or," he added with a bitter smile, "as though I was poor again. There is something afoot here tonight that I hadn't noticed. It's certainly time for us to go. I want to hear everything you can tell me."

They ducked out of the great house as latecomers were still streaming in. A footman gave Hannah her wrap; another called for their coach. They stood outside in the evening air, the bright lights of the house pouring out from the door and windows, illuminating the lawns, sending long bright streamers of light as far as the road, with strains of lovely music pouring out into the night as well.

"A party seems so much merrier when you're on the outside looking in," Hannah said wistfully.

"It should have been merrier inside for you," Ian said curtly.

He handed her into the coach and sat next to her. "Now," he said as their coach rolled off into the night, "tell me everything, please. And with all the names you can remember."

She did, only pausing to wonder if she should recount the story of poor little Lady Harkness's confession about her marital woes. She had promised that she wouldn't tell them to anyone else. Still, a husband and wife were considered one flesh and no sane person would ever expect someone to keep things from their spouse, especially on such short acquaintance. But it was too painful to talk about just yet; it was too close to her own fears.

When they arrived home so early, with Hannah so subdued and Ian frowning so darkly, Hannah's father and sisters were alarmed. They leapt from their chairs in the front salon, and clamored for information.

Ian held up a hand. "Hannah is just depressed. The ball wasn't pleasant for her. I think you talking to her will help a great deal. As for me," he took Hannah's hand in his, "I'm going back. Not to be the belle of the ball, but to try to find out what the devil is going on. I'll be back with some answers, I hope. Hannah," he said seriously, looking down at her, "I hope you know I'd never do anything to make you feel even momentarily unhappy. I'll see you again soon."

He kissed her hand, turned, and left the house.

"What?" Anthea cried as soon as he'd gone. "Sit down at once. We'll get you some tea. Or sherry or whatever. And then, tell all."

"Do sit down," Jessica said, "before you swoon. I vow you're white as my gown!"

"Sit, my dear," her father said sadly as her sisters steered her to a settee and settled on either side of her. "I would hear it too. I've had some regrets about this union. Not about your husband, but about his world and how they would accept you. Now it seems that my worst fears may have come to pass. Relax, sit with us a while, catch your breath. And then tell me, please."

"It wasn't that bad," Hannah said calmly, and then ruined the effect by beginning to weep.

Ian stalked into the ballroom again, and stood watching the crowd. They had shunned him, but worse, they had insulted Hannah. He wanted to wreck mayhem. But he knew better. There were subtler ways to find revenge.

The music that was being played now was incidental. There was no more dancing. A late supper was being served. His eyes raked the tables filled with merrily chatting diners and then the crowd around the serving tables. Finally, his eyes narrowed. He saw what he needed, and sauntered into the room.

"Good evening," he said as he approached one of the tables. The guests seated there went still. "I wonder," he asked, "is there room for one more?"

"Of course," a portly gentleman said as he stood to greet him. "Heard you were here, Sutcombe, but didn't see you in the crush. Thought you'd left, or would have looked for you to join us." He signaled to a footman for another chair.

"Thank you, Oscar, I know you would have," Ian said smoothly. "We often dined together back at school," he told the others at the table as he took the chair the footman offered.

But the chatter didn't resume. Ian raised an eyebrow. "Oh dear," he said too sweetly. "I seemed to have killed your appetites as well as your conversation. Tell me, how have I offended?" His smile was not kindly.

"Not at all, not at all," another gentleman said quickly. "In fact, we were just talking about you."

The sound of many indrawn breaths came from round the table. The guests, ladies and gentlemen, looked stricken.

"Yes, yes," the gentleman went on quickly. "We were all commenting on how lovely your bride is."

Ian could hear the exhalations as everyone breathed out again. "Too true," he said with a smile.

All the guests then pretended great interest in what was on their plates and in their glasses. Ian arose. "How foolish of me," he said, "I forgot to graze at the buffet before joining you. I have nothing on my plate. Oscar, old friend, will you come with me and recommend what's delicious? You were always a gourmet."

This was so patently untrue that some of the company at the table snickered. Sir Oscar Wentworth was pink-faced, plump and growing plumper every year. Everyone knew he'd no discrimination, at least so far as food was concerned. He'd eat anything on the table, or under it, as some cruel wit had once commented. He was a nice enough fellow otherwise, a staple of the *ton*, and well liked everywhere. He'd also always been in awe of Ian. Few but the marquis himself knew that.

Oscar rose from the table immediately. He and Ian ambled over to the buffet. "Glad to help," Oscar said.

"I hope you mean that," Ian said. "I'm not in search of food. No, nor money neither. Not any more. I need some information. My good lady left early tonight, because she felt cast out. That's intolerable. I found myself shunned as well. What's happening, Oscar? I need to know."

"Of course," Oscar said sadly.

They spoke in low tones as they hovered over the buffet table, Oscar loading up his plate, Ian taking a few things for the look of it.

"The Dowager Sutcombe, your father's widow, has been saying terrible things," Oscar said.

"That's no surprise. But why should anyone believe her?"

Oscar's face grew redder as he speared another lobster patty. "Well," he said, seeming to address his plate, "she says you married for money because you were a bankrupt, or nearly so, and your lady's a common tradesman's daughter."

"All true," Ian said, nodding. "Except for the common part. She's an uncommon delight."

Oscar forgot the food on the buffet as he spun around to stare, open mouthed, at Ian.

"You look as though I've threatened to murder you; keep selecting delicacies," Ian chided him.

His friend dutifully turned his attention to the buffet again.

"The fact is I was not almost bankrupt, I was totally bankrupt, thanks to the dowager widow," Ian said. "She pried all the coins from my father's pockets and then looted the estate when he died. My lady is a tradesman's daughter, and he's rich as Midas, and an uncommon fellow because obviously, unlike the king with the golden touch, he is eminently touchable. Just look at me now." Ian smiled. "But the further truth is that my lady is lovelier than all the gold coins my stepmama stole, clever as her father, and the chiefest treasure of my heart. Since I refuse to fund the dowager anymore or give her houseroom, she's busy trying to destroy my reputation and slander my lady. Were she a gentleman, I'd challenge her to swords or pistols at dawn. As she is nominally a lady, all I can do is ignore her. As I wish you and everyone else would do."

Oscar paid too much attention to the choices on the table before him.

"Think on, my friend," Ian said with a chuckle, "can you imagine *me* doing anything I don't really want to do?"

Oscar began to grin, and Ian watched as it bloomed into a huge smile. "No, Sutcombe, I can't, and that's certain," Oscar said happily. "That witch of a stepmother of yours is spreading preposterous rumors. I'll see it stopped."

"Thank you," Ian said. "Now some other names I need to know about: Lady Harkness."

"Harkness? Pretty little thing," Oscar said. "Apple of the young baron's eye. She's sitting with him, there, near the entrance. Girl with lemon yellow hair. He dotes on her, and she on him. And she's not only a commoner born, but a Jewess as well." He winced. "No offense meant. No insult to the lady meant, or to yours."

"I know," Ian said calmly. "And a certain Mr. Timothy Adkins? What do you know of him? Good-looking fellow, black hair, blue eyes. He was here tonight."

Oscar frowned. "Haven't heard of him."

"And Auntie." Ian persisted. "What the devil is going on with her?"

"Oh, that's a long story," Oscar said. "Take our plates to an empty corner and I'll tell you all. Always liked you, Sutcombe. Glad you'd come back to Town. But then you suddenly disappeared. Next thing I heard you were married."

"I'm back," Ian said, putting his hand on Oscar's shoulder. "Let's talk."

Hannah sat up in bed, waiting for her husband to return. She'd had plenty of time to think and talk about the events of the night. The time for tears was over. She had accepted everything, and had only to know what Ian thought of it. It was hours past her bedtime, her father and sisters were in their own beds at last, and the night was fading. But she couldn't sleep until she'd spoken to Ian, and she'd heard that London's great parties lasted until dawn. She waited. She couldn't have slept anyway.

Now doubts filled her head, replacing the fears she'd felt before. Her own family had been comforting; her sisters vowing they wanted no great London debuts after all, but only a chance to meet some kind and decent, educated gentlemen. Surely they could find such men either in London or in the countryside. They swore they didn't need to go to great balls or be accepted by the *ton* in order to do that. Her father steadfastly defended Ian, saying that he always thought a country life would be better for his daughters.

She didn't know if any of them meant what they said, but Hannah did know that events of the night had set a seal on any idea she had about being accepted in Ian's world.

She hadn't told any of them about Timothy's sudden reappearance, and not because she wanted to take up where they'd left off. She didn't want her family even mentioning the name, lest Ian grow more suspicious of her. She knew how Anthea could prattle. Even her father might say something. Best that the subject was dropped, and buried, along with the foolishness of her youthful infatuation.

She hoped Ian had believed her, that it was a chance encounter. Well, it had been. Now she only wanted to avoid any further complications in her life. Her infatuation with Timothy had been calf love, a romance of youth. She knew that now. Seeing him in a new setting had been a startling revelation for her. It had healed whatever lingering yearnings she had for him. She realized she'd grown far past him.

Ian was the only love in her heart now and so she'd tell Timothy if she ever saw him again. She'd also tell him she never wanted to see him again. Not just because of her morals, but because it was low and unworthy of a man for him to be delighted that his love had married so that he'd be able to sneak around with her. However things turned out with Ian, she couldn't cheat. Nor could she now imagine any other lover but him.

She wondered what he'd think of her after this debacle tonight. Would he decide his newfound wealth was a fair price to pay for losing his friends and place in Society? Had he lingered at the ball because he found better company there with his peers?

"Hannah?"

She looked up to see him standing in the doorway of their connecting rooms.

"Oh, Ian," she cried, sitting bolt upright. She put out her arms. "Come in, please tell me what happened."

He looked elegant, although weary. He hadn't undressed for bed, and still wore his evening dress. But his face was solemn and in the rising dawn light she could see that his expression was sad. He came to her with the scent of the night still on him and without any ceremony sat on the bed beside her and took her in his arms.

"Forgive me," he sighed, holding her tightly. "Forgive me for exposing you to that nonsense tonight, and for causing anything that upset you."

And then he kissed her and she forgot every other thing that had happened except for the warmth and joy she found in his arms and on his lips. He drew back for a moment. She lay content in his arms, waiting for him to start building a fire in her again. When he didn't, she kissed his neck, and his cheek, and then his mouth again.

"I'd love to," he murmured, moving away. "We will, and soon. But first, before you tire me out, you wretch, I want to tell you what happened tonight so you can rest easy and relax completely with me, with no shadow in your mind."

"Oh, all right," she said, trying to grumble as she lay back in his arms, and succeeding only in laughing. "Tell me, and get on with it, please."

That made him laugh. "Now, you've ruined my concentration," he said, drawing her closer again.

"And you've aroused my curiosity," she countered.

He sighed. "That's not the only thing aroused, but yes, I'll tell all, and quickly. And then you can remind me of what I was doing."

Chapter 19

"I'm sorry," Ian said. "You were right, Hannah. I don't know why I doubted you and your perceptions tonight. They were cruel to you, and they acted like beasts. If I'd known . . ." His voice trailed off and she could feel the tension in his body against her own. "But if it's any comfort," he went on, "I realized that those people were never my friends. We went to the ball because I was told everyone would be there. That was true. But they were sheep, not friends. I met one old friend I could talk to, and he hadn't seen us earlier. He told me what was happening. I regret subjecting you to the others."

"And that *Auntie* person?" Hannah asked.

He groaned. "Whatever she once was, she's now a pathetic and unconscionable creature, and so I told her. My friend Oscar told me that she fell into debt and will do anything for money, and has done. She has half London under her thumb.

Which is why none of my so-called friends dared defy her. Someone wanted to humiliate me and so paid her to humiliate you since they realized that's the only way to hurt me."

"Who could it be?" Hannah asked, drawing away from him in order to watch his expression.

"I have a good idea, but no proof," he said grimly. "Even Auntie wouldn't tell me, with all my threats. But until I know I'm right I can't make an accusation. In truth, it might have been anyone at that wretched ball. Some of the established gentry we saw tonight aren't in good financial condition. I am now, because of you. There are some who resent that as well as the fact that their world is changing so quickly. One day, Hannah, people like your father, clever men with a knack for getting ahead in the world, will form their own society and not need the old one anymore. More than that, they will certainly grow ever richer, while the gentry who aren't wise will grow ever poorer, as witness me and my poor father and the state he left me in.

"The world's changing and so the only way the established gentry can try to stop it is by showing spite to those who are helping the process along and trying to keep them out of their sacred precincts. But it's like trying to hold back the rain, or the snow, as on our wedding day," he added with a slight smile. "Change is part of nature. Don't let it worry you."

"But it's not fair to you," she told him earnestly. "Restoring your place in the world meant as much to you as restoring your fortune."

"Hannah," he said softly, stroking her hair gently, "that isn't true. I have what I wanted, and more than that. I have my home, or shall I say 'homes'? They've been restored to a state they hadn't been in for years, if ever. Now I can take care of my brother without stripping my home. I no longer have to worry about my tenants. I took care of my debts and obligations that weighed on me so heavily. I was never the sort of fellow who felt good about not paying my bills on time, and never wanted to be one. So whether or not I'm invited to Society's parties and balls was never a consideration. But you are.

"I'm only sorry I can't totally fulfill my pledge to your father," he said with genuine sorrow. "I don't know if we can launch your sisters in Society after all. And I'm sorry the people I thought I knew hurt you tonight. For that, I can't forgive them. I wish tonight had never happened. As time goes by and the bad memory of this night fades, we ourselves will give a greater and more gala ball, right here. We'll invite only those I know can be happy for us. And believe me, the invitation will be looked on as a great honor. The more exclusive any event is, the more it matters to that kind of person. But know that those people you saw tonight do not and never will matter to me. You do. They didn't want me before, when I had no money, and I don't need them now. I do need you."

He kissed her again. And she kissed him back with all the love and loneliness and ardor that she felt.

"No wonder we females are so susceptible to seduction," she finally whispered, giggling as she tugged on his sleeve to help him rid himself of the tightly fitted jacket he was struggling to shuck off. "When we need to be close to someone, it's simply a matter of bits of gauze and muslin for us to raise, or lower."

"*'Be close to someone'?*" he asked with a tilted smile. "What a nice euphemism. But wrong. Think about it, my delicately spoken lady, without being vulgar I must remind you that it's even simpler for men to ready themselves for love," he said as he finally cast the jacket to the floor to follow his discarded neckcloth. "But not now, and not me with you. That's for strangers. I want to feel my skin against yours," he added as he bent and tugged his evening slippers off.

They didn't speak for a while. She was too entranced by his kisses and the way he slowly unveiled his body to her. He pulled his shirt over his head, revealing his taut muscled chest, and stripped off his hose and breeches to display his flat abdomen and obvious eagerness for her before he returned to her embrace.

They writhed against each other, discovering more and more ways to pleasure each other. He was too interested in touching her, holding her, readying her to speak to her. And she, too thrilled by them and the feel of him to even think of it.

When at last they were damp, tingling, and flushed with desire, he raised himself on his elbows over her.

"Forgive me, excuse me," he said, punctuating each statement with a kiss on the tip of her nose. "I never meant to bring you sorrow, I hope I never will again. Make love to me, Hannah, and know that."

He brought his body to hers, and she raised herself to assist him. She held him in her arms, and this time greeted his entry with a sigh of pleasure. Her hands went to the small of his back to still him there for a moment and clasp him close.

"Where do you leave off and I begin?" she asked in wonder as she stroked the small of his back.

"I never want to leave," he whispered, as he began to move, "but I soon must. First, I want you to begin to feel what I do."

He couldn't say more. He held her and moved within her, and smiled when she moved with him. He didn't leave off touching her and so when at last he stroked that small hidden part of her above his entry and she gasped aloud, he finally allowed himself to strive against her as he had to do.

She heard him growl his rising pleasure when her own began to ebb to quivering. Then she felt a new pulsing sensation gathering deep within her body, and held her breath and let it begin . . .

Until he suddenly pulled away and fell to the bed beside her, face down. He groaned, his body buckled, and he spent himself on the bedclothes. It was a while before he could catch his breath and speak. It was longer before she dared to.

He sat up beside her holding a ball of crumpled material he'd scooped up from beneath him. "It's only your discarded night shift," he murmured, tossing it away. "Everything else is dry. Are you all right?"

"Why did you do that?" she asked.

"To keep you from the consequences until you're more sure of me," he said, lying down and taking her in his arms again.

Her body stiffened. So did her voice. "You mean having a baby? I'm a country girl. I do understand. But we are wed. Such consequences are to be expected."

"Now?" he asked. "When you suspect everyone around me of hating you? I want you to have time to come to know the world you've entered, be easy in it, and accepted: to be sure of yourself before I ask you to bear my child. You have enough on your plate. What's the matter?"

"I think," she said slowly, pulling herself away from him, sitting up and crossing her arms over her naked breasts, "that I'm insulted."

"That's ridiculous," he said, sitting upright as well.

"Is it?" she asked, gathering the coverlet and pulling it over her. "I met a lady at the ball who was distressed because her husband, who had married her for money, gave her pleasure but refused to give her a babe because of her lower station in life."

He struck the side of his head with his palm, and groaned. "You seduced the thought out of my head. I was too entranced and involved with your lovemaking to remember to tell you that. I spoke to Lady Harkness. When I introduced myself to the baron, she looked petrified with fear. She's a shy little thing. So I didn't go on, not there. But she put her hand up and begged me to speak to her, privately. With her husband as well, of course.

"We went to a corner of the room, near the windows. She told her husband that her heart was heavy with remorse. She regretted the lies she told you. Seems she'd done something he didn't know about, and Auntie was blackmailing her for it. The baron vowed he knew something was wrong and thought she'd been sickening. She was *enceinte* with their first child, he said proudly."

Hannah gasped, and put her hand to her mouth.

"They are very much in love, Hannah. They can scarcely keep their hands off each other. She told us what Auntie made her tell you. And wept as she did."

"What could she have done that was so terrible?" Hannah asked. "Gambling debts? I heard some of the older Society ladies like to get newcomers enmeshed in their card games and win their quarterly allowances and more from them."

"Nothing of the sort. Lady Harkness has always had money and being a sensible creature, disapproves of gambling it away, unless on bonds or investments in real estate. No, Auntie had got the poor girl aside and told her that she'd make her an outcast in the Society her husband loved to travel in if she didn't obey. She'd only one task, she was told: to tell you that faradiddle.

"The lady thought it would be terrible but that she could do it because she didn't know you, would only meet you that once and never again. But she'd been grieving about it and was going to come see you tomorrow, to explain. And she assured her baron she was nerving herself to tell him that very night. He calmed her, calling her 'poor puss,' and 'silly lamb,' and said nothing mattered to him as much as she did. He also vowed to ruin Auntie forever. I told him I'd do it. But you, Hannah? A stranger told you intimate details of her husband and her marriage at first acquaintance, at a Society ball. And you believed her?"

Hannah looked down at the coverlets. "I suppose I was even more foolish than poor Lady Harkness." She could see him clearly in the rising morning light. His expression was stony. "When you protected me from begetting your baby, I thought you were doing the same thing . . . that the baron didn't do," she finished weakly. But she soon fired up again. "What was I to think anyway? I told you I wanted a baby. And you know you told me you didn't want one."

He sighed again. "Hannah, many educated, knowledgeable husbands of our class do the same when they are newly wed; some from a wish to protect their ladies from too early an obligation. Others because they wish to be sure that the babe, when it comes, is their own. But wait. When you spoke to the poor lady, did you reciprocate? What did you tell her about your own marriage?"

"Nothing!" she gasped. "Nothing intimate at all."

"Thank you," he said. "But maybe, some day," he continued in a cool, contained voice, "you'll also tell me more about that fellow *Timothy*, and why he was so sure you'd welcome his advances last night. I heard more than I revealed. I've been waiting for you to tell me. I thought you would, and then convinced myself that it was of no matter, because you likely forgot and would soon remember. He left too quickly for a final answer, didn't he? What would it have been?"

She sat stock-still.

He nodded. "And you tell me you wonder why some newly wedded husbands delay love-making that might result in a child? Now, that *is* amusing."

"And so that means you don't trust me any more than you said I trust you!" she retorted in shame and anger.

He paused. "Perhaps not. A perfect marriage of true minds we have here, don't we?"

"Why did you make love to me at all, if you were thinking dreadful things like that?" she cried.

He smiled. But it wasn't from amusement. The increasing light showed it was merely a matter of his lips curling. "Because whatever your morals or plans, or thoughts, your body calls to mine. I wonder that I was able to restrain myself as well as I did."

She flared up at him. "I do too! I wonder why you didn't do the same before this."

"Because I hadn't seen your Timothy then."

"That's vile!" she cried.

"Aye," he said, rubbing his forehead. "Forgive me. I should never have said or thought it. But I'm so drawn to you, and you, so responsive to me. I thought maybe I was just lucky. Then I saw him. Maybe that's why I said it."

"I think," she said in measured tones, "that is hateful too."

"Under the circumstances," he said sadly,

"you're right. Will you forgive me? Will you let me love you again? I trust you, Hannah. But I wish I knew more about you."

"Timothy means nothing to me now," she said stiffly. "When I was a girl, I was infatuated with him. He seeks to renew our acquaintance. I do not. That I vow. And we never . . . well, you certainly should know that!" she exclaimed.

"Yes. Again, my apologies, sincerely."

He held out his arms. She moved into them and rested her head against his chest so she could hear his beating heart.

"When?" she said softly.

"When what?" he asked, craning his head to look at her.

"When can we make love, again?" she whispered.

"Oh, Hannah," he said. She felt his chest moving with suppressed laughter. "I've been up all night. I could, I expect, and would, if I were sure I could. Can we wait a little while, do you think?"

She was glad he couldn't see her face, but was sure he could feel the heat rising in it.

"Never fear," he added. "We will as soon as I can. Such invitations are not forgotten."

She nodded, and didn't see his grin.

After a while, as the room filled with morning sunlight, he kissed her and left, quietly closing the door between their rooms. Her maid wouldn't be in for a few more hours, but Hannah had a difficult time getting to sleep again because she was mulling over all that had been said, and unsaid, done and undone.

And even though he was exhausted, so did Ian, because he was thinking about the same things.

"I think we should go home," Jessica said the next morning, looking across the breakfast table from her host's frozen expression to her newly-wed sister's astonished eyes. "After all, it's clear we don't fit here."

"I wonder how much room you think you need," Ian answered, looking up from his breakfast with a small smile.

"It's not the room, my lord," Anthea said. "It's the fact that we don't wish to be an embarrassment to you, or for that matter, to ourselves."

"You aren't, you won't be," Ian said. "But if you continue to call me 'my lord,' when we're in private you may well be. I told you, the ball we went to last night was in the way of being a trap. I'd no idea of the reception we'd get. Someone chose to try to humiliate your sister, and I was too stupid to see it. I should never have left her side, so I suppose I'm equally at fault.

"In future," he said, "I'll choose our adventures with more care. And there will be a future. In the meanwhile," he said as he laid his fork down, folded his napery and put it on the table, "I think you girls should explore London with me. It's a remarkable city. I'll be careful to see that no one insults or distresses you. Since the weather is holding, I thought we'd see the Tower today. I have some influence and we may get to see some interesting sights apart from the menagerie. You might wish to come along," he told their father.

"Not I," the elder Leeds said. "I saw the Tower years ago when I was a lad. But it's an excellent outing for the girls, thank you."

"So we'll go," Ian said as he rose from the table. "I promise, there won't be a Society snob in sight. Not one of them visits their own city's wonders. In fact, most are ignorant as geese about many things. About noon then, shall we say? I'll have the coach readied."

He sketched a bow, and left them.

"You don't seem happy," Anthea said to Hannah.

"It's early," Hannah lied. "My mood will rise with the sun. He's right. We don't often get such clear days. Wear slippers you can walk in. I'll meet you in the salon when it's time to go."

She rose, and left the table.

Her sisters watched her go, both of them looking troubled.

"Newlyweds," their father sighed. "Don't try to understand them, my dears. Doubtless, they don't themselves."

* * *

It was a bright, mild, totally delicious day for a tour. But the Leeds girls weren't enjoying it, because neither was their older sister or their host. Oh, the marquis was polite, courteous, and conversational but they knew him well enough now to know that he was preoccupied and, as Jessica later put it, "sitting on thorns." And Hannah was uncharacteristically silent. She passed most of the trip biting her lower lip until Jessica leaned over and whispered that they were red enough, so she ought to stop.

Still, when they reached the Tower complex itself, with its famous towers, and its glorious reflections in the Thames, they were thrilled enough to forget their host's and their sister's problems for a while. They crossed over the smelly moat with handkerchiefs to nose, as Ian suggested, but then forgot everything but the Tower itself as they walked historic paths. They were delighted by the sight of the polite, stalwart Beefeaters, guardians of the Tower, in their dazzling red uniforms; some young enough to be almost more thrilling to the girls than the Tower itself.

It was a city in itself, a complete and separate world, as it had been in its days of greatest glory and infamy. There were many impressive towers within the compound, each famous. Paths led them past shops and outbuildings, gardens and dairies, bakeries and homes, as well as places they'd read about in history texts. Ian took them every place where they could ogle and goggle to their heart's content. It would have been even better if they had failed to notice what happened every time their host and his bride happened to meet alone, by a display case or in a corner, and thought no one else could hear them whispering and snarling to each other.

Anthea managed to desert the fabulous crown jewel display and edge close enough to hear Hannah whisper to Ian, with ferocity: "Why did you make love to me at all? Even with all your control, surely it was a risk, thinking that I might have betrayed you?"

He was still a moment. "Because I hoped you had not."

They parted then, both red-faced when they realized that Anthea was standing nearby, enthralled.

But it didn't stop them for long.

Jessica managed to creep away stealthily, leaving the path to the Prison Tower, lingering long enough to hear Hannah hiss to Ian when they thought they were alone: "And now, my lord? What do you think now?"

"I want to believe you," he said.

"I should think you would. I've never lied to you," she retorted.

His eyebrow went up. "Really?" he said coldly. "Have you told all then?"

Before Hannah could answer she caught sight of Jessica's enraptured face. The newlyweds walked on in silence the rest of the way, both of them glowering.

The girls caught hints of accusations and snippets of spite, and were both alarmed and perturbed.

"Let them be," Anthea finally said. "Perhaps if they can talk it out they can work it through. There are other things that you and I can do here."

But Ian and Hannah had stopped communicating. They walked behind the girls, silently. There was no more they dared say to each other and much more that they wanted to. So they walked on, noticing nothing and remembering everything—until they heard Anthea cry out.

They ran ahead, their own trials forgotten. They found her leaning on a handsome young Beefeater's arm, bawling, her handkerchief to her face. They'd have been terrified if they hadn't seen Jessica's expression. Instead of being worried, she was definitely put out and actually rolling her eyes.

The young Beefeater looked embarrassed and helpless, a strange sight in such a brawny fellow. Anthea was sobbing, and not as a sham, because when she moved the handkerchief her eyes and nose were red as his coat, and they knew she'd never have wanted a fine young fellow to see that.

Jessica had been trying to comfort her, to no avail. She looked up with dawning hope as her sister and brother-in-law ran toward them.

"This is Tower Green," Jessica said wearily. "She found out this is where enemies of the kingdom were beheaded."

"I dinna mean to frash her," the Beefeater said miserably, his Scots accent broadening in his own distress. "I told her some tales of the history and she started greeting. I dinna know the child had such tender feelings."

"I am not a child," Anthea said suddenly, her wailing abruptly stopped. She sniffed. "Anyone's heart would be wrenched. The poor harmless earl of Warwick had his head removed right here," she said, pointing with a shaking finger. "As well as Anne Boleyn and others. Here's the *very* block where so many heads rolled and brave souls perished."

"And traitorous ones as well," Ian muttered. "That's enough history for today, I think. We will not proceed to the Traitor's Gate as planned. Instead, I think we should visit the menagerie and see some exotic animals."

"A grand idea," the Beefeater said with obvious relief, handing Anthea to her sisters. "We have some bonny specimens, my lord."

When Anthea had composed herself, she walked on, arm in arm with Jessica again, ahead of her sister and brother-in-law.

"You only did that because he was so charming and handsome," Ian heard Jessica accuse her younger sister in a hissing whisper as they walked forward.

"That's a terrible lie," Anthea said, although her cheeks did turn red. "You know I have sensibilities."

"But you didn't succumb to them when that fat, jolly old Beefeater told you some even worse stories about the prison," Jessica said.

Anthea pointed her nose to the sky. "I may have no control over my emotions, but at least I have emotions. You didn't so much as frown."

Hannah turned to Ian just in time to see him grinning at her even as she was at him.

He put his hand over hers where it lay on his arm. "Yes. We've been setting a terrible example. Our mood was contagious. No more today then."

"Yes," she said, "no more today. We have a lot to talk about, but you're right. This isn't the time or place. I wish we didn't have to, though," she added on a sigh.

He patted her hand. "I agree. We'll try to iron things out, but in private. We must, for their sakes, and our own."

They smiled at each other and walked on in companionable silence, wishing it would last. *If only every moment with him could be like this*, Hannah thought. She felt secure, and warm, and protected.

She did, that is, until she saw someone on the path ahead of them, someone who quickly walked away and out of sight. And then she wished for all the world that she were able to cry out and weep as Anthea had done. Because something as fatal to her hopes for the future as a chopping block was following them.

Chapter 20

Ian knew something had gone even more wrong with the day. Hannah's smiles were suddenly forced, and it wasn't because of the delicate situation between them. She fairly vibrated with a new unease. And, he thought with sinking heart, he knew why. He hadn't missed the man who had been ghosting across their paths today. In fact, he thought he'd seen him even sooner than Hannah, and then again as soon as she had. He'd felt the jolt of anxiety tighten her arm when she'd first seen the shadow of the fellow as they were strolling. But much as he wanted to, Ian couldn't break away, run, and catch the man. He had no reason to accost an innocent stranger, even though he knew that this was no innocent stranger. He was Timothy Adkins.

And yet, Ian thought, Hannah still didn't say a word to him about her Timothy, even now. She probably hoped he hadn't noticed. Ian was glad the girls were with them. Because if they hadn't

been he might have been tempted to walk away
and leave Hannah to herself, and her Timothy,
forever.

He'd taken careful notice of the fellow in the
glimpses he'd gotten. Here in the bold sunlight,
he got a better look than the night of the ball. Timothy was a young man, handsome, and dressed
decently. He was guarded, ducking away whenever he thought he was sighted. It was obvious
he was smart enough to know that he'd been noticed. He looked clever, he seemed alert, and was
determined to follow them everywhere. Hannah
looked away when she spied him, even as he faded
back into the shrubbery.

Ian stood heartsick as they watched an old
lion pacing his cage. He'd wanted to trust her.
This struck his hopes a deadening blow. So she'd
already begun to lie to him, because not saying
something was in his opinion as good, or bad, as
a lie. Ian supposed he could nab the fellow and
demand to know why he was spying on them,
and so bring the whole thing out into the light.
But what was the use? If Hannah wanted to see
him without anyone knowing, she'd eventually
go to him in secret.

Now he remembered how she'd asked him
early on, about what arrangements men and
women made for sex in marriages of convenience.
He'd thought she was only asking what he'd do in
the matter of taking a mistress. He'd been an idiot

and might soon be a cuckold. Such was the fate, he thought with a twisted smile, of men who held themselves too high.

And why should that matter? Ian had few illusions. He had a wife; he'd begun to believe he might have more than that. But he didn't have a real marriage. He'd been bought and paid for, but not by her. She should have some joy out of life and if he couldn't give it to her, why should she suffer? He thought about that in silence as Hannah and the girls strolled to the bank of the Thames to watch the boats that sailed past.

What did matter was that it meant he couldn't trust her, and that he'd never have a real marriage with her. He hadn't cared about that before. Now, as they'd seemed to be reaching a new understanding, he did. It also meant he couldn't make love to her again; he wouldn't give his birthright to an imposter, which their son would surely be.

She'd told him that Timothy had only been an infatuation. Now her face told more. She was obviously silently sorrowing even more than her silly sister had done in the arms of the Beefeater. Ian didn't know whom her sorrow was for. Herself? For him? For the man she might have loved out in the open before she'd married him? That was a thing he'd find out, Ian promised himself. He'd know this very day, by means of the best way he could. He'd ask Hannah. Many things she was, or he thought she was or could be. But he knew her long enough to know she wouldn't lie to him directly.

They left the menagerie and paced along a road by the great white parapets that enclosed the complex. There, at last, they stood by the great river and watched the big-bellied, high-masted ships and little skiffs sail by, the gulls wheeling above and crying foul, as always when the men in fishing boats threw them no entrails. They breathed in the scents of the Thames, the smell of salty sea and lake, land, fish, human waste, and mud. Still, it was a lively breeze and a curiously bracing scent. No one spoke for a while.

"May we please go for a stroll?" Jessica suddenly asked. "We won't go out of sight, or fall in the river, or collapse in tears in the arms of handsome guardsmen."

"That is unjust!" Anthea fired back.

"But true," Jessica said serenely. "No one died here, so you'd have no excuses, even if you see a Beefeater that looks like Adonis."

"Much you know!" Anthea said darkly. "Many have drowned here in the night in sinister and mysterious circumstances."

"But we won't," Jessica said calmly. "May we go?" she asked her brother-in-law again. "We have things to discuss."

"And discuss them you shall," Ian said. "But I think it's time we returned home. You two can discuss everything you like in perfect secrecy there. We've stayed for longer than I thought we would. Your father might be worrying. What do you say?" he asked Hannah.

She looked surprised that he had deferred to her about such a small thing, but forced a smile, and said, "Yes, of course."

He noted that she only looked over her shoulder twice as they walked back.

"May we talk?" Ian asked Hannah.

She sat up in her bed. She put down her book. She saw him clearly in the lamplight. He stood in the doorway between their rooms, wearing a red banyan, a long elegant robe she hadn't seen before. He also wore a grave expression.

"I saw the light under your door," he explained, "and knew you weren't sleeping. Your sisters thought they needed private time to sort things out. We do too. You know that, Hannah."

"Yes, we do," she said softly.

He came into the room, and sat beside her on the bed as he always did. But tonight she didn't feel any thrill of excitement or expectation. She felt only dread, because he was right. He had eyes and was no fool. They had to talk. It was time, past time.

"The man who followed us today," she said at once, looking at Ian. "I know you saw him. And it was Timothy Adkins. His father was a draper, and he had few chances to really rise in the world. But no one cared a snap for that as far as his marital prospects went, at least the girls in the village didn't, they all adored him. And when he came courting me, I was flattered and astonished and in the end, thought myself the luckiest girl in the land. I wasn't a great beauty, as you can see."

She held up a hand to stop whatever he might say. "Please, I wasn't asking you to argue the point. Nor was I popular with the local lads." She gave a little laugh. "Much chance I had of that! My father watched all of us carefully. He was richer than anyone in the vicinity, indeed, maybe in the whole country, and he mistrusted any man who made up to us. And so, none dared. Except for Timothy, and since he knew my father's protectiveness, we met in secret. I . . ." she hesitated.

Then she looked straight at Ian and went on, "I wasn't young anymore, but I behaved like a girl. In short, I soon thought I was in love with him. But I knew my father would disapprove, so I did all sorts of reprehensible things."

His eyebrow lifted.

She ducked her head and traced a pattern on the cover of the book that lay on the bedcovers. "I stole out in the night as well as the days to meet him. I lied about where I had gone." When she looked up again, there was entreaty in her eyes.

"I was quite out of my mind with desire for him that summer."

"I see," he said.

"No, I don't think you do, my lord. You've never been a young woman growing older and wondering if anyone would ever love her. You never suffered such a lack of freedom. You never knew so little about the other gender, or the world, I think. I might have thoroughly disgraced myself," she went on softly, "but you of all people know I didn't. Don't credit me. It wasn't because I was so virtuous or sensible. But because he never took it that far. He just kept raising me to a higher pitch of desire.

"And then he came to meet me one day and told me that he loved another; a woman of beauty and wealth. He said all that had happened that summer was just sport to him. He said good-bye. I cannot tell you how I felt, I think because I don't want to remember such pain. I do know I felt a fool and a dupe and an idiot, and thoroughly broken."

She raised her head. "So when my father saw me languishing, he decided it was time for me to marry. He asked if I had anyone in my eye. As if he would have listened if I had told him I had." She sighed. "But truth is that I didn't anymore. I was done with love and through with illusion, and only wanted to be far away."

The room was silent for a few moments.

"And so," he said, "you agreed to marry me." He took a deep breath. "I should have asked you why?"

"You did."

He shook his head. "Not really. Or if I did, I wasn't prepared to believe you. I thought it was all for the title. But you aren't your father, and I was the fool. You came to me with a crippled heart, and I married you without bothering myself with doubts about it, and to cap it all, when you saw Adkins again, I reacted with distrust." He rose and paced a step, his mouth twisted in revulsion at himself.

She gestured as though she were brushing away a cobweb. "I was walking in my sleep when we married, I think," she said. "It made me gather my wits and try to decide my future."

He came back to her and sat beside her again. "Hannah. What's to do? All isn't mended, not even with the whole story. You didn't tell me all about him until you had to."

"I was ashamed," she said.

"For having loved him? I'd hope you know me better than that. Did you think I'd hurt him?"

"No!" she said immediately, eyes wide.

"So, is it that you want to leave with the fellow? Is there still a place in your heart for him? I'll let you go, but I cannot let you bear his child. I've shown little mettle and less pride, but that, I can't and won't accept."

"That," she said, "I would not do."

"We can't divorce," he went on. "The scandal would forever blacken my name. And yours. It's a long, complicated, expensive and public process, and a shocking one that no one will ever forgive or forget. Neither of us deserves that. But if you can't live without him, you may go off with him, to a foreign land, preferably. Except, as I said, I won't accept any child you may bear."

She looked into his eyes. "I don't want to see him, much less go with him. I don't love him. If I thought I did once upon a time, I didn't know what love was."

"And you do now?" he asked sadly.

She looked up at his still, handsome face, and almost said yes. But she couldn't give so much without getting anything in return. Perhaps he wasn't furious because he was remorseful. That wasn't the same as loving. That much, she had learned.

"I know I don't love him," she repeated. "I'm very glad, now, that he dismissed me then. In fact, I'm grateful to him. I don't know why he's following me. There's no blackmail to be done. He surely can't think I would forgive him, and anyway, I'm married now."

"Some men," Ian said carefully, "think females in unhappy marriages would give anything to have what passes for love."

"Oh. You mean his own love affair may have come to grief? And since he heard about some Society marriages, he believes I'd still want him? So now he wants me, at least in his bed? That may be it, of course," she finally said. "But I don't know. At any rate, you know I'm not unhappy. Don't you?"

He shrugged.

"You don't believe me?"

"Hannah," he said, "how can I?"

"Because I tell you so. I want nothing to do with him. You heard me the night of the ball."

He nodded, and his expression lightened a little. "Then if you fear he won't talk with you when I'm near, then meet him with me nearby, speak to him, and tell him that again," Ian said, rising from the bedside.

"Ian," she said, putting out a hand. "Can you . . . could you stay awhile? If not for love, then for company? I've grown accustomed to falling asleep with you nearby."

He didn't move for a moment, and then sat down again. "You look very pretty tonight," he said as he did. "That pink robe suits you, and the sun you got today caused tiny freckles to bloom on your cheeks and the bridge of your nose. It looks charming."

"Thank you," she said with a small laugh. "*Exactly* not the thing to say to a lady, my lord. Freckles are poison to the ladies of the *ton*. Luckily, I'm not one of them. And you looked very elegant at the Tower today. I don't doubt your size and obvious fitness was what kept Timothy away."

"We approve of each other then," he said, lying back, plumping up a pillow, and settling himself beside her.

"We do," she said, and wished she could say more.

"That's a beginning," he said. After a moment's consideration, he added, "Tomorrow bids to be fair again. We can take the girls to the park, and let them stroll the lake path and see the fashionable at play. And at some time, I can walk with them and at some point you may trail behind us. Mind, I won't let you out of my sight. But you will be out of my hearing. I can't think of any other way you can talk to your Timothy unless you invite him here. I don't think I'd care for that."

"Nor I," she whispered, lying beside him, but careful not to touch him in any way. "Ian? Shall you ever trust me again?"

"I don't know," he said. "It's a thing we both need time to discover. You gave your hand and your fortune to a man you didn't know. I should have expected disaster from my foolishness in knowing that and accepting it even so. But I believed I was trapped, with few possibilities. The other females I met were impossible. You weren't. I chose you. And so even if you don't love your old beau, I closed the door on your chances at finding a true love. I'm not a poet or a sentimentalist, but I believe you should have had a chance at that."

"I find myself growing daily more content," she said. "If you pardon me my folly for marrying in a daze and not thinking ahead, things will be better for us both. I acted like a child, but maybe it's just as well. I wasn't in any state to make a good choice for myself."

"And you are now?" he asked.

She thought about it. The bedchamber was still. They were both tiptoeing around their feelings as well as each other's. *I said I grow more content daily. You have said nothing like. I don't believe I can bear your suspicion much longer.* She wanted to say it. She couldn't, it was too soon or too late. And she believed he was the one who should give her some hint of how he felt about her before she laid her heart before him.

"Ian?" Hannah finally said, when she thought she had a well-considered thing to say that wouldn't cause more pain or doubt.

But she got no answer. He'd fallen asleep. She could hear his steady breathing. It comforted her. She rose and turned down the light. Then she lay back on the bed again, carefully as a woman sleeping next to a newborn babe, and closed her eyes. He hadn't said he trusted her. But he hadn't said he didn't.

Ian lay quietly until he finally heard her even breathing and knew she was asleep. Then he opened his eyes and stared into the night until it was dawn, never knowing that his wife was doing the same.

The lake in Hyde Park glittered blue, the trees were in full leaf and the grass was stunningly green, dappled with flat white daisies. It was a small lake, but wonderful to see in the heart of London town. Rowboats plied their way around it, and children threw their toys and beheaded daisies into it. The lake was surrounded by a path shaded by ancient copses of towering trees. In other places it was bare except for grass, so one could see the green slopes leading to meadows far beyond. The path was also dotted with benches and arbors for those who simply wanted to sit and relax.

Commoners might sit on the grass in their parks, this one, so near to the palace, was for the gentry. Of course, there was no way of keeping the rest of London out. This was, after all, a public park in a free country. But on a sunny weekday working morning there were few commoners to be seen apart from those on their way to or from errands, as well as those who worked here: flower sellers, food vendors, and the myriad nurses and companions with their young and old charges.

Some of the *ton* paraded the paths. Some rode their horses or carriages on by. But in all, it was a quiet, peaceful morning, made for quiet enjoyment.

Hannah, her husband and sisters walked two by two, the younger sisters in front. Jessica was dressed beautifully. She wore a new dark red walking dress, a saucy bonnet tied under her chin by a red ribbon, and carried a cherry-colored parasol to save her face from the ruinous effects of the sunlight. Her attire suited her dark looks perfectly.

Her sister Anthea wore a saffron-colored walking dress and a charming straw bonnet perched on her blond curls. She kept her parasol folded, so everyone could see how the sun made her fair hair gleam. They linked arms and perambulated along the banks of the lake in the park.

"One doesn't just walk here," Anthea explained. "Not if one wants to be seen to be as elegant and privileged as any of the other fashionable souls strolling here on a glorious morning."

"Well," Hannah said, "I don't think I have the knack of perambulating just yet, so I'll walk, thank you."

This made Ian and the sisters grin. But almost anything could reduce the girls to giggles this beautiful morning. It would have made her smile too, Hannah thought, if she weren't strung tight as a wire, wondering if Timothy would be on their trail again this morning. If he were, then she'd have to confront him. That wasn't a problem. Timothy along with the memories of their furtive lovemaking were now like the rapidly fading wisps of a strangely tangled erotic dream she'd had in the night. It was nothing like the incredible feeling of what had happened to her in Ian's arms.

Timothy couldn't compare to her husband. Not in looks or manners, intelligence or charm. No one could. She knew it and others could see it. She caught the sidewise glances Ian received from passing females of all classes. He got a nod from the ladies, if they recognized him, and interested stares even if they didn't. She also noted the many smiles and winks he got from the common lasses who were also moving along the paths. He was dressed casually, but elegantly as always, in a dark brown jacket and dun unmentionables, with brown half-boots. A glimpse of his mustard-colored vest could be seen beneath his carelessly and artfully tied neckcloth. But Ian would have shone in any garb. Hannah was proud to walk along with him.

It wasn't only his appearance. It was, she thought, the entire makeup of the man. He didn't rage at her or scorn her for her confession. In fact, she thought sadly, she wished he had. Nor did he entirely believe it. She'd have to prove herself to him. She had to dismiss Timothy from their sight, and Ian's mind. He'd married her for profit; she'd wed him for escape. But now she loved him. And only the lord above knew if he cared for her for more than courtesy's sake. He was, she thought sadly, far too much of a gentleman.

She felt secure in her appearance today, though. She wore a new dark green walking dress, very dashing in its military cut and bright brass buttons. It looked almost like a riding habit and rather like a fashion plate, and she was thrilled with the effect. A small shako-styled confection of a hat sat tilted on her hair, and she hoped she appeared to be just as dashing and confident as she didn't feel.

The problem was wondering what Timothy wanted and why he was behaving with such stealth. It made it look as though he was waiting for a secret planned assignation with her. Now she walked in the sunlight and waited.

She saw Timothy out of the corner of her eye, standing beside thorn bushes by the path, and when she turned her head he was gone.

"He's gone behind the big bank of trees, to the right," Ian told her quietly. "I can walk to the water's edge with the girls, point out the rowboats and ask them if they want me to rent a boat for us. I'll stay there while you sit on that bench to the right and try to get the pebble out of your slipper that's making you limp. Remember to limp on your way there, please. And if you happen to slip behind the tree behind the bench when I've gone, how should I know? But I'll be within call and I'll know where you are, *if* you want me to be. Do you want to do that? Or," he asked more softly, "would you rather meet with him when I am nowhere to be found?"

What she wanted was to slap him. He saw it in her eyes.

"Very well," he said. "I'll escort you to the bench, and then go stand with the girls. Hannah?"

She looked up at him.

"Good luck in whatever you decide to do."

"Do you have any doubt?" she asked.

He smiled. "Yes. Of course I do. Wouldn't you?"

She cast down her gaze, and limping, made her way to the bench to the right.

When Ian and the girls returned, Hannah was sitting on the bench, looking nonplussed. She glanced up at Ian, shook her head, and then rose and took his arm again.

"No one," she said as they continued walking. "Do you think that means he's given up whatever he was about to do?"

"No," Ian said calmly. "I think he's determined not to be seen by anyone but you. There'll be other times. Do you want me to do anything to stop that possibility?"

"No," she said, shaking her head, watching the path ahead. "And not for the reason you may believe. Thank you, but now I think I must know what is going on."

He said nothing to that, and they kept on walking.

Chapter 21

For the rest of that day and on into the evening, there was little chance for Hannah to talk to Ian alone. But they didn't have a chance to be alone. They had tickets to the theater. That meant that from the moment they returned to the town house, they were in a flurry. They had to bathe and dress for it, which was no small feat. Hannah's maid, and Mr. Baker, as well as the girls' maids, were in a tizzy, getting everyone ready for the event. But they were no more fevered than Anthea and Jessica were.

"Everyone knows that the theater is *the* place to be seen!" Anthea burbled as she spun in front of Hannah's tall looking glass, showing her finery off to her sisters. But since we aren't out yet, there's little to see," she added, staring at her reflection. "White! Ugh. It does nothing for me."

"But if you aren't 'out' you can't wear jewel colors to any place where you expect to be seen," Jessica said, noting with satisfaction how her white gown complemented her glossy dark curls. "It must be white."

"The pearls look lovely at your throat, Jess," Hannah said. "Your hair is dressed beautifully, and that camellia set in it is a lovely touch."

"Yes." Jessica sighed. "But that's easy for you to say, in your beautiful apple green gown, with that pink sash beneath your breasts."

"Which look lovely too," Anthea commented with a grin.

Hannah tugged at her low neckline. She looked down. "I suppose they are rather on display, but I'm assured that's the style."

"You look like an apple tree in spring bloom," Anthea said enthusiastically.

"Just exactly what every lady wants to hear," Hannah said. "I suppose I look like a country girl come straight from the fair."

"And what's wrong with that?" Ian asked, from where he stood in the doorway watching them.

"Not fair!" Anthea cried. "We were going to make a grand entrance to show you how we look. We were planning to float down the stair and amaze you."

"I promise you if you did that, you still would," Ian told the girls with a laugh. "Your maids assured me you were ready. So I came to tell you that our carriage awaits, princesses, and it's time for us to be off."

"I wish Father had agreed to come," Jessica said

as they filed down the stair. "He'd be so proud to see how we look."

"He was anxious to dine with his old friend," Hannah said. "It would have been selfish for us to insist."

"I think," Jessica said from behind her, "that's not it at all. He still wants us accepted by Society and I think he's afraid his very presence will assure that won't ever happen. They think he's a 'mushroom,' and well he knows it."

Ian didn't say anything to that, so Hannah realized it was probably true.

The footmen assisted them with their wraps, Mr. Baker beamed, and their maids watched from the upper stair. The group, accompanied by a retired elderly governess who hired herself out for such purposes, since no respectable young females went anywhere without a proper female chaperone, sailed out into the London night, accompanied by a hearty young footman, who sat up with their driver.

They didn't talk much in the carriage. The governess was, after all, not one of the family. But even if they could have spoken they wouldn't have. Hannah was worrying about what Ian thought of her aborted meeting with Timothy, and now wondering if she ought to tell him to call in someone to stop his shadowing her. She was also upset because since that first glance at her this evening, he hadn't looked at her. Her sisters were on fire to know if they'd be noted, smiled upon, or snubbed. And Ian was deep in his own thoughts.

The theater was a blazing fortress, a bastion of light on the dark crowded London streets. Torches flamed to show the huge play boards announcing the night's entertainment. Linkboys led theatergoers in from nearby streets; gas lamps glowed high on the theater's outer walls and the gas lighter had every streetlamp blazing.

"They're all dressed beautifully," Anthea whispered, watching the crowds.

"What good eyes you have," Ian commented as their coach stopped to stand in a line that would let playgoers off at the front of the theater. "All I can see from here in this crush are hats, capes, and wraps."

Anthea giggled. "It doesn't matter. I'll just bet you they are dressed in the height of fashion."

"And you'd win," Ian said. "Although not all the audience is. But you're right; this is a good place for you to be seen. The Season will be ending soon, so everyone's trying to get in last looks at the prospects they might have ignored before. Prospects for invitations to summer homes, courtships, marriage, and such," he added. "Which you young ladies are not yet ready for. Consider this a night for amusement, and for letting people see you are here, in my company, under my aegis. Don't worry. My name still stands for something. Thanks to your father," he added.

The coach stopped, and the party was let out onto the teeming pavement. They stood there for a moment, and then followed Ian inside.

Once inside, the girls gasped. Hannah herself held her breath. The place was done up in gleaming gilt and rich gold and red fabrics. There were chandeliers radiating more light with their hundreds of candles. In the midst of it all was a magnificent curved and winding marble stair leading to the second floor. The playgoers promenaded up the stair, where many of their kind already stood hanging over the railings, looking down at the crowds below.

"How can anyone see anyone here?" Jessica whispered.

"They can be seen, which is what they care about most," Ian answered. "I have a box for us. An old friend lent it to me for the night. We'll go there and watch the play and the playgoers, which is usually the whole point of the night, if Mrs. Siddons or Mr. Kemble aren't performing. There's an intermission. Then the play goes on, and after that, another intermission, and the farce. It's usually broad, but your father seems a broad-minded man. Just don't fall off your chairs laughing at the vulgar bits," he told the girls. "The correct thing is to look amused. Not beside yourself with laughter, although if we're lucky, that will be a difficult thing to do."

They proceeded up the stair in silence, aware

that hundreds of pairs of eyes were observing them.

"Head high," Ian whispered to his party. "They don't know you, that's why they stare. Don't try to stare them down. They've more experience. Be actresses tonight. Pretend you don't give a snap of your fingers for their opinions. You can look enchanted with me," he added to Hannah at last, "if you like."

She grinned.

"And watch your step," he warned her. "This is a highly polished and very crafty stair. It's famous. Caricatures have been made of the ladies, upended and bare-bottomed, tumbling down it."

Hannah held on to his arm and took the stairs with what she hoped was regal indifference, hoping she wouldn't stumble, or meet anyone from that ill-fated ball. Both events would be disastrous for her pride. She didn't dare look behind to see how the girls were faring. When they reached the top, she turned at last. The girls were born actresses. They looked amused, and a bit bored.

Nevertheless Hannah breathed a sigh of relief as Ian led them down a long corridor to a curtained alcove. He nodded at a gorgeously dressed footman standing in front of it, then handed him a note and some coins. The footman bowed and swept back the curtain. Hannah and the girls, in spite of their fine acting, genuinely gaped at what they saw.

The view from the private box was of the entire theater. It lay before them in all its glory. Drawn curtains covered the stage; footlights flared on the stage perimeters. But the theater itself was filling with all the drama, color, and noise anyone could want.

There was a roisterous crowd milling in the very front seats, which seemed to be all benches. It was easy to see that though they were dressed in their finest, those patrons' clothes weren't very fine. They were bright and colorful, not fashionable or elegant. From their behavior and their dress, Hannah guessed these were people of the common class of London out for a night on the Town. They were enjoying themselves mightily, even though the play hadn't started yet.

Farther back, separate from those boisterous playgoers, the seats were being filled by men and women who were nicely dressed and more sober in their behavior. Clerks and physicians, men at law and financiers, Hannah guessed, sober and respectable, but never people of Fashion. Behind them, though, sat more elegant clientele, using quizzing glasses to inspect all the people above, behind, and around them. Some stood in order to better see and be seen. These were obviously flamboyant men about Town, gentlemen with ladies, or at least, females, who wished to be seen. The women wore feathers, tiaras, and jewels in their hair; the men were togged out in the latest styles.

High above in the balcony, and in the rings of side boxes surrounding the audience, Hannah saw the most elegant patrons of all. They were dressed exquisitely, although they behaved with all the open curiosity of anyone else in the place. *Nobility*, she thought, *gentlepersons*, *Society*, all looking down on the audience, like the painted gods on the ceiling high above even them.

To the left and the right of their box, separated only by waist-high padded partitions covered with silk, were other boxes filled with smartly dressed patrons. There should have been no privacy but as the boxes were built so as to form a ring, each box was set back a bit from the others, and each had a shadowed section to the rear.

Their footman settled the aged governess in one of the gilded chairs in their box, as Ian seated Hannah. Ian also made sure that the girls were sitting, composed and delighted beyond words, before he sat beside his wife. Then their footman folded his arms, and stood in the back of the box, by the curtains, as though on guard.

Hannah was made speechless by all this show of privilege.

"Well, what do you think?" Ian asked her in a low voice.

"It's like seeing our world laid out before us, in the order in which we put them," she said. "I don't think they can put anything on the stage half as fascinating."

"Which is why going to the theater is so popular," he said. "If the play is good, they'll watch it. If it isn't, they'll be very happy watching each other."

"No one paid undue attention to the girls," she whispered. "Is that good or bad?"

"Neither," he said. "Which is good. They haven't ogled you either, if you noticed. That's also good. You are behaving with *bon ton*, and my name is yet known. Our wealth is even better known, and my wrath at what happened at the ball is becoming very well known. We yet may get through all this unscathed."

"*This*?" she asked.

"Being accepted, as your father wanted, for the girls' sake."

"Oh," she said.

"I pay my debts," he added.

Hannah bit her lip. How much of what he did was for her and genuine feeling he felt for her? And how much to pay that ever-present debt? Would she ever know? With all that had happened, with all the distrust and suspicion, could they stay together that long?

"Ah, the curtains are stirring," he said, sitting back. "Soon, we'll see a rehearsed performance."

It was hard to do that. The actors bellowed at each other as they stalked the stage, or posed in classical positions denoting hate and love, joy and grief. But it was hard to understand anything going on onstage. Soon, dissatisfied with the players and the play, the audience became loud; the sound they made overwhelmed the actors. Which was just as well. From what could be heard, it was a trite and badly performed bit of drama. Hannah was glad when the curtains finally fell, to the general relief and obvious approval of the audience.

The lights in the theater itself grew brighter as chandeliers were lowered and wall lanterns turned high.

Hannah glanced around the box. The aged governess was sleeping peacefully.

Ian stood. The girls looked at him expectantly. "Now," he said, "the promenade. This is when everyone gets up and walks around the corridors, or up and down the stairs on some pretense, greeting each other and comparing their finery. Some actually use the withdrawing rooms. Would you care to do that?" he asked the girls.

They leapt from their seats and shook out their skirts.

"And you, my dear?" he asked Hannah, who was sitting and watching them.

"I think I'd like to stay," she said. She couldn't tell him that she didn't want to risk anything that could cloud this evening. Meeting up with Auntie, or Lady Harkness, or any of the other spiteful ladies from that ball would be disastrous to her hard-won composure. Seeing Timothy would be disastrous. "May I?"

"You may," he answered.

"It won't hurt your reputation?"

"It will show you are a lady of taste and reserve. Would you like me to bring you an ice?"

"Oh, yes, thank you," she said.

He nodded, and crooked his elbows so the girls could put a hand on each arm. "We'll be back presently." He signaled their footman, who drew back their curtain, and then followed the trio out into the corridor.

Hannah sat back and sighed with relief. She felt a bit of a coward, though. And as the minutes wore on and she saw how the entire audience was using this intermission as an opportunity to socialize, she began to feel even more craven, and ever more nervous. People were popping in and out of each other's boxes, greeting each other, visiting, and signaling from all parts of the theater.

Hannah rose, shook out her own skirts, took a deep breath, and moved toward the shadows at the back of the box. She knew she'd never find her husband and sisters in the mad crush of milling theatergoers. But she could stand in the corridor by her box and wait for them there. She'd also be unobserved by the throng. It was a coward's compromise, or not even that. It was actually a retreat, she thought, but better than sitting and hiding in plain sight.

She drew back the curtain and then stepped back in shock.

"Hello, Nan," Timothy said.

He wore correct evening dress. This close, she could see that his boyish good looks were fading and becoming less beguiling. At least, she no longer found them so. In fact, with his pomaded black curls and newly pale face, he looked more commonplace.

"At last!" he said, advancing a step until he stood in the box, half in shadow. "I've been waiting for a chance to talk to you again, alone. I have to talk with you."

She stepped back again. "We *have* spoken," she said coldly. "I find your intentions objectionable. Please believe me when I tell you that."

"Objectionable?" he asked. "Not as I remember. We can have that again."

"Never, ever," she said. "Please go away. Our time is as over as that summer is. I've a new life now. And," she added, as she couldn't yet to Ian, "a husband I love and respect."

Timothy was about to speak, when they both heard the increasing sounds of the audience returning to the theater. He looked over his shoulder. "Good night, then," he said hurriedly. "But not for the last time. I can't bring myself to call you, 'my lady,' because you aren't. Not yet."

"Or ever will be!" she exclaimed furiously. "You have to stop following me. You must believe me. I—don't—want—to—see—you again! Understand?"

He paused. He smiled. "Not at all. You don't know what you're saying, Nan. You still have such . . ." he seemed to search for a word, "bourgeois ideas. Life with your milord will soon teach you differently. Didn't you learn anything at that ball? I heard what they were talking about. He used you to pay his debts. You used him to get over me. His debts are paid. Yours are not. You still want me, poor girl. I know that."

He turned to go again. She grabbed his sleeve. It was either that or slap his face. "Well, you're wrong," she said angrily as she confronted him. She didn't like his disbelieving, smug smile. "Listen!" she said imperatively. "I don't know who's been filling your head with nonsense. I do know that you forgot who I am."

He looked at her again. "I haven't forgotten how much you wanted me," he said with a smile, looking at her hand where it clutched him.

She dropped his sleeve. Her color rose. "I was a girl. A foolish, lonely girl. I'm a woman now, and I don't want you to go until you understand that I don't want you. I want my husband, no one else. Nor do I want to play games, and definitely none with you."

"I only left because I wanted to spare you," he said with a radiant smile. "Now I'll stay because I want to save you."

"I think not," Ian said from behind him.

Chapter 22

Timothy's eyes widened and he froze. Then he began to sidle away, toward the next box. Ian stopped him by grabbing his shoulder in a steely grip.

Hannah couldn't speak because she didn't know what to say. Surely Ian had heard it all and couldn't distrust her anymore? Still, she had been a fool. What could she say now without making matters worse?

Anthea burst into speech.

"Of all the liars," she said angrily, "*You*, Timothy Adkins, are the worst! You did *not* leave Nan because you went to make your fortune so you could marry her!"

"Absolutely not!" Jessica agreed with heat.

"Shh, girls," Ian said. "Speak quietly if you must, and smile while you're at it. Pretend you're jesting. But speak again, bright angel," he told Anthea with a real smile.

Anthea glowered at Timothy, bristling like an

angry sparrow ruffling her feathers. But when she spoke again it was in a harsh whisper, and she curled her lips in a cold smile. "You always were a liar and a cheat, Timothy, but this is the end of enough. You left because our papa thwarted you. You left because he threatened to cut Nan off without a penny piece if you ever married her. No dowry, no houseroom, nothing. He said he meant it, no matter how much he loved her, because you didn't, and he'd rather see her starve than be married to you. He said he knew that telling her that would only make her rebel against him and favor you. He said he reckoned that telling you would end it because you were only after money."

"And he told you he'd see to it you'd be aboard a ship in two snaps if you seduced her," Jessica snarled, "and signed up as a petty seaman for years to boot!"

"What?" Hannah gasped. "How do you know that?"

"Because we were there, when Papa said it," Anthea said. "Although he didn't know it."

"We were usually there whenever we heard anything that had to do with you last summer, Nan," Jessica admitted quietly. "Especially you and that creature," she added, smiling at Timothy with gritted teeth.

"Oh," Hannah said. She didn't know whether to laugh or weep, or blush ruby red with embarrassment.

Timothy had grown pale.

"No more explanations. Not here," Ian muttered. "We'll go home. With you," he told Timothy. He signaled to his own footman, who was standing nearby watching with fascination.

"Take this fellow in hand, James," Ian said, "and see that he doesn't get away. He's slippery."

The footman put his arm around Timothy's neck and pulled him close. He bent Timothy's arm behind his back, and held on. "Aye, but I'm strong as an ox, milord. If he tries anything, it's that sorry he'll be."

"Good," Ian said. "Make it look like he's taken ill and you're helping him to the carriage. You can actually make him sick if he tries to escape, so that won't be a lie. For now, we wait. When the farce begins everyone will be seated again. Then we leave under cover of laugher, and we leave quickly. Wake Mrs. Alter," he told Jessica, gesturing to the old governess, "but gently. See to it that she's ready to go when we are. And keep smiling, everyone. Stay together. We'll have time enough to sort things out when we get home."

They stood quietly at the back of their box, false smiles pasted on their faces, just in case anyone in the theater could see them. Jessica gently roused the old governess. Timothy tried to move once, but the pain that showed on his face when he did proved that the footman hadn't lied about his strength.

At last, they heard the sounds of laughter and conversation in the corridors and the theater lower to a murmur, and fade to silence. Then the lights on the stage bloomed bright, and they heard applause, soon followed by a great gust of laughter filling the theater.

Ian nodded. "Now," he said, taking Hannah's hand.

The group moved as one out of the box, and proceeded slowly down the long corridor toward the great stair.

They heard riotous laughter from the theater audience, but the only sound they made was when the footman muttered to his captive as they approached the great stair. "Aye, it's slippery, and so are you, but I'll break both your arms and a leg if you try it. I've got a firm footing, and a terrible temper."

Then they stopped, because Ian did. He looked into the recess in the wall, the entry to a box, near the stair. "Come out, dear Stepmama," he said wearily. "I see you, and I know you've been watching, and much more than that. Come with us, or suffer the consequences."

"Whatever are you talking about, my lord?" his stepmother asked as she came out of the shadowed alcove.

She wore an exquisite white gown with black panels, a matching crown of feathers in her hair. Her face bore faint traces of rouge. There were diamonds at her throat and on her fingers. She looked world-weary rather than old; a fashionable and handsome woman of middle age.

"Let's not play any more games," Ian said wearily. "Just come along. I'll call for another carriage for some of the others. You can travel with my lady and me. That way, anyone seeing us will never guess what's been afoot. You wouldn't want them to, would you?"

"Thank you," the lady said in a normal tone of voice. "How kind of you to note that I was feeling faint, my lord, and offer me an invitation to your home. I think I will come, at that. I just must go and make my farewells to my party."

"Do that," Ian said.

"My maid must accompany me," she said.

"Of course," he answered. "But no others. Be in front of the theater in five minutes. We won't wait, and I know you won't want to miss a word."

She nodded, and turned back into the box she'd exited.

"Now." Ian sighed. "We move on." He looked down at Hannah. "The truth," he said, "can only set us free."

But she didn't want to be free of him, so she only gripped his arm tightly, and followed him down the grand stair.

They sat in Ian's library so that if Hannah's father returned earlier than expected he wouldn't see the company assembled there. Two footmen stood on guard to make sure that no one in that assembled company made for the door.

Ian paced.

Hannah perched on a settee, between Anthea and Jessica. None of them spoke. Their eyes followed Ian's pacing. His stepmother sat upright on a chair before the hearth. Timothy sat motionless in a straight-back chair near Ian's desk, but his eyes darted back and forth.

Finally, Ian spoke. "I discovered all about you and Mr. Adkins today," he told his stepmother. "Servants, when paid enough, do talk. Though why you should ally yourself with him puzzles me. There's certainly no financial gain to be had from . . . Oh," he said, stopping in his tracks. "I *am* a fool. Hannah would have funds even if she left me for him. You realized she'd never go penniless, at least not from me.

"And this fellow," he said, inclining a shoulder toward Timothy, "would share some with you for information and entrée. That's why he was invited to the ball. And that's how he was able to follow us everywhere, from the Tower to the park, and the theater. I will soon discover who in my household was foolish enough to sell that information to you. The rest of my staff is loyal. I'll know before we're done here tonight. So, as ever, dear Stepmama, it was for the money, wasn't it?"

His stepmother shifted in her chair. "Since you

know everything," she said loftily, "I wonder why you asked me here tonight."

"To insist that you stop," Ian said. "To warn you, actually. I told you I'm not funding you, and you must believe that. You beggared me once because my father was bewitched by you. I'm not. So, never again. The next time I find you trying anything to interfere in my life, I'll call in the runners. I don't want gossip but I'm willing to make some to be sure you go away. Are you as willing, my dear?" he asked Hannah.

She was taken by surprise, but her answer was automatic. "Of course," she said. "Certainly." Then her wits returned as she spoke. "Can you also convince Mr. Adkins that I don't want his company? And tell that miserable little sneak that I wouldn't even if my sisters hadn't spied on us, and told me everything?"

"Oh, I say!" Anthea exclaimed. "We weren't spying . . . exactly. We worried about you because we knew what a snake Timothy was. You didn't believe us. But when we told Papa, he agreed. And you can see we were right, can't you?"

"I can," Hannah said. "But I wish you'd said something to me sooner. Certainly I would have been crushed. But, believe me, giving someone up is so much easier than being given up."

"They're very young," Ian said. "They meant the best for you."

"We did," Jessica said. "We just were so happy

Timothy had gone we didn't think it through. For-give us, Nan, please."

"Of course," Hannah said, because she did. If they had told her, she mightn't have agreed to a marriage of convenience. She'd never have met Ian at all. She still didn't know if that was a good or a bad thing, considering all their problems and misunderstandings. But however it turned out, she was glad it had happened.

"But I did care for you, Nan," Timothy said sud-denly. "I couldn't pretend the emotions I felt when you were in my arms. Can you doubt that?"

"*Emotions?*" Hannah scoffed. "That's a new word for it. Most men don't call it that. You were a healthy young man, and I was a pliant female. Only thank heavens, not that pliant, after all. Go away, Timothy. I've grown up. Not only don't you thrill me anymore, not one bit, but now I know that my purse excited you more than my charms."

His eyes narrowed. His face grew ruddy. He obviously forgot the company he was in in his rage. "But the same can be said for the man who did marry you, can't it?" he asked spitefully. "At least, that's what everyone says. So what's the dif-ference, your father's approval? Didn't you have a mind of your own?"

The room was still. Ian clenched his fists and took a step closer to Timothy, but stopped when Hannah answered Timothy, in cool, even tones.

"I didn't know you'd asked Papa, or the extent

of his disapproval," she said, rising to her feet in her anger. "Nor would it have mattered to me then. Obviously, it certainly did to you. But are you mad to compare yourself to my husband? He's a man of elegance and manners, an educated gentleman."

Timothy sat back, his eyes wide.

Ian watched her, his expression still.

"Most of all," Hannah went on, raising her chin, "he's honest in all his dealings. He never vowed love when there was none, tried to seduce me, or made promises he didn't know if he could keep. But he's made me very happy. It was a marriage of convenience, and he never pretended otherwise. But it has become something far more. I love him with all my heart, you see. I could never have loved you half so well. I'm grateful and lucky beyond my desserts that you lied and cheated, Timothy, because as it turns out you only cheated yourself. You actually did an incredible favor for me. But I don't think you should be rewarded for it."

She fell still, suddenly raising her eyes to Ian. He was gazing at her with an expression she couldn't read. It was disbelief and rising delight. She sat abruptly and closed her lips tight. She hadn't declared her love to him as she'd wanted to, which would have been only after he'd declared his own feelings. She'd blurted it out in anger in front of everyone. She closed her eyes as well. Would she never learn to control her emotions?

"But I'm not lying now," Timothy persisted. "You really did grow up to be a beautiful woman," he protested.

"A smarter one, that's certain," she said, opening her eyes to do battle again. "Timothy, listen. I don't even like you anymore. And I wouldn't even if my sisters hadn't told me the whole sordid story. Imagine! Coming to London, knowing I was married and still trying to be my lover! Have you no eyes as well as no wits? Look at my husband, and then take a look in the mirror. Hear him speak, and then listen to yourself. How could any woman be stupid enough to even *compare* the two of you? Oh, you make me ill."

"I heard your marriage was a failure," Timothy protested. "I was only trying to help—"

"Yourself," Hannah said, finishing his sentence. "You believed what you wanted to hear. And you've no business snaking about asking about my marriage anyway. I tell you that even if my lord left me I wouldn't take a lover, and *certainly* not one such as you. You really never knew me, did you, Timothy? Now go away, will you?"

"You heard my lady," Ian told Timothy. "Go away. If you're ever found within six feet of her again, be sure I'll be more than annoyed."

"I don't see how he can help it," his stepmother said, "considering that we two have come to an understanding."

The room fell still. Even Timothy looked shocked.

"We get along well," she said. "I've been thinking of going to the Continent when the war wears down."

"Unthink any trip to Italy, whatever happens with the war," Ian said grimly. "Because my letter to my brother will get there before you do. It's hardly necessary; he liked you less than I did. You'll find no welcome there."

She shrugged.

"Nor any at my homes here anywhere," Ian added. "Or the dower house. Not any more. I don't care what the gossips say about that."

"Nor I," his stepmother said. She rose. "There are other places I can prosper. I'm not too old. But now you say my reputation will precede me?"

"Depend on it," Ian said tightly.

"Then perhaps it's time for me to travel to America," she said lightly. "I've heard there is a civilized Society being built there. There are certainly riches, and they do so admire us, even if we were at war only a generation past. I'll need a masculine traveling companion. I believe Mr. Adkins would suit me. He needs only to acquire more polish, he's already learned to ape manners; he has a ready mind, and is young and attractive. That won't hurt my standing at all. Now, are we done with this rude interview?"

"Done and done," Ian said. "Good night and good-bye. And please take Mr. Adkins with you, before I lose more of my temper and have the honor of tossing him out."

Timothy rose, and as though sleepwalking, went to the lady.

"She's a hard taskmaster," Ian told him. "Watch yourself, Mr. Adkins."

"I'll do that for him," his stepmother said. She put her hand on Timothy's arm and they went to the door. She looked back once. "You never forgave me for trying to seduce you while your father was still alive, did you?"

"Or after," Ian said. "Actually, I never forgave you for marrying him in the first place. But once you did, you should have been content with the title and the money."

"Ah well," she said, with a tiny smile. "But the money ran out. You were right about me, you see. *Au revoir*, my son," she said sarcastically.

He laughed. "You mean, *adieu*," he said. "Or at least, you had better, for now and forever."

The lady winced. Then her face became a smooth mask again. "Done," she said, and left the house, head high.

Hannah went to Ian after the pair had left. "I never knew," she said, looking into his eyes. "She's dreadful. But so was I, in a different way, before I met you."

"Young," he said, touching a finger to her chin. His gaze was soft as he looked at her. "You were only very young, and lonely. There's no crime in that." He straightened. "I must go make sure that pair does what I asked, and immediately. I have to wait for your father too, and make sure he knows all. I'll leave you ladies to talk it over, and if you have any questions, please let me know."

Anthea and Jessica got up and went to Hannah's side.

"I mean that," Ian added. "Jessica and Anthea? If you've any compassion, please don't keep me under observation as you did that fool Adkins. You two are better than Bow Street, you know. Just ask me and I'll tell you anything you want to know, within reason, of course."

They laughingly agreed, and linking arms, left the room.

"We'll go with you to your room," Anthea told Hannah. "Poor girl, you've had a lot of shocks tonight, haven't you?"

She didn't answer as they mounted the stair. But once they'd followed her into her bedchamber and clambered up on her bed, making themselves comfortable, obviously ready to have a nice, long cozy chat, Hannah spoke.

"You were the ones who tipped the milk can that night in the barn, weren't you?" she asked them. "The night that I took fright at the noise, and thinking someone was coming in, ran out of the hayloft, leaving Timothy alone."

"We didn't want things getting out of hand," Jessica said. "And that was before we even knew everything about him."

"In fact," Anthea put in, "we didn't tell a soul about that. Even Papa didn't know about you and Timothy until just before your last meeting with him, when he left you. We just made sure Timothy didn't take advantage of you until then."

"So you were the footsteps in the orchard that moonlit night?" Hannah said slowly. "And the whistling in the stables that rainy afternoon?"

"Don't be angry," Jessica said, looking worried.

"We meant it for the best," Anthea protested anxiously.

"I know, and you did the best. I thank you." Hannah put her hands to her head. "But, oh lord, what an example I set for you! What a debauched sister you must have thought you had. I apologize to you."

"Never," Anthea cried, holding out her arms to her sister. "You were only under a midsummer's spell."

"And who could blame you?" Jessica asked. "Papa didn't want to let you go, I think, and he never introduced you to anyone. Because he didn't think anyone was good enough."

"But then, after he banished Timothy, when he saw you were obviously stricken," Anthea said, putting a hand on her heart, "so quiet and dull, and unlike yourself, we all worried. Then Papa really started looking for a husband for you."

"We told him that buying into the nobility was a bad idea," Jessica said. "But this time, he was right. Ian is perfect for you! We all adore him, and only hope we find someone half as good for ourselves."

"I do too," Hannah said softly, coming to sit on the bed with them. "But this time, my dears, don't let Papa buy you anything but wedding gowns."

Hannah lay in her bed, the lamps were lit, and her eyes were open. She rehearsed what to say to Ian should he come into her room tonight. Her emotions ran from anger to self-pity, from fear to defiance.

There was nothing new to tell Ian now. All had been discovered. Surely, now he must realize she'd never lied to him. And whatever feverish embraces she'd shared with Timothy, they'd never actually made love and well Ian knew that.

Hannah sat up and smote her pillow to plump it and to release her anger. What nonsense a bride's virginity was, after all. Now she knew that a woman and a man could do many lovely things with each other's bodies, and yet leave the woman a virgin. And well Ian knew that too!

It was just her bad luck that in her youth and loneliness she'd fallen victim to a cad. But what if Ian disagreed? What if he thought her low and conniving, to have been so willing to literally romp in the hay with another man? That's why she hadn't told him in the first place, and why she hadn't told him she'd seen Timothy following them. She was still embarrassed about how wanton she'd been with him.

She wept a little. When she stopped, she gave up preparing a speech. Because when all was said and with all that had been done, the fact was that she loved her husband. Did Ian feel anything like that? She knew he wouldn't say it unless he believed it. She hadn't told him because as she'd announced this evening, she loved him with all her heart. But a heart could be broken only so many times before it was impossible to put back together again.

He came to her after midnight. He wore that handsome red banyan again, and without a word, he went to her bed and sat beside her. He looked grave.

Hannah's breathing became shallow because she was suffused with dread.

"Your father sent me to tell you that he deeply regrets everything," Ian said. "I assume that means even me. Nan . . ." he said, using the pet name everyone but he had always used. He paused. "May I call you that now? Your family does."

"You may, you should," she said quickly.

"Nan," he said again as though relishing the word, "I think that if you decided to leave me now your father would even forgive that. And in fact, so would I. It was wrong of me to simply accept all the good fortune that fell to me. After knowing you for five minutes, I could have seen that you weren't after a title. But I didn't want those five minutes."

"You're apologizing to me?" she asked.

"Why not? What do you have to apologize for? Almost falling under the influence of a charming cad?"

She lowered her gaze. "I think that if my sisters weren't mixing in all the time I might have fallen all the way."

"Then, knowing your morals, you'd have felt bound to marry him, and that at least, you were spared."

"I didn't tell you that I saw him following us at first."

"You turned pink," he said, smiling at her. "You aren't good at secrets. No wonder your sisters knew everything you were up to." His expression sobered. "What's to do, Nan? What do we do now?"

She couldn't tell him. But she could move into his arms and rest her head on his chest. She breathed in the spicy scent of him and sighed from the bottom of her soul. And then, without a word, she tried to tell him all she felt for him.

She kissed his neck, then his dented chin and then, his lips. He broke from his passivity and held her close, and kissed her back with such passion that she could forget her fears and doubts, and lose herself.

He cast off his robe, and helped her out of her night shift. But then he stopped. She looked at him with inquiry.

"Not another embrace, not another kiss until I confess," he said.

She wrapped her arms around herself and looked at him wide-eyed.

"I want to make love to you and hold back nothing," he said. "So first, I have to tell you I love you dearly." He smiled. "That wasn't so hard, but I've never said it to anyone else, and doubt I ever will, unless I speak to you . . . or our child, if we are so blessed. I'll never leave you for another, not for an hour. Nor do I want you to ever leave me."

"I wouldn't let you go," she said, laughing. "I'd cling to you like a thistle. I only worried because I thought you might leave me."

"I'd sooner leave this earth," he said, and took her into his arms.

They kissed, and touched, and then lay down together, and at last, they smiled. Then they were much too busy touching and sighing, admiring and congratulating each other, to think or speak another word.

But what they did spoke volumes.

"Nan," he whispered into her hair, at last, "I married for convenience and found the missing part of myself. I thought it was for money, but I got something far more important. You are my treasure."

She sighed. "I married you blindly, because I didn't care. Do you know how lucky I am?"

"Are you sure you are?" he asked, delighted to feel his desire rising once more. "Let me try to convince you again."

She balled up a small fist and pounded him, and then kissed the place she might have hurt. They laughed before they found themselves too ecstatic for mere laughter.

"You're pleased?" he asked, when he could, when they were at last done.

"I didn't know it could be that way for women too," she said in continued awe.

"Legend says it's even better for your fair sex," he said. "Although I don't know how that can be."

"We can keep trying to find out," she said.

They were weary now, too tired even for laughter, and so they grinned, and lay together until they were asleep.

When Hannah woke, she found Ian propped on his elbow, gazing down at her in the morning light. "It's nice not to have to hop out of a warm bed and shiver down by myself to sleep every night," he said when he saw her expression. "It's nicer still to wake beside you in the sunlight. I don't know how it's done in your family, but may we please share one bed, and one bedchamber, from now on?"

"Oh yes," she said, with heartfelt glee.

"Good," he said, wrapping her in his arms. "Mr. Baker," he said, "will be ecstatic."

Chapter 23

The first things to be carried from the Marquis Sutcombe's London town house were his personal effects and clothing. His lady and her family's personal items were next to go. Only the kitchens and a small dining parlor were left in working order, so that the marquis could have a last breakfast there.

A beaming Mr. Baker ordered the day. Coaches were loaded, servants scuttled, housemaids packed. Dust covers were thrown over furniture. The town house was being closed for the season. Summer was upon them, and Londoners who could afford it, and precious few they were, were leaving the city.

The butler delivered the morning posts to his master.

"Forgive me," Ian told Hannah and her family, "but I must read these now, in case there's something yet for me to do before I leave."

They nodded their approval, and went on

describing all the things they meant to do this summer.

"It's wonderful that we are to have garden parties and picnics and guests all summer," Jessica said.

"I looked at the guest list," Anthea said. "It's such a good idea to introduce us to the *ton* slowly, so that when we come back to London we'll feel comfortable. There's not a soul we know in Society now but Ian."

"That's 'my lord' in company," Hannah said.

"I know, but we aren't in anyone's company but our own right now," Anthea protested.

Ian was too occupied with reading to make any comment.

"I'm still not sure we should all move in with you," their father said.

"There's room for ten more of you," Hannah said, "and Ian said that way you will become familiar to everyone we know as well."

"That's 'my lord,'" Jessica said with a grin.

"Yes," Hannah said with a glowing smile, looking at Ian, "*my* lord."

But Ian still wasn't paying attention to their conversation. He was rereading the paper, his expression slowly changing to one of glee. He leapt from his chair.

"I must go!" he said. "There's something I have to do before we leave London. Excuse me, but this is essential to my happiness. I'll return as soon as I can. If worse comes to worse, we'll stay at an inn on the road tonight, but I still think we can leave at a decent hour. They're still packing up the coaches. I must be off."

He dropped a kiss on his wife's forehead, and before she could ask a question, headed out the door.

"Well, at least he was happy," Anthea said in puzzlement.

"So he was," Hannah answered slowly. She was nervous. After what had happened such a short time ago, any unlooked-for event struck fear into her heart. "So he was," she repeated, as she wondered what could have made him so merry.

The coaches were all packed and Hannah was pacing when Ian returned. If anything, he looked even happier than when he'd left.

"Come," he said, taking Hannah's hand, "we must go. I'll tell all when we stop to dine. I'll ride part of the way, following your coach, because it's a glorious day and I want the sun on my back and the breeze on my face. But I want us all together for my news. Don't worry. It's all good, for all of us." He grinned like a boy. "And I want to build up some suspense. It's not every day I have such news."

"I don't need suspense," Hannah wailed.

He laughed and hugged her. "Yes, you do. You need a good surprise for a change, my love," he whispered in her ear. "And that you shall have, never fear."

The inn the coaches stopped at was an ancient one. The Rose and Thistle had carefully preserved that aura. But inside Hannah found the place to be modernized and clean. The private dining parlor Mr. Baker had rode on ahead to reserve had its original thick-paned windows, but they shone with light like a cathedral's rose panels.

Hannah and her family sat quietly. For once, the girls didn't clamor to see what was being offered on the dining card. They all sat, breathless, until Ian entered the room, and seated himself at the head of the table. He was grinning.

Before he could speak, the landlord entered with a dusty bottle. He wrapped a towel around it, and it opened with a loud pop.

"Champagne?" Hannah asked.

"As much as you like," Ian said as their glasses were filled.

He raised his glass. "To good fortune, good bargains, love and marriage," he said.

The others raised their glasses and drank with him.

"Now," he said, putting his hands on the table. "The news. That letter I got this morning was from my brother, in Italy. His lungs have healed."

"Huzzah!" Anthea cried, raising her empty glass.

Everyone smiled at that. They all knew she had nurtured romantic notions about Ian's younger brother, so sadly alone and ailing in a foreign land.

Ian smiled. "Sorry to douse your hopes, my girl, but part of the news is that he's married. Not only married, but to a neighbor, a widowed countess whose villa, he tells me, can accommodate us all when it's safe to travel. And the lady is not only beautiful, young, and loving, but she's rich as she can hold together. She came to visit when he was recuperating, and came back more often every week. And now they are blissfully wed."

"That *is* good news," Hannah said with relief.

"There's more," Ian said. "This is for you, sir," he told Hannah's father as he handed him a document.

Though obviously confused, Mr. Leeds took the paper, and taking his spectacles from his pocket, scanned it. He looked up, his wide eyes magnified even larger by the spectacles. "But this is a fortune!" he said. "Whatever is it for?"

"It's a settlement on your daughter, sir. I wish it were as large as the amount you paid to me on our marriage, but think of it as a first payment. In time, I will refund it all. But I keep the bride, of course. You see, now that my brother is married wealthily, he and his bride insisted on repaying me for sending him to Italy, paying for his rooms, medicines, physicians, and treatments. He sent me a bank draft. I didn't realize the costs had gone that high." He smiled again and looked at Hannah. "My brother and I seem to gravitate to beautiful, wealthy young women. I hope our sons inherit the knack of it."

"But you needn't pay me, my lord," Mr. Leeds said. "Ours was an honest trade, and is complete."

"Never," Ian said, rising and going to Hannah's side. "You restored my financial health and also brought me love and joy, and unexpected delight."

He put his hands on Hannah's shoulders and gazed down at her. "Turn about is fair play," he told her. "This time, I'm buying you back."

She rose so quickly her chair fell over. She flung herself into his waiting arms. "Too bad," she said when she drew back from his kiss. "Because in your case, my love, I'm absolutely free."

It was a while until they were all calm enough to dine. They laughed and even sang, and in time, they went on. But none of them ever forgot that day, or the bliss of a debt paid in full, with interest and joy.

Next month, don't miss these exciting new love stories only from Avon Books

Between the Devil and Desire by Lorraine Heath

Olivia, Duchess of Lovingdon, would never associate with such a rogue as Jack Dodger, a wealthy gentleman's club owner. Yet when Jack is named sole heir to the duke's personal possessions, Olivia is forced to share her beloved home with this despicable, yet desirable man . . .

Simply Irresistible by Rachel Gibson

Georgeanne Howard leaves her fiancé at the altar when she realizes she can't marry a man old enough to be her grandfather, no matter how rich he is. Hockey superstar John Kowalsky unknowingly helps her escape, and only later does he realize he has absconded with his boss's bride.

The Highland Groom by Sarah Gabriel

To claim her inheritance, Fiona MacCarran must marry a wealthy Highlander, and soon. Arriving in the misty Highlands as a schoolteacher, she despairs of finding an acceptable groom . . . until she meets Dougal MacGregor.

Wild by Margo Maguire

For Grace Hawthorne, the new stranger is unlike any man she has ever known. Proud, defiant, and mesmerizingly masculine, he flouts convention and refuses to enter into proper society. Is he the real Anthony Maddox, heir to a glittering earldom? Or an arrogant imposter, sworn to claim what doesn't belong to him?

Visit www.AuthorTracker.com for exclusive information on your favorite HarperCollins authors.

REL 1208

Available wherever books are sold or please call 1-800-331-3761 to order.

At Avon Books, we know your passion for romance—once you finish one of our novels, you find yourself wanting more.

May we tempt you with . . .

- **Excerpts** from our upcoming releases.

- Entertaining **extras**, including authors' personal photo albums and book lists.

- Behind-the-scenes **scoop** on your favorite characters and series.

- **Sweepstakes** for the chance to win free books, romantic getaways, and other fun prizes.

- Writing **tips** from our authors and editors.

- **Blog** with our authors and find out why they love to write romance.

- **Exclusive content** that's not contained within the pages of our novels.

Join us at
www.avonbooks.com

AVON
An Imprint of HarperCollins*Publishers*
www.avonromance.com

Available wherever books are sold or please call 1-800-331-3761 to order.